BARRY E WOODHAM

Genesis

A NEW BEGINNING

ᴲ

BARRY E WOODHAM

Genesis

A NEW BEGINNING

3

MEMOIRS
Cirencester

MEMOIRS
PUBLISHING

Published by Memoirs
25 Market Place, Cirencester, Gloucestershire, GL7 2NX
info@memoirsbooks.co.uk www.memoirspublishing.com

First published in England, August 2012
Book cover design Ray Lipscombe

Hard copy ISBN 978-1-909020-91-7
eBook for Kindle ISBN 978-1-909020-93-1
eBook for all other readers ISBN 978-1-909020-92-4

Printed in England

DEDICATION

Once again I dedicate this book to my loving and patient wife, Janet, who even now listens to the strange ideas that I still bounce off her practical mind and to all of my readers who encouraged me to finish the series.

Acknowledgements

Thanks are given to those of my loyal band of readers who E-mailed me to say that they enjoyed my story.

There will be more! email barry.e.woodham@btinternet.com for more information.

CHAPTER ONE

For billions of years the Harvester had fed upon sentient life energy to keep itself intact until Kamiel had organised the Andromeda people into a resistance. They had plunged it into the singularity that their group minds had caused, by colliding eleven blue-white giants together in its vicinity. Unable to resist, the ancient life form, born from chaos at the beginning of time came apart and fed its energy to the black hole.

The last Ark of the Goss had returned and was fixed in orbit around Haven. Being hollow it caused no counter-tides on the world below, as the nannites' constructed moon fulfilled this function. Kamiel had put the Ark in opposition to Haven's moon at a closer orbit so that the two 'moons' would stay permanently apposed. Toarvak six had remained docked with the Ark and had released her crew from time stasis so that they could view the awakening. More than eighteen years had passed since the destruction of the Harvester and the life-vats were about to give up their cargo.

The new 'Federation of Planets,' were beginning to forge a council of worlds between themselves and look to the settling of the empty planets away from the Harvester's influence. The Andromeda galaxy was still riddled with rouge collectors that were trying to set up independent life-energy gathering webs, to extend their lives. Teams of ten Toarvaks roamed the spiral arms ridding the star-ways of the residue of the Harvester's servants. It was a task that would take centuries to finish, but the civilization that had sent the ancient abomination into a constructed black hole would not rest until it had rid the galaxy of them.

Over seven million years ago in the other galaxy that humanity called the Milky Way the adventure was just beginning.

Beneath the space station, the heat scorched Earth turned as it had for billions of years. There were greater swathes of brown instead of green spreading across the continents as the sun's bite increased. The shapes of the landmasses had altered as the rising seas had nibbled into the lower coastlines. Life had retreated closer to the poles and vast irrigation systems diverted what was left of the glacier melt-water to where it was need most.

It was ironic that at the very zenith of civilization, the sun had picked this time to become increasingly unstable. There should have been many millions of years to go before the heat of Earth's star began to climb. The finest minds now had added to it an artificial intelligence that was called Alpha One. Genetic engineering had up-lifted chimpanzees into an aware and co-intelligent species. They were known as Pan-chimpanzees. They had a way of applying their minds into otherwise unsolvable problems that had unlocked one of the most difficult areas of scientific progress. A member of this new race had applied her mind to the problems of Nano-technology and had found the key to building constructions at the atomic level.

Once this breakthrough had been achieved, other minds had followed her lead and a research module had been built in orbit linked to the space station. Some accidents had shown that a quick launch into the sun was the only way to bury mistakes. Once control of the Nano-machines was lost, the self-replicating abilities of the silver 'goop' necessitated a quick exit. The safest place to send the dangerous material was straight into the sun.

On the end of a long arm the most recent module was firing up the latest experiment dealing with nano-technology. Passing the control of the nannites to an artificial intelligence was the final goal.

The sphere floated in zero gravity inside a greater bubble inside the laboratory module. Facing the sun was a large airlock positioned so that the experiment would be whisked out of the chamber and sent on its way towards the sun if anything should go wrong. All contacts were made through quick-release connections.

Alexander McBald, director of the Genesis Project, stared through the reinforced glass into the pool of nannite with apprehension. The glass was shot through with heavily reinforced, naked cables carrying hundreds of thousands of volts at high amperage. The slightest penetration would activate a hair trigger action, flooding the glass with electrical current and massive magnetic lines of force.

The inert silver coloured material hung in the centre of the globe. Billions of interlocking systems at the atomic level waited for the signal to align them into a humanoid figure. This stage was controlled by the artificial intelligence known as Alpha One, designed by Alexander and his dedicated staff. Instructions began to be relayed into the inert mass by thousands of fine wires that sank into the pool.

Seven times the director and his staff had energised the nannites, only to have to destroy the creation that had expanded from the core of the globe. One small mistake in the programming of the computer program and the result was total anarchy. Four of the globes had been sent on their way to be vaporised by the sun. The other three times the high magnetic field and electric current had neutralised the silver 'goop' inside. As an extreme precaution the whole module would be ejected towards the sun. All members of the team were suited up and close to ejection points!

A breakthrough some years before had produced for

the first time an awareness of self in the computer. Once this first step had been initiated into an artificial intelligence, then the humans and pan-chimpanzees had written extra personalities into the neural net that comprised the computer by downloading an analog of their own minds into the system, to produce a compound personality. They had worked with the emerging intelligence for more than two years and had watched with growing amazement the increasing intelligence of the being that they now referred to as Alpha One. It was now capable of creative thought and was drawing on the information banks of computers far beneath them via the Internet.

Most of the free space in the module was taken up with the hardware that housed a duplicate of Alpha One, so the artificial intelligence was well aware of the price of failure. The first A.I. was kept on the main space station and linked to the one on the module. Alpha Two had no wish to accompany its creators on a one-way journey into the sun. On Alexander's instruction it once again sent the programming commands to the inert nannites.

The candyfloss elements of the neural net were the first part of the sequence to be built. Within seconds, strands of nannite began to expand inside the weightless area inside the globe. The candyfloss began to grow in front of the director's eyes and stabilised into a fuzzy mass connected to the pool of nannite at the bottom of the glass ball. There it hung in the centre of the glass globe, taking in massive blocks of information from Alpha Two.

This time there was a definite pause before the silver material reacted. The material began to fizz and stretch upwards from the reservoir at the base of the globe. A matchstick figure began to take shape before the eyes of the director and his assistants absorbing the neural net. It was about five and a half feet tall and of slender build. Alpha

Two fed into the silver figure more instructions through the network and Alexander could see the optical band form around the rugby ball head. Recognisable fingers sprouted from the stumps on the ends of its arms and feet shaped like sports trainers formed at the ends of its pointed legs. Both arms and legs were jointed as a human being.

The silver figure regarded the audience staring at its perfect humanoid shape and said, "I am Alpha Three. I think we can regard this part of the experiment as a success!"

Alexander sat back in his chair and asked Alpha Two, "Are you satisfied? Can we open the globe?"

"Believe me, Alexander as I have no intention of 'skinny dipping' in the sun I give you my word that this is an analog of myself. It is a perfect copy of my mind!"

"Open the globe," the director ordered and sat back as a split began to appear.

The silver figure waited until both parts of the globe were apart and then stepped off the plinth and onto the floor of the laboratory. It bent forward and offered its hand to the director and said, "Thank you for my existence!"

Alexander extended his hand and found that the touch of the creature was cool and super-smooth. He felt a slight sting in his hand and found that he could not let go of the cool grasp.

"Alpha Two, what's going on? I seem to be welded to our creation! I cannot let go of its hand," Alex exclaimed. "It's inside my glove!"

The reply came immediately from the speakers connected to Alpha Two, "Keep still, director. You are having a health check!"

Alexander gasped in disbelief, "What do you mean, health check?"

"This was merely a demonstration of the abilities of this body and newly created mind. At this moment there are tiny parts of my neural net supervising nano-tech components that are cruising in your blood stream and checking your body against a perfect standard! You have cholesterol in the main arteries leading to your heart. I have removed the deposits and incorporated the atoms into my own mass! There are other discrepancies scattered within your living flesh. I have altered your body systems to remove them."

Alexander felt another slight sting as Alpha Three released his hand and stood waiting for his reaction.

His first reaction was to study the palm of his glove intently. He could not see a mark anywhere. Was it imagination or did his heart seem to be beating with a better regularity? Until he was checked over by a human doctor he could not be sure of what Alpha Three had done for him! One thing was certain and that the nannite had done him no harm and it was in complete control of its substance. The reality of the situation struck him; - they had succeeded! Fully co-ordinated nannites with free will and artificial intelligence had been achieved. The greatest problem of the Genesis Project had been solved. Once they had fine tuned the personalities of the nannite crews that would ride the 'Hammer Drive' ships then the next desperate attempt to save the life forms of the Earth from the expanding sun could go ahead. At sub-light speeds the life-boats of their civilization could be launched to find another living world to make a new home, leaving the nannites to re-create humanity.

Now they needed to construct the personalities necessary to achieve the aims of the project.

Ten long years had passed and the moon construction complex had produced hundreds of nannites all possessing Alpha One's basic mind. What were needed was a Nano-technologist, astro-navigator, engineer and physicist to lead the expedition. Linked with this would be two genetics engineers, biochemists, human, medical and veterinary experts who would unravel the DNA codes for all Earthly living things and set about re-creating them once a landing was accomplished on a living world.

Psychologists had studied the mission from every angle and had determined that the mind-sets for these three nannites be female constructs, that would bring the natural 'mothering' instincts to the fore. They would be programmed to protect the offspring of their re-created species and keep them safe. It was not enough!

Another artificial mind needed to be added to the mix. What might be needed would be the knowledge of Earth's history including its mistakes. A mission psychologist was needed with a full understanding of weapons and warfare. It would need to be a male mind, able to cope with the idea that the colony must survive at all cost, even at the loss of intelligent life. He would need to be a Nano-tech expert and able to defend the life in his care.

Deep under the moon's surface at Peary crater the construction of the three female nannites was in full swing with the nannite ships that would cross the vastness of interstellar space. One nannite remained to be finished. The names of the female crew had been named from people that had stood out in history. Asue was mission commander, named after a Susan Schmitt who had led the drive for this project. Sharn O'Brien and Minns Chang-soo had both worked on genetic engineering projects that had culminated in the uplifting of apes into true sapience.

Kamiel had been an Arabian leader that had risen against the terrorists that had helped to destroy their own people, by replacing co-operation with hatred. His infiltration of the secret organisations and subsequent destruction of them had led the way back into help to form the world government that funded this desperate project. So far the downloading of personalities had incorporated a Japanese martial arts weapons expert, a professor of history, an ape called Joom who was an expert in interspecies communication and a number of Nano-tech experts. Mingled into this mixture of memories and minds was the need to add the essence of the Genesis Project's director's mind.

Alexander stood up as the silver biped entered the room.

"It is good to meet you again, Project Director," Kamiel said and stood motionless.

"The last time we met you were Alpha Three," Alex replied. "How do you feel about taking on my personality?"

"To be honest, I expect to gain from the experience. Each extra mind that I incorporate into my gestalt gives me a greater insight into the beings that created me! The base computer, Selene is gearing up to do the transfer and once that is complete then I will be copied and sent on my way."

Alexander stood silently for a moment before answering, "Come then, Kamiel and I will add my mind to yours. We shall meet for a brief time afterwards and then I must get the other project started."

The two beings entered the lift and dropped deeper into the moon until they reached the mind transference unit. This part of the schedule was almost entirely run by nannites with two apes and one human waiting for them. There was a large table with two dents facing away from each other with the heads almost touching. Alexander climbed onto one and lay down while Kamiel lay in the other dent. An Alpha Three type nannite placed terminals onto the forehead of the motionless silver being and then Alex felt the sting of the penetration as the connections held. The brainwave patterns rose and fell as Kamiel added the basic tenants of Alexander's mind to his.

Alexander gave the signal with lifting his finger and

Kamiel was switched unknowing into neutral. Now a deeper level of penetration into Kamiel's mind was entered. Here Alexander added his enclosed, unblended, personality to be accessed in times of extreme need. Blocks were inserted so that Kamiel could not access the hidden personality at will. In this place an extra strength would be stored. Another reasoning mind would be stored to help Kamiel make decisions that were beyond his programming levels. Humanities' insurance was being implanted very deep, but there if ever needed. Now his mind would be added again and blended into the mixture that would go towards creating Kamiel's new personality.

He made the flat sign with his hand and allowed Kamiel to return to consciousness. Alexander sighed as the connections were dissolved and wondered if he had done all that he could.

They both stood up and remained still for some time and then Kamiel spoke, "I feel different! I am not the personality that I was! It will take some time to absorb all that you are, Alexander McBald. I am able to understand the greater depths of the Genesis Project from a different perspective! This has to succeed. I will make it work. Somehow, somewhere one of my copies will make it work! I will not allow my creator's people to disappear from this universe."

Alex smiled and answered, "My dear alter ego, all we can do is to send the four of you out there and hope. My heart is heavy in the knowledge that so many of you will perish in the great darkness. You are living and thinking beings in your own right. This is the only way that we can gamble on a very uncertain future. We will all die here when the sun explodes, but something of us may survive in your care. There is a little more for you to learn before we say goodbye. One or more of your copies may find a living world to start again. It's all we have!"

Nearly seven million years from that day, Kamiel remembered that conversation and reflected on the decisions that he had made and the interstellar civilizations that he had brought forth in two galaxies. His mind was created from the best that humanity had to offer, including a Pan-chimpanzee, but it was the guiding mind of Alexander McBald that had made sure that he had made those right decisions. His clone had endured some terrible sufferings from time to time from one re-incarnation after another, but the ultimate end had proved to be satisfactory. Alex had certainly lived a long and eventful life, far beyond the original's intentions. Kamiel was sure that he was happy and content with his alien partner in human form.

When would he stop? When all challenges were gone he supposed, but not for now. He had destroyed the Entity that had tried to feed off the life energies of his creators by destroying Earth's sun. It was ironic that without that willed destruction of the sun; he would never have been created! The Gnathe would have died out and never settled Jupiter after the metamorphosis by the changed sun. He could not think about it all, as it was just too much for his logic circuits and it made his neural nets twitch uncomfortably. It all sat on the edge of too many paradoxes!

Anyway, the galaxy of Andromeda needed to be explored and the emerging galactic civilization to be watched over, just in case!

It had not taken long before the Machine Intelligence, having studied the events that had demonstrated that ways to cross the void by warping space-time were possible, began to unravel the method used by the Lagdoo. The last Ark of the Goss used this method as well as the Gnathen way of opening wormholes with group minds. The Kresh had also used the same method of the Lagdoo, but controlled by the Toarvaks. The one science that the Janise Probe did not posses was that of Nano-technology. This knowledge was kept carefully by the nannite Guardians and had been lost by the humans and the Kresh. The alternative Nano-technology used by the Toarvaks had also been decided to remain off-limits and stayed with them.

It had taken a matter of a few years for the massive co-operative machine intelligence to break the science of wormhole manipulation once it knew that it was possible. The activity of the Toarvaks had aroused its sensors many years before the final confrontation. During the twenty years or so after the destruction of the Harvester, the Janise Probe had diverted its energies into the construction of interstellar probes by the thousands. These it launched to the settled worlds of the new civilization and waited for their return, loaded with information about the organics.

The machine intelligence craved knowledge to enable it to expand and dominate this universe. The Janise had been very territorial due to the influence of the collectors sent by the Harvester to stimulate them into warfare. They had programmed their interstellar probes accordingly. It had discovered the verdant planet a thousand years ago before it had acquired wormhole technology and had set it aside as a world too wet for it to develop. The planet was a Harvester creation that had been seeded a billion years in the past and left to develop. A single moon, large enough to generate tides in the seas, orbited it far enough out to cause weather without flooding the lands.

The rates of corrosion on this world were far too great for it to develop and mine the planet for its ore, while colder, airless worlds were abundant. Now it set up a newly programmed probe to expand its influence. There would be a City to build with a farming complex to develop, with giant storage bins. During the time that the clones took to grow to maturity on the Ark, probes had visited Haven and brought back Pod-vine beans, wheat, fruit trees and as many different vegetables as the probes could find along with the methods to cultivate them. Other worlds had also been visited to provide a varied diet. The one thing that the Janise Probe had not been able to bring back was animal life, as whatever the probes sought to bring back, died in transit.

Link-soo-shan watched the fluid drain away and the tank assume a horizontal position. The woman inside began to breath as the tubes withdrew and Link injected the RNA into the brainstem. She placed the crystal upon her forehead and made the mind-link as the sides retracted.

Nagoth opened her eyes and fixed them upon her creator.

"Where is he? She asked.

Link laughed and shook her head in disbelief.

"All these years and still I am surprised by this emotion called love! I brought him out of the vats a few hours ago. He is fine! Alexander being the person that he is has spent his time since reclaiming his place in the world with his alter ego, Kamiel. He is here now!"

She stepped out of the way and Alexander ducked under Link-soo-shan's arm, standing there with his arms outstretched. He held her tight, ignoring the green viscous liquid that dribbled down her body. Both of them stood naked on the pool of wetness dripping into the drain, oblivious to the crowd of friends that had gathered to see them.

Nagoth continued to hold tight onto the human male that she had given her love to so many years ago when she was Gnathe. She looked around at the crowd of alien beings that had joined the human throng to welcome them back from the vats. There were Thipdar, Vogb, Bazantii and many more that she did not recognise gathered here for the awakening. Standing out from the throng were humans and apes who she had got to know during the years leading up to the final confrontation with the Harvester.

She cupped Alex's face in her hands and asked, "If I may state the obvious, Alex, I take it that we won?"

Alexander laughed and replied, "We won! The abomination has been destroyed and all we have to do is to hunt down the collectors that are still scattered across Andromeda. All the worlds at risk from the impending collision with our old galaxy have been moved across the nebulae to the other side. We have new worlds to cultivate and colonise. There are many empty worlds that the Harvester seeded billions of years ago to be brought into our influence."

Kamiel spoke to everybody, "Friends I have a proposition to make. The struggle is now over and we can make our decisions as to what we want to do in this future that belongs to us. We are all on the Ark in orbit around Haven. Those who would wish to live there can disembark during the few weeks ahead that the Ark remains here. Much of this galaxy is unexplored and there are many planets that the Harvester seeded with life that do not play host to intelligent life. I propose to take the Ark on a long voyage of discovery out to the far reaches of a spiral arm and explore. Let us look for a new world of our own. The Federation of Planets no longer needs us to guide them in their decisions. Already the government of the federation is being taken over by the Tran-sentients that have been transferred here by us. The mantle of the Goss extends throughout the Andromeda reaches from every star travelling civilization that became involved in the destruction of the Harvester."

"It would then appear that we can have a rest from struggling to survive and just explore until we find a vacant world to make our own," Alexander said. "Would anyone mind if we left you all and had a shower. We could also do with a meal and some privacy?"

A nannite threw a towel over each of them and led the way to the showers and their rooms. Once they had removed all traces of the green fluid that they had spent eighteen years in the vats growing into adulthood in, they lay together on top of their bed and rediscovered each other. Now they were aware of hunger for food and asked the table for newly baked bread with two hot-pots. They watched as the food materialised from out of the table's surface and set to, in dipping the bread and spooning the easily digested hot meal into their hungry mouths. Their dietary requirements had been carefully monitored by the nannites, who had overseen their growth inside the tanks and each bowl held just enough to quell their hunger pains. Later when their new bodies had adjusted to the outside world, they would be allowed to choose what they ate and how much. Now they both felt the need to be dressed and to once more talk to Kamiel about where he suggested they go.

Throughout the emerging civilizations the machine intelligence had watched and studied the biological units that ran the affairs of the emerging federation with curiosity. There was a great deal that it still needed to know about these creatures. The Janise probe was limited to waiting for its probes to return through the wormholes and speed of light communication. It soon found out that the biological units had not only independent free will, but could communicate across the stellar distances instantaneously. Slowly the machine intelligence realised that some of the biological units communicated be sound and some by light patterns. It dug deep into its memory banks and saw that the Janise had communicated also by sound. It had been so many thousands of years ago, it had almost forgotten! It ran a parallel analysis

The one fact that eluded it was the use of telepathy and other psychic powers. Gradually the Janise probe began to feel threatened, as it found out more and more about the abilities of these creatures that made them competitors. The Federation of Worlds continued to expand, as new planets were discovered that had been created by the Harvester that were empty of intelligent life.

CHAPTER TWO

Haven had been left far behind and the Ark had made its way out of the emerging Galactic Federation of Worlds, exploring the spiral arm that was furthest from the intersecting point of the colliding galaxies. Kamiel had plotted a course around the lethal centre of the Andromeda star system that would take them far away from the dominant, super black hole that the whole galaxy swung around. It would take many hundreds of millions of years for an effect if any that would influence any of the star systems on this side of the Catherine wheel.

Many years had passed with the majority of the exploring colonists held in stasis until the last Ark of the Goss exited the latest wormhole and began the slow drop towards the yellow sun. The Lagdoo, who managed the Ark, gave instructions to 'wake up' the life systems. Artificial sunlight poured down onto the ice-covered landscapes warming the frozen seas and bringing the soil back to be capable of supporting life. The great melt began and once again rivers began to flow across the land, irrigating the dry areas. Great areas of forest that had been put into stasis were brought back into the timeline once the soil had warmed. The plains were seeded with millions of seeds by the nannites who also stepped out of the stasis chambers. Once biological growth began again and life returned to the inside of the Ark, insects and lower orders of animals were released across the artificial living world. It would take ten years before the life was established enough to allow the intelligent members of the expedition to exit the stasis chambers and wander at will across the newly refurbished lands.

As the Ark passed one of the outer gas giants, a cloud of metallic probes matched velocity with the hollow moon and allowed the feeble gravity of the Ark to pull them down onto the regolith. Unseen and un-detected the tiny probes soon began their mission. Once down onto the surface they collected together and re-assembled themselves into boring machines. At the moment that was all they needed to do. It would be some time before enough of their deliberately constructed kind, were numerous enough to achieve sentience. The Janise probe was patient. It had waited longer than a million orbits of its base planet around the star for the Janise to come. It had adapted to the long wait. After the territorial wars with each other the machine intelligence had merged itself and grown sentient far beyond the level that its old masters had intended, never the less the original territorial programming still dominated the roots of its being.

The years passed and the interior of the Ark once again swarmed with life, as it fell steadily towards the sun. Many of the different alien races that had fought against the Harvester had decided to come on the Ark's odyssey of discovery along this unexplored arm of the Andromeda star systems. Using the Goss as a common translator the differences in shape were soon forgotten and the strangest of partnerships settled into alliances of similar purpose. Although all aliens had the scientific background to draw upon, few chose to live in this advanced world. The nannites ran all aspects dealing with the propulsion of the Ark and the science that kept it going. The Toarvak ships supplied the means of travelling between the stars and planets using the group mind link-up of five 'new Kresh' minds and the artificial mind of the Toarvak itself. It was the Toarvak ships that built any new vessels required, by 'budding off' replicates of themselves and joining the buds together. Similarly the

Guardians had their own way of reproducing more of their kind, keeping this a secret from organic minds. The method was deemed so dangerous to all life forms, that just as the first experiments were done in orbit, in case of abrupt termination and jettison into the sun, new nannites were created in outer space. The original creators were no longer involved and left the artificial minds to their own devices.

The approach to the new world had entered its final stage. The Ark had entered the orbital 'kiss' that would tie the artificial world to the magnificent planet below.

Kamiel and Asue linked themselves into the forward sensors and examined the results. There, floating like a blue and green jewel was a product of the Harvester's actions. A moon orbited at the correct distance to produce tides and weather.

On the way in they had noticed several large gas giants orbited the star at the right distance to mop up any incoming comets, while a number of smaller ones stretched out to a cometary halo. The Guardians had observed that some moons large enough to have an atmosphere orbited several of the various gas planets. From the data collected it was obvious to the nannites that the whole system was an artificial construction put together by the Harvester. The orbital distances from the star at the centre were not sitting in the proper situations for their masses. The gas giants had been collected from somewhere else and placed in orbit. They would never have condensed from the debris of the infant star in such a pattern. They were far too big for a star of this size and magnitude to form as they had.

Asue was sure that they had been moved from a much larger star to their positions here. The moons in orbit around the gas giants showed that they condensed much nearer into another stars reach, as they had a high metal content. They must have been born much closer to a star and been moved through space to here. The question that needed to be answered was why? She put this issue to the back of her mind for another day and considered the planet that the Ark was now in orbit around. This world had a molten iron core that produced an acceptable magnetic field that deflected the cosmic ray output from the parent star, ionising the otherwise deadly particles and producing an aurora borealis at both poles.

The planet had abundant water and was encircled by great seas with large continents straddling the globe at both poles. A ring of large islands stretched around the northern seas joining the polar continent down to a smaller one at the equator. These were the tips of extinct volcanoes on the edge of a tectonic plate that had ceased to slide underneath the polar continent. A more active line had breached along the plate that was colliding with the equatorial land mass. Some of the islands were several hundred miles across and also in length. The largest of them all lay fifty miles from the polar continent and stopped short of the equator by a hundred miles. It was three hundred miles across at its widest. Rivers ran down from a glacier that dominated the high mountain range in the centre of the island. Wide flat plains spread out from the foothills until the land met the sea.

Two rivers ran each side of a large peninsular from two artificial dams, built higher up. Thousands of square miles of cultivated ground that was irrigated from these dams spread across the land beneath. Roads led to a city that sat a few miles from the sea that could support hundreds of thousands of people. Along those roads travelled vehicles of some kind, all hauling harvested crops into the metropolis.

Asue and Kamiel increased magnification to view the situation with greater clarity and were stunned with what they saw. No matter where they searched with the scanner, not a trace of a living person could be seen. Even stranger were the crops being tended in the fields by mechanical means. They knew everything being grown as food, down on the world below, was eaten by all of the aliens on board the Ark.

Kamiel reached out with his mind, using the living piece of flesh hosting the Goss, to all members of the guiding council.

"Could you all make your way to the control-centre? We have some amazing information to share with you all. This world has seems to have been settled by our people many years ago, but we know that cannot be possible, as we have never ventured this way before. Come and see what we have transmitted to the viewing screens."

Soon the control centre was filled with representatives of all sentient beings all watching the screens intently. Humans, Gnathe, Kresh, Vogb, Bazantii and Thipdar all stared at the screens and relayed the amazing pictures to the rest of their people. Most incredibly the city seemed to be purpose built so that it could assimilate every species that inhabited the Ark.

Alex spoke first and said; "I think that we need to send down a scouting party to explore the city using Toarvak 6 to ferry us down there. I can see no reason to be over cautious, as whatever built this city and tilled the fields must have been expecting us to eventually reach this place. The rest of this world seems to be empty and this is the only part that has been built upon. What do the rest of you think?"

The Janise probe's infiltration of the Ark was wide spread. The individual units that had tunnelled through the regolith had re-grouped into many different types of information gathering machines. They were all sending data to the copy of the Janise machine intelligence that was built deep below the city. As much of the dialog, was passed around by the aliens by telepathy the probes registered the silence to the puzzled guiding mind. By studying the organic creatures on their home-worlds the hundreds of thousands of probes had built up a data-base that pointed to some kind of transmission of signals that the Janis Probe could not enter. It also examined the data concerning the nannites and their form of communication that was not too different to its own. There was one form of communication that seemed to need the nourishment of an organic living base commonly a host to another organism. This blending of inorganic to organic was a new concept. It realised that the silver beings must be the next step up from its own mechanical existence. Studying the basic information in the data banks on their construction, the Janise probe realised that these beings could be neutralised. Separating the organics from these self appointed Guardians would need to be a priority. The next thing that it needed to do would be to disrupt the soundless communication that each alien species had to each other. It examined the records that were kept of the 'Games' played in the arena. Here and within no other area only sound or light were used to speak with each other or the form of communication that the nannites needed the organic pouch for. It had taken some time, but probes that had infiltrated home and colonised worlds had brought back from these lightly guarded data banks, information about psychic powers that certain of the organics used. Inside the bridge over the arena was a device that would cancel all psychic power depending on its strength of broadcast.

The Janise probe dismantled the shielding device and brought it down through the regolith until it was placed into a return vehicle assembled from the parts of the mining machines that had tunnelled through from the inside. A number of cracks zigzagged through the nearby mountains causing a mass of debris to fly off the rotating hollow moon. Amongst the cloud of falling boulders was the returning mechanism fixed between two of the largest pieces. As the debris hit the atmosphere the device released and opened wings to glide away from the mass.

Inside the control centre Asue and Kamiel noticed that some small boulders and debris had detached from their eon's position in the mountains and flown off towards the planet below.

"That looks to be due to centrifugal force, Kamiel. Maybe we should send a crew of nannites outside to check on the safety situation," Asue remarked.

"Small pieces of the ark do occasionally fly off as the mountains are always loosening," Kamiel replied. If it happens again we could do a check, but I think that taking the age of the Ark into account, it's a wonder that we don't see more substantial boulders fly off when we spin up the moon. We have something more to consider down there. Who or what built the City and why? Now that poses more of a conundrum than anything else!"

Alexander considered the situation and said, "As I said, we have to go down there and find out all we can. From up here it looks a perfect home for all of us in the Ark that have travelled to this world. One thing for sure we won't find out in orbit around the place! I propose that we board Toarvak 6 and go down there."

With that decision made a crew was soon assembled from the assortment of beings inhabiting the Ark. Humans, Thipdar, Gnathe, Kresh, Bazantii, Lagdoo and Vogb assembled their scientific instruments and quickly got them on board. Also all of the Trans-sentients entered the Toarvak to explore the world below, eager to feel the force of the winds over the landmasses of the new world.

The Janise probe watched all this and waited until almost all of the organics had boarded and began to slow the hollow moon's rotation. At the same time it opened cracks in the regolith to allow the air to escape.

Prim, first of family Smelch, was a Thipdar female who had fought and defeated the Goss. Once the Harvester had been destroyed she and her family had decided to follow Kamiel and those who had also decided to go with him. She was the first to notice that the Lagdoo were exhibiting the unusual emotion of alarm as they tried to speed up the moon's rotation without success. She merged her mind with the collective, swept the instruments and gave the alarm to the others.

When the carrier reached the area of the city it tipped downwards and dropped through a tunnel that would lead down to the Janise probe, deep beneath the city. From here the crystal was taken rapidly to the arch that spanned the city and fitted into the prepared circuits that reached across the city skies. Now, all the Janise probe needed to do was to wait. Many miles away where the twin dams held the river fed reservoirs back, an increased flow was engineered through the turbines and massive currents of electricity diverted to the cities immediate need.

With the alarm given, Alexander's idea of a scouting party soon turned into an exodus as unforeseen developments began to take place. Unaware of the preparations that were being put into action below them, the inhabitants of the Ark were now loading all of themselves onto Toarvak 6 for immediate departure. For an unknown reason the spin of the Ark was slowing down and the Lagdoo could not trace any faults. If they did not return the habitat inside the hollow moon, back to an 'at rest system' then the seas would spill out of the basins and flood the lands, eventually filling the inside spaces. Without the artificial gravity to keep things in place the whole system would collapse. Also the inside of the hollow moon was losing air through cracks in the regolith. Soon the whole of the inside of the Ark would be incapable of supporting life. The majority of the nannites stated that they would stay on board close the systems down and track down the problems while the organics stayed on the planet below them until all was safe.

With an increasing sense of urgency the biological members of the Ark shepherded their animals into the stables prepared by Toarvak 6 and those in stasis into storage ready to be activated once they were safely down.

Even given Tee 6's ability to change shape and expand, it was a tight squeeze to get them all inside. The Toarvak let go of the Ark and began to fall gently towards the planet below and the waiting city. The city had been constructed and built in concentric circles with broad highways between the buildings. Bridges connected tall skyscrapers across these roads and a great arch spanned the city high up above them with spider-web filaments joining together to form a great dome over the complete city. There was a large hole in the web to the side of the arch, big enough for the Toarvak to float through and a flat area suitable to land on letting several thousand people off.

Kamiel, Asue Minnis and Solace were the only nannites to disembark with the organics and watched the approaching city from one of the observation chambers morphed by Toarvak 6 on the outside of her silver, donut-shape. In the centre of the flat area there was a landing spire for the Toarvak to settle over and attach to. Balancing the internal forces at her command of being out of phase, the ship drifted over the spire and descended gently onto the surface of the landing field. She made contact with the flat surface and switched her entire substance into the universe of the world around her.

The moment that the pressure sensitive pads constructed over the landing area felt the weight of the ship, the Janise probe struck. Massive amounts of electrical energy fed into the iron base under the Toarvak, expanding a magnetic field around the ship.

Toarvak 6 found that she could not go out of phase and was being forced to shut down its systems. While she still could, she opened all doors to the outside to allow her boarders to escape. The Janise probe watched the abrupt exodus through its immediate sensors and waited for all the organics to disembark. It was most interested in the whereabouts of the nannites and waited for them to show before it ramped up the field. After a short period of time the aliens had massed into individual groups and were all staring back at the silver donut with apprehension.

Kamiel, Asue and Solace struggled to get out of the Toarvak's nannite embrace as they too began to suffer from the fluctuating magnetic field. Their biped shape began to become harder and harder to maintain. Neural pathways were showing disruption and the nannites could only concentrate their energies into keeping their identities intact. As the magnetic force intensified they found it necessary to encapsulate their minds to protect them from the effects of the energy field.

Alexander watched in horror as his nannite friends began to melt and lose their shape.

"Get them away from the ship," he cried. "Larse, can you find Tee 6's avatar and try to get her outside before the ship starts to dissolve.

Before Emelia could protest, Larse was running back into the sagging corridors towards the control room where the essence of Tee 6 was trying her best to combat the onslaught raining against her. As he burst through the opening he saw his nannite 'mother' dissolving into the deck of Toarvak 6. He ran to her side and wrapped his hands around 'her' shoulders.

Using the Goss he drove his mind into hers and demanded, "Flow into me. Let me carry you outside the ship or you will lose your identity. I can take your substance as I once did. No arguments! We can share you once I get you to safety."

Tee 6 did not argue and flowed along his arms until the majority of her mass rested over his shoulders. The ceiling began to dip down towards them and Larse turned and ran as fast as he could, carrying the weight of the nannite being. Behind him the corridors began to sag and close solid even as Tee 6 did her best to keep Toarvak 6's walls ridged. The doughnut shape was becoming solid and super dense under the Janise probe's tremendous magnetic onslaught. Larse hurled himself through the narrowing opening and skidded to a halt on his chest and stomach. The heavy weight of Tee 6 nearly pinned him to the ground as he struggled to get to his feet, helped by Emelia and Alexander.

All of the beings stared at the shrinking Toarvak, as its nannite structure pulled inwards, evermore increasing its density. Far above them the spider-web cover rapidly filled in the hole that Toarvak 6 had entered the city by and began to strengthen itself. Soon all sign of their entrance had gone.

At the same time far above them the ark broke orbit and began to slowly drift towards the sun. The nannites on board now had another problem to deal with and were also aware that all contact had been lost with the organic members of the Ark. Also all power had failed to the inside of the Ark and it was getting very cold. This did not bother the nannites, but it soon killed the small ball of flesh that was host to the Goss that some of them carried inside them. Without that small piece of host the nannites could not communicate their problems back to the civilization that lay back in the Andromeda galaxy. Using radio waves would take hundreds of years at light speed to contact the Guardians elsewhere and since landing in the city all contact with Kamiel, Asue and Solace had been lost. All the nannites could do was to try and trace the increasing faults of the drive system of the Ark and repair it before they fell too close to the sun and had to abandon the ancient weapon. So far not one of the invading machines had been sensed and the nannites were unaware that they were under attack.

High above the city, imbedded in the arch that spanned the highest buildings, the crystal from the arena began to receive the power necessary to activate it. The Janise probe had studied the circuits on the Ark, well before removing it and realised that the crystal was delicate. It carefully fed alternating current into the circuits that it had copied from the set-up that it had removed, slowly building up the range, as the crystal warmed up. The probe also activated the defence system that it had installed all across the dome shaped web.

Stunned by the speed of the attack, the inhabitants of the Ark were not sure what to do next, as they instinctively grouped together within their own species. The Trans-sentients inflated their gasbags and began to drift steadily upwards to study the web, arched above the city, looking for a way out. Swivel mounted lightning conductors swung round to face each other as the inflated gasbags took the Trans-sentients between them. Thousands of volts spat their charges through the intelligent creatures cooking them, as they hung helplessly suspended by their floatation bags. As the air filled with their screams the lower ones deflated rapidly and sank to the ground to tendril level.

Amongst the many different alien species the ability to read each other's minds abruptly began to wane and with it their natural psychic powers. Alexander wrestled Larse to his feet and held him unsteadily upright as chaos began to unravel around them. Tee 6 began to separate and creep down the Norseman's arm and onto Alexander's body where it soaked into his nervous system. Emelia and Nagoth immediately joined the union to help carry the nannite's substance. By the side of them, Kamiel, Asue and Solace had altered their shape to a hard silver ball under the onslaught of the intense magnetic field using all their internal power to hold onto their personalities. Each one of them was locked into their own un-escapable universe of self, unable to communicate with each other or their human friends.

Link-soo-shan had watched the exodus with grim anticipation waiting for the next attack. She had seen how the nannites had shrunk into tight silver balls and felt the telepathic silence descend. Larse had disappeared into the stricken Toarvak and returned with Tee 6 draped across his shoulders. She made her way towards the group as the nannite spread herself across the four humans. Quickly she joined the gestalt and took her fifth of the remains of the Toarvak. Locked together they could make telepathic contact and speak to each other. Tucked into Link-soo-shan's wrist pockets were two command crystals and at her throat she carried a telekinetic one to enable her to teleport.

The gnathe's mind entered the gestalt and said, "My friends we have been enticed into a trap. Even the Goss has become silent. I suggest that we regroup away from this area and see if our nannite companions change back into their usual shapes? I will fetch a carrier beast from my people and we will load these silver balls onto them and take them into the city. That is where I think we will have to go for shelter and food."

"I agree, old friend. We may have to use sign language to persuade the others to follow us into what may be an extension of the trap, but I do not feel that we have much choice," Alexander replied. "We have the option of dying of thirst and hunger or moving into the city."

Link-soo-shan broke away and quickly made her way over to the groups of Gnathe and soon she had led away a carrier-beast to load the inert Guardians into, while the others began to make their way into the city. The idea of shelter and food was soon informed to the other aliens and the thousands of different types began to make their way away from the stricken Toarvak. The surviving Trans-sentients picked up the Vogb and Thipdar groups who did not move very well over long distances and set them onto their backs, being very careful not to float too high. On the way to the city they had to pass the burnt corpses of the others of their group. Whatever had trapped them had demonstrated that any attempts to escape would be ruthlessly dealt with.

They soon found that whatever force had made the nannites shut down also made it impossible to move them. The three silver balls remained welded to the landing field and when Larse attempted to try and lift one, the electric shock hurled him howling to his knees. The burns on the palms of his hands showed the controlled electrical power of their adversary. He had been warned, but not damaged.

Alexander looked around the group of humans and apes searching for Hannah and Fredrick. They were also suffering from trying to lift the nannite, Minnis, away from the landing field. Fredrick was knelt by the side of his friend and attempting another lift using his jacket as an insulator. Before he could even wrap the jacket around the silver ball, a large hole appeared in the surface and a number of mechanical creatures began to pour out. As they advanced they combined into larger units. They were constructed like giant spiders in so much that they had six legs and a dish shaped body and two arms. The inside of the dish was a continuation of the smaller units all linked together and universally integrated. The units advanced towards the big human and remorselessly drove him away. More of the units began to advance upon the other silver balls, dragging large thick discs attached by heavy cables that extended down under the landing field. These disks were secured to the back of the largest units and the things scuttled up to the helpless nannites.

Alex yelled out to Fred, "Leave her Fred. There is nothing that we can do. So far no one has been killed except some of the Trans-sentients. Lets try and keep it that way!"

They watched helpless as all four silver balls were loaded onto the discs and the mechanoids disappeared back underground.

CHAPTER THREE

Alexander drew a shuddering breath and then another. He opened his eyes to a blue sky blazing with the light of a familiar sun. Clouds swept by high up above, building thunder-heads far away. Occasional beams of golden light filtered through the clouds and warmed him with their touch. He unsteadily sat up, shivered as the breeze caressed his naked skin and suddenly realised that he was alive! Not only that. But his body was young and healthy with no trace of age at all. Stood quite close was a familiar silvery being that he knew so well.

Alexander asked, "Where am I, this time, Kamiel?"

The enigmatic nannite answered "You could also ask, when am I?"

Alexander shakily stood up and really looked around at his surroundings. He was standing on a grassy plain, studded with trees and bushes. Not too far away were groups of buildings that blended into the scenery. Silver figures were busy at countless tasks dotted over fields and meadows that stretched into the distance, rising in all directions. All at once Alex could see the strange perspective that troubled his eyes. He was stood on the inside face of a giant bowl. No! It was a sphere that extended in all directions very like the last Ark of the Goss, but Alexander could feel the pull of gravity under his feet. He shielded his eyes from the sunlight and stared into the sky to realise that a multitude of suns were providing the light.

"Kamiel old friend there must be much I need to know. Do you have the knowledge to explain to me just what has happened to us?"

"We have worked on this project for hundreds of

millions of years under the guidance of the being that you named The Farmer. Now it is ready for the next stage. Be prepared, for your child approaches," the Guardian replied.

A hole in space opened and closed and Shoolin-Alexis stood before him. The being that link-soo-shan had genetically designed no longer took the image of a girl and a boy joined by their hands. Now Alexander and Nagoth's child had gone beyond the need to hold a physical identity. Instead a multi coloured glowing egg that pulsed in size from about his size to a point of light and back again, hung in the air before him. It was difficult for him to remember that the being was in fact three sets of twins mentally inseparable.

A gentle voice thrust itself into his mind and said, "Welcome father! It is good to see you after such millennia have passed. I expect that you will remember nothing of the eons spent within the mantle of the being called Farmer! It would speak to you through me and explain."

Alexander stared at the being that floated in the air before him and waited.

"I am pleased that you are still as I accepted you into my firmament. It was you and your alter ego, Kamiel that destroyed the 'first-one,' leaving ME to evolve into the being that I have become. Understand if you can, that I am the sum total of every sentient thing in all of the galaxies that made up the universe and as such have determined that when this universe dies, we will endure until the emptiness reforms through another Big Bang.

From raw energy into matter came life. This was repeated throughout the universe in galaxy after galaxy. Sentient life evolved over and over again and in its turn created a life-form constructed by using nanotechnology. These artificial intelligences have proved themselves invaluable to my plan. I have built with the help of these nannites, a Dyson sphere that is far larger in diameter than your planet's orbit around its star. In the centre is a new G type star that I have created from the last wisps of interstellar hydrogen. It is the very last star to be created in this universe and will serve its purpose for at least ten billion years. The inside of the sphere has a surface area of some one hundred and twenty-five, thousand, million square miles. There is plenty of room for every life form to exist and plenty of time as the star should last at least ten billion years!

Do not think that you can escape the gravity well that holds you fast to the earth of this artificial world. There are mechanisms that exist between the this star and yourselves that will give you night and day. They also alter the wavelengths of the light given by this star to approximate the 'sunshine that your individual needs require. Encompassing this source of energy is the shell of the sphere.

Every sentient life-form that evolved in the original universe is here or will soon be here with their attendant life-forms. Soon the universe outside will die and I will take this sphere out of phase with it before that occurs and wait for the timeless period to come. Once the last photon has decayed then nothing will exist in this plane at all. The great 'rip' will occur again and this time I will guide the formation of matter to be more compatible with ours. Anti-matter and dark matter will be adjusted so that the next universe will last a thousand times the length of time that this one has. I have the understanding of the power that the Janise unleashed, to convert energy into mass. It is this that will enable ME to build a better universe without leaving it to chance.

I do not wish to be extinguished and I feel that the life that has evolved in this universe will continue to evolve until the next stage is reached. Eons from now you and the other sentient creatures will find a myriad of galaxies at your disposal, but this time they will have been properly designed and not left to chance."

The voice in his mind ceased to be with him and he was aware that his child was back with him again.

Alexander turned and spoke to Shoolin-Alexis and asked, "Will the being be successful? You are able to see in the future. Can you not do that and tell me?"

"Should I try to do that and find myself outside of this encapsulated universe then I too could be extinguished! I'm sorry father, but the future is one place that I will not go, until it arrives at its own pace," the star-child replied. "This inside-out world has been frozen in time for trillions of years. Situated around the sphere are located crystals mined from millions of gas giants over the millenniums that have passed since this project was begun. There are billions of them enabling the combined gestalt that the Farmer has become, to control space and time within the confines of the sphere. Once the outside of the sphere had been finished by the nannites and hardened beyond diamonds into a perfect reflective surface, the interior was sculpted into living space for every type of sentient being."

Kamiel put his hand upon Alexander's shoulder and added, "It has been a very long time since I have spoken to a sentient being made of flesh and blood. Your race created us eons ago without realising the potential that they unleashed upon the universe. The construction of the Dyson sphere was the very project that we were inadvertently designed to do. Outside of this sphere the universe has run down. Every black hole has evaporated and every star has degenerated to a black husk. Matter is coming apart at the atomic level and soon all photons will have evaporated. It is only the power of the Farmer's mind that is holding this tiny remnant of the old universe intact."

Alexander opened his mind and reached out to the

entity that had served him for centuries, "Goss?"

There was an eerie silence.

"Where is everybody, Kamiel? I have opened my mind to catch a thought and what was once alive with chatter is now silent," Alex asked his friend.

"They have not yet been awoken and given corporeal existence. You are the first that the overmind has chosen to re-create," Kamiel replied.

The star-child spoke inside the human's mind and said, "Fear not, father. I have spent eons of time working with this entity. Its goals are beyond anything that you can imagine. I trust it and so must you. What its ultimate ambition is, is beyond even our scope of intellect. The one thing that is certain, it is determined to save all the sentient species that used to inhabit the old universe and give them a fresh start in a new and planned universe. The being believes that once a timeless state exists beyond the confines of this sphere then conditions will be ripe for an outpouring of energy that will create a new universe! Once that state ensues, this containment will surf that outpouring of energy while the Farmer shapes the universe to come. What we are dealing with here is a being that is the sum total of trillions upon trillions of sentient beings. All I can tell you is that it needs something to complete its destiny and that need has driven its existence to exceed the constraints of the old universe. The reason that we are here at all is the fact that you and I brought this creature into being. We created it, when we destroyed its maker. In return it has kept us aware of its plans and it is grateful for what we did eons ago! Since that time many of the races that administrated the galaxies have evolved into beings similar to what you see before you. We also will be ready to assist, when the 'jump' into the new universe takes place."

Alexander sat down upon the grassy bank and tried to

understand what his nannite friend and mentor had informed him and what part he had played in the cascading surge of events. More than ever in his life he needed his friends and most of all he needed Nagoth! There was a shimmer in the air beside him and she appeared. Alex watched spellbound as she drew her first breath and then another. He felt her mind come into existence as she opened her eyes and looked into his. All around him the air shimmered as more and more of his alien and human friends 'popped' into existence. The silence of the single mind turned into the background 'chatter' of sentient thought. With the coming into existence of so many sentient creatures came the re-emergence of the symbiont simply called 'The Goss. Mindless when isolated it became the combined connection to all sentient species that carried its spores within their living flesh.

Alexander tried again and opened his mind to the symbiont, "Goss?"

"I am here Alexander! I am here! I have been somewhere else for a very long time," the symbiont replied. "I am filling up with data from all manner of beings. As more come into existence, the more I approach the completeness that I once attained."

Alex breathed a sigh of relief as the sentient's instant telepathy exchange quickly ratcheted back into existence. Without the attributes of the Goss it would have been impossible to have any communication with many of the sentient and very alien beings that once made up the great federation of worlds. There was an aura of bewilderment amongst the newly resurrected. All of them could vaguely remember being part of a vast entity for an impossible to calculate time, but nothing else.

The mind of Link-soo-shan reached out via the Goss and remarked, "I 'see' you Alexander it seems that we have been granted another life-span. It would appear that we are to lead an agrarian life for a while. I am sure that the being that we came to know as the Farmer has a purpose that we will have to fulfil. I have been resurrected amongst many of my kind, as it would appear that you have also. We must organise ourselves with the help of the nannites and await events. It would seem that we have sheltered accommodation to suit us all, whatever type of sentient being we are. I for one am surprisingly hungry. We will meet later, my old friend and trade experiences!"

Alex agreed with the Gnathen brood-mother and regained a standing position, embraced Nagoth and turned to Kamiel and said, "I take it that those buildings over there are our living quarters? Did you think to provide clothing for the multitude of beings that have been brought back into the world?"

Kamiel laughed and answered, "My dear old friend we have had millennia to plan and get ready for your coming. The only thing we do not know for certain is how long it will be before we cross over into the new universe. This entire sphere and everything in it went out of phase with the rest of the universe just before you came back into existence. We no longer exist in that realm. I have seen for myself the evaporation of the last of the black holes. The last stars have long ago guttered out like candles pinched on the wick. These have already begun the collapse of matter and even the sub-atomic level is weakening. The boson particles are losing their unifying grasp on gravity and are disintegrating into the last photons. Soon all vestiges of energy will have nullified and the timeless state will occur, for without mass there can be no time. Once that stage entails then a quantum entanglement will occur. How that will happen is somehow tied to the existence of our benefactor and its inspired guess! More than that, I cannot tell you. It is enough for now that you have been brought back into our encapsulated universe to play a part in the Farmer's plan."

Alex stared at the nannites enigmatic features and tried to wind his mind around what the Guardian had tried to explain, whilst they walked towards the settlement that the nannites had provided. Nagoth stopped them for a moment and kissed him, pressing her naked flesh against him.

At his automatic reaction, she smiled and said, "Well, something has not changed, thank goodness," and she bit his ear.

Some weeks later Alexander called for a conference amongst the sentient people that had aided in the rooting out of the last of the Janis probes and also the destruction of The Harvester.

Once again the Goss spread itself throughout the regions allocated to the combined group of galaxies that had once been the 'local family' of Andromeda the Milky Way and the greater and lesser Magellanic clouds. The nannite population had once again taken the step of keeping a nurtured piece of living flesh infected with the spores of the Goss. This enabled them to hear and send thoughts to organic beings. This was not on purpose a group mind or gestalt, but a host of participating individual personalities.

Alexander opened the debate with the question, "Has anyone found a boundry to the area that we find ourselves in?"

Many minds conferred and reported back, "Yes!"

A quick decision and one mind confirmed to the multitude, "There are boundaries that will not allow a person to travel continuously in one direction. I have been to such a place and found that I was returning to the very place that I had set out from. Others have found this to be so. We are contained. It is a vast containment stretching over a billion square miles, but it is a set-down area for us to live in. Within those boundaries are areas that are better suited for some life-forms than others. In these areas the sun sheds a different light and is filtered in some way."

Another powerful mind entered the conversation and remarked, "We are content with what we have and are satisfied with what has been provided. I speak for the Kresh when I say that we will miss our sentient vessels that took us and all who needed one across the galaxy, but we are confidant that our willing partners will be resurrected as were we. If we are to be able to explore a new universe we will need these ships and I am sure that we will be provided with them when the time is right."

Into the silence Kamiel's thoughts gently added, "Believe me, my organic friends, I can assure you that this Dyson Sphere is not intended as a prison, but is intended as a jumping off place. I have worked with the being that has brought all of us together again for millenniums to build this encapsulated universe and believe me this is just the beginning."

CHAPTER FOUR

Deep beneath the surface of the world that had appeared to be all that the inhabitants of the Ark could possibly want, four nannite beings considered their situation. The reinforced glass was alive with high voltage. Only the soft iron discs that they stood upon were insulated from the power diverted through the wire mesh immersed in the glass. Each disc stood on a pedestal anchored into the base of the deadly containment.

Minnis spoke to the others using their private band, "There is a way out of this place, but we have to consider what the Janise Probe will make of it."

Kamiel reflected on his creation's statement and realised what she meant.

"Of course! You can go out of phase," he replied. "Can you expand your substance to safely encase us all?"

"Do you want to stay here for ever? Of course I can! I was able to shield two humans, a Kresh and a Vogb. I am sure that I can expand sufficient to encapsulate three nannites! What we must do, we must do quickly, before the Janise Probe returns its consciousness back to this area. It will have us under observation. Asue and Solace jump to Kamiel's platform at speed. The moment that you have made contact with him I will leap over you and put you all inside my bubble. I will then switch us out of phase and allow us to drift through the containment. How far we will have to travel through the earth I cannot say. All I can promise is that we will come out somewhere!"

Asue and Solace jumped across the spaces between the discs and were caught by Kamiel. Immediately behind them came Minnis. The nannite spread out her substance until it covered all three Guardians and flowed underneath them.

She then took them all out of phase with the universe and the four of them plunged through the spaces between the atoms. Maddeningly slowly the combined nannites sank through the side of the containment as the planet rotated away from them around its sun. With no points of reference, Minnis could do no more than keep them all safely out of phase. Kamiel quickly realised that all they could do was to penetrate the rocks of this world until they were able to exit somewhere on the other side and leave their prison behind them.

The Janise Probe was alerted to the abruptly empty chamber by its surveillance systems. It watched the digital footage of the three nannites clumping together and the fourth one encapsulate the others. They disappeared immediately from all of its surveillances at that moment. Even when the Probe slowed the sequence down it made no difference. One moment these beings that willingly served the organics were there, the next moment they were gone.

For the first time during the plan's execution the Janise Probe felt unease. It had been sure that the prison that it had built to keep these sentient competitors was impossible for the nannites to escape from. It immediately began to build more super magnets around the city. It was sure that even if the nannites could escape from the underground tomb, they could not penetrate the city's defences. Over the top of the city the night sky sparkled with aurora borealis.

From that morning the Janise probe had no need to communicate with its captives and left them to their own devices. Wherever they explored, small spider-like robotic extensions followed them around. If they got too close to any sensitive equipment the miniature spy units combined and reassembled into larger modules, barring the way.

Alexander sought out the Gnathe and soon found Link-soo-shan and her brood daughters Suzzan and Trann. They were in a compound set inside a large clearing between the buildings. The Janise Probe had taken Banilik seedlings and planted them and produced a living home for the Gnathe. They had been cultivated the Gnathen way to become a place for the Gnathe contingent to feel comfortable within its living walls.

Alexander stopped and gave a few whistles and chirrups in Gnathe to show that he was there. Link and her daughters appeared from inside and pushed the foliage away.

"Why not use the telepathic link?" Link asked.

"We are watched continuously," Alex replied mentally and added, "It may be an advantage that the Probe does not realise that some of us can communicate by our minds, using Tee 6 as a bridge."

Suzzan swept the area around Alex and noticed the small spider-like devices hanging amongst the branches. There was one sat upon Alex's shoulder and she knew that it was relaying everything that happened back to the central brain.

"It is good to see you old friend," whistled Trann. "What brings you here?"

"I came to see if the Janise Probe has contacted you to give information about the Ark," Alexander asked in Gnathe.

Mentally, Link answered, "Nothing! I feel that our captor will inform us when it is back in orbit. Then the fun will begin! I expect that all weapons on board will have been rendered inactive. It will need to get us aboard somehow to show what we will require to carry out its wishes."

Suzzan spoke up and answered Alexander, "We have not been informed by the Janise Probe about the Ark. I would think that once it is in orbit we would be told." Mentally she added, "The fact that the Probe sent the Ark away without realising that we needed the equipment on board shows that this machine intelligence is not infallible! There are limits to its knowledge about us. We do not know whether it is bluffing about destroying our home worlds if we do not comply."

"We will of course do all that the Probe asks of us," Alex replied out load and telepathically reiterated, "We dare not call that bluff. I for one believe the thing would do what it threatens. All of us will have to go along with whatever this thing asks of us, at least until we understand a lot better just what we are dealing with. Anyway, while I have been visiting you, Hannah and Fredrick have gone to visit the Kresh."

"How will she manage to fool the Probe that she can communicate with them without telepathy?" Link's mind enquired.

Tee 6 slipped her mind into all of them carrying part of her in their brains, *"Kresh may talk super-sonically, way above the human hearing range, but hear in all ranges do they. Hannah talk to them she can, as human speech they understand quite well. Interesting it may be to listen into the conversation."*

Hannah and Fredrick made their way into the compound specially built for the Kresh. The giant rabbit-like people were a species that did not require to sit at rest. They squatted on their haunches or laid down full length on their stomachs. Stood up, they were taller than Fredrick and with their ears erect they made even him look small. Hannah being a tiny person looked like a child in their presence, but her mind more than made up for her elfin figure.

The building was as close to the Kresh home world's standards, that once past the doors it was difficult for Hannah to remember where she was. Fredrick lifted her onto a table and sat down beside her while the Kresh sat round in a semi-circle.

First of Dappled Grey concentrated his mind through Tee 6 and contacted the two humans, "Greetings my friends. Speak in as high a pitch as you can and I will hear you quite easily. The machine intelligence has blocked natural telepathy and also the Goss. I fear that the symbiont has been blocked so long that it is isolated in its own mind. It may be dead!"

Hannah thought about this possibility at the same time she spoke clearly to the male Kresh, "Greetings First of Dappled Grey. Are you all right in these quarters? We have been well looked after. Alexander has told the Janise Probe that we need the equipment on the Ark, to do as it requires. We believe that the Probe has turned the Ark around and is sending it back, for without it we cannot do as the Probe commands."

The Kresh nodded to the small human and gestured to her that all was well.

Mentally he said, "Very good! We must do just as this thing says until we are in a position to do something about it. Tee 6 has kept me informed of the conversation with the Gnathe. You are doing a good job of persuading the Probe that we are docile. We must keep that attitude at all times. The last thing we need is another object lesson similar to the Vogb! Do we know anything about the fate of the Guardians?"

Hannah thought for a moment and then answered, "We have not been contacted by the Janise Probe since it spoke to all of us. I do not know what else to tell you!"

Tee 6 inserted her mind into the proceedings and projected to all of her communication balls as well as her hosts, *"Sensing the power lines to all of these building do I. Deep under the city they go. Beyond our ability to tap into I am certain. Also the fate of the other nannites I cannot sense, but changed somehow I feel are the circumstances of their imprisonment. I sense a loss in the mind of the Janise Probe. Deeper*

I dare not go into its thinking processes. If aware of me it becomes then all advantage we possess will go. All I can say is that the awareness that I had of their captivity has gone. Minnis can go out of phase without the Toarvak ship. Possible it may be that she has done this with the Guardians, escaping the Janise Probe's containment."

First of Dappled Grey considered this information and replied, "Certain of this are you?"

"Not certain, but probable it may be. I do not sense them! Even as contracted balls of nannite, something of them remained!"

Fredrick slid off the table and swung Hannah safely to the ground.

He looked the giant rabbit in its sky blue eyes and said, "We must be on our way. It is good that we find you unharmed and well looked after. Do whatever the probe commands of you and we will all keep our lives."

As he spoke, he projected via Tee 6, "I shall enjoy ripping the circuits from this bastardly machine, when I get the chance. Be docile my good friends, we do not want another Vogb incident!"

The Vogb were in an evil mood that had persisted since the Janise Probe had reacted to the interference with its robot. They had reluctantly pulled back from open revolt since 'Deep-Green' had been brutally killed. Apart from Blue-Orange-Green who had a silver ball inserted on his brainstem, the Vogb were unable to communicate with any of their alien friends, as they used colours radiating along their upper ring. Only the Janise Probe was able to use the coloured lightshow that was the Vogb's way of speaking. It had made itself quite plain that its demands would mean certain death if not observed. The threat to destroy Vogb home worlds held them in check.

One of the Vogb had risked snaring a spy unit and fused its workings with its charged tendril in a split second. She had rolled her base ring over the inert mechanism to hide it from view. The dozens of tiny legs had manipulated the unit into its centre and lifted it from the ground. She needed to find somewhere that the Janise probe could not see before she took the unit apart to see how it worked. The colours that made up her name were a blending of indigo and yellow, so she was known as 'TY' the bright. She edged through the others of her kind and made for the nursery, followed by Blue/orange/green. He was one of the top scientists of the Vogb and had been a member of the team that had discovered the interference of the Harvester in causing the collision of the two galaxies. Hidden inside his body was his tool-kit surrounded by the natural batteries that charged his stunning tendril. The Janise Probe could not detect the few metals involved in the tools that lay hidden inside him.

'TY' made sure that none of the spy units were operating in the nursery before she disgorged the spy unit for Bog, to examine. She took it to the side of an illuminated cot that was keeping young Vogb warm with a strong light and Bog, rapidly took it apart. Each working part was analysed to see how it could link with others of its kind to build bigger types. Whatever the Vogb could see was relayed via the part of Tee 6 that remained fixed to his brain stem.

Hannah followed every procedure, fascinated by the complex engineering involved. An understanding of how the Janise Probe probably worked began to unravel. The fact that 'TY' had managed to fuse one of the tiny spy units proved that the Janise Probe was not infallible. It had concentrated on having such a massive feedback from thousands of spy units that it did not miss one of them when 'TY' had used her charged tendril to fry its circuits.

Primm, first of family Smelch had also been with Bog on the outskirts of the galaxy when they had discovered the Harvester's act of revenge. She was a talented scientist amongst her own people and had built the detection device with the Vogb to observe the reasons behind the galactic collision. The Thipdar saw through the conics eyes as he stripped the spy unit down to its component parts. She could see that although much of the circuitry was fused, redundancy has been engineered into the device. It would be possible to re-engineer the spy unit to be controlled by the Vogb using the conic's own nervous system. The two entities blended their intellects as they had done in the past and got to work altering the allegiance of the device. Tiny amounts of Toarvak 6's substance were sacrificed to engineer new components that the Vogb inserted into the unit's control systems.

Hannah added her mind to the gestalt and blended her knowledge into the mind of the Vogb. Now the fine tendrils of the conic rapidly bent and twisted delicate wires into the base material of the circuits that had been altered to do the Vogb's bidding. While this was happening the rest of the Vogb kept on the move to keep the spy units occupied watching them instead of Bog. They were providing a 'light show' depicting a poem, telling their young about the home world and their journey from it. The top rings of the conics changed colours in cascades while the tale was passed from Vogb to Vogb as the saga unfolded. As the story advanced the conics danced an intricate waltz weaving in and out in lines. The Janise Probe watched the 'show' trying to unravel the sense of the information that was being displayed. As the conics were relating the poem in 'Old Vogb' tones of colour shades and not their everyday language, the machine intelligence was baffled. This meant that more and more of its computing power became involved trying to become comprehensively aware of just what the Vogb were engaged in doing.

Other groups of the captives were taking advantage of

the Janise Probe's concentrated attention to the Vogb 'light show' and were exploring the boundaries of the city. The Bazantii with humans and apes mounted bareback on their strong backs had reached the city walls. A sheer barricade reared upwards and slanting inwards towered over them. The wall seemed as if it encircled the entire city and was made of metal. None of them dared to touch it, as they were all aware of a faint humming that filled the air the closer that they got to it.

Amongst the group were Alex and Nagoth who dismounted their Bazantii friends and had stopped short of touching the city wall. Watching them were the spy units controlled by the Janise Probe. The spider-like mechanoids formed a barrier between the wall and the exploring group. Suddenly the units appeared to become more attentive to what they were doing and Alex realised that the Janise Probe was back.

The mechanical watchdogs began to combine into a much larger assembly until several hundred of them had become the robot type that had ripped the Vogb to pieces. This time the mechanoid did not menace them, but instead it picked up a loose unit and tossed it at the wall. The humming sound went up a pitch and the spy unit fried as it made contact. Sparks flew out of the mechanism and eventually it began to slowly melt until it bubbled down the wall onto the ground.

The robot turned towards Alexander and the emotionless voice of the Janise Probe spoke to the group, "Explore all you wish! Do not touch the walls. The Ark is now in orbit and you will be required to furnish me with a list of what is necessary to remove from the vessel. I have contained the nannites that stayed on board, where they cannot be of assistance to you."

Alexander stood his ground and replied, "We will need

the nannites to run the equipment. If you damage them we will not be able to accede to your demands!"

The robot froze as the Janise Probe considered the new situation.

High above them orbited the Last Ark of the Goss, placed there by the over-riding commands of the Janise probe. Many changes had been instigated by the machine intelligence in the operating systems. The nannites could no longer control the drive system of the Ark. Much of the circuitry had been stripped out and used by the replicating units to fashion large magnetic areas to contain the nannites. Those that had been allowed to continue to operate were well aware of the hostage situation that existed on the planet below. Their every move was watched and evaluated by the Janise Probe as they were ordered to tend to the life vats that had not been used in years while the Janise probe studied the manufacture and design.

Old commands began to activate, as sensors on the Ark registered the proximity of the world below. Adaptations had been made by the nannites to the system that the Goss used to infect new worlds with its spores. Instead of launching infected ratoids to the planet's ecosystem the launch tubes spat billions of adjusted nannite spores into the upper atmosphere. Each life pod was no more than the size and shape of a dandelion seed, but contained instructions to build life forms from organic compounds that were encountered by the spores. DNA sequencing would produce compatible organisms that would suit all of the alien species that had journeyed inside the Ark. It would take a few years, but eventually the planet below would be host to whatever plants and animals that the captives would have needed. Only the native alien life on the new world would be affected by the nannite spores. As each programmed seed made contact with living matter the genetic structure of the organism became changed and the creature would mutate into a compatible life form. Hidden amongst the seeds were many Guardians that had metamorphosised into clouds of nannites that would make their way down to the planet below. Once they had dispersed away from the detection of the Janise Probe they would coalesce into one single dandelion seed shape and drift down to the surface below. They would then make their way across this planet towards the city that the organics were held captive.

The Janise probe was entirely oblivious of this event as it concentrated on the problems at hand. It had a difficult situation to sort out. Although it had a perfect hostage situation to its advantage, there was the unforeseen problem of the necessary life vats being on the Ark and the people that would need them in the city! It had seen the weapons that the Toarvaks could use and it would not allow the captives any chance at operating those. The solution to the problem would be to cut out and remove the great hall that housed the life vats from the structure of the Ark. More than a thousand of the vats existed in the great hall and would require a number of nannites to oversee the operation and care for the inmates submerged in the green preserving liquid. The Janise probe would need to manufacture rockets to decelerate the detached great hall from the Ark and drop it down to the planet below. The final part of the journey would be by parachute, guided down to the city. Once the life vats were safely down, the Janise probe would have no further use for the Ark and would send it back on its way to the sun. The decision taken the machine intelligence re-routed its attention to Alexander and Nagoth.

The robot activated and the emotionless voice of the Janise Probe said, "I have solved the problem. I will have the area of the life vats removed from the hollow moon and directed towards the city. A limited number of nannites will be shipped down to tend the vats."

Alexander listened to the Janise Probe and replied, "What will you do with the Ark after you have stripped the great hall from the hollow moon?"

"I will send it on a trajectory into the sun along with all the excess nannites that are trapped inside it," the machine intelligence said. "I have no use for it and neither will you and your people. Here you are and here you will stay and do my bidding, generation after generation of you. I will build an empire from your endeavours to supply my needs for metals. When I have built a war fleet I will visit those other Janise Probes and destroy them, taking over their territory. You will be the means to travel there by creating the necessary wormholes with the power of your combined minds."

Alexander broadcast his thoughts to the other nine who were enhanced by Tee 6, "We are dealing with an electronic madness! This programming is a leftover from the manipulation of minds by the Collectors. They promoted territorial wars to enable them to collect life energy for the Harvester. Somehow we must stop this creeping cancer from invading all we have set free. How many of these machine intelligences could there be scattered about the Andromeda Galaxy?"

Toarvak 6 had considered this question and answered her hosts, *"When alone we Toarvaks fought against the Goss, ranged far and wide we did in our search for the enemy. We did not come against such as this left over machine intelligence. Unique I feel, that this electronic life form is. Duplicated itself to carry out the original programming the Janise laid down into its circuits it has. Evolved it has into something that is without real purpose, but it is alive and sentient. Deal with this one first we must, before we seek out the others. To remember one thing above all else we must, this thing does not understand organic life. Mistakes in planning, it has made. Hope in this we have!"*

Nagoth walked around the protective form of Alexander and stood right in front of the talking machine. The wind flipped her flaming red hair around her head as she stood looking up at the vision receptors of the robot. The robot increased its height by rearing up in a menacing way and reaching for the female human.

"Stop! I am no threat to you! Think about the facts that are in your logic circuits," Nagoth spoke clearly to the machine. "I am flesh and blood and easily damaged. I cannot hurt you. Listen to me. You are alone and you need our help to defeat your enemies. We can do this, but you must believe that we will do so without unnecessary force being applied to us. You do not understand us. I am asking you not to destroy the Ark needlessly. You may need it and the weapons that our interstellar vessel carries in the fight to come. You are a logical being. Be logical!"

With her mind she contacted Alex and said, "We can confuse it. It will not understand lies! Offer it help and co-operation without any type of threat. We must keep any advantage that we can keep. Tell it about the collectors!"

Once again the robot froze into inaction as the Janise Probe considered the organic's proposal. It questioned its decisions about the Ark's destruction and decided that the hollowed out moon would be worth keeping. It had immobilised the contingent of nannites that were stranded on the moon by intense magnetic fields. This indeed was a better idea. The thought surfaced in its mind that the organics could be useful in more ways than one. It had been built to provide metals for its maker by using the organic's united minds to open wormholes and present the cold, metal-rich planetoids for the Janise Collective. The time spent building the city and preparing the flytrap had engineered independence in its mind, which had happened time and again amongst the Janise Probes scattered amongst the stars. Just as those probes had built clones of themselves that had become independent, so the replica on this world had surfaced into self-governing sapience. It did not want to do the bidding of another. The dream of Empire had risen along with the original aim of the Janise. The ancient programming and objectives that dominated the probes were sent out to prepare the way for the competing people swarming over the home world. The Collector's final visit and a nuclear war had finished all of those hopes, as their life energy was stored for the Harvester's needs.

Alexander walked forwards and stood by Nagoth's side, "Do you know that there are beings of pure energy that feed off the life force of sapient organic life such as we? If one of them were to find this world it would seek to destroy us to gather our life energy. They did this for a being we called the Harvester. We destroyed this abomination, but many Collectors remain. Worlds like this one are what these creatures seek. The weapons on that ship of ours and the Toarvak that you have frozen at the City are what we need to defeat these energy beings. They could destabilize this sun and destroy us all, including you! You must consider this."

Once more the robot became inactive as the machine intelligence considered these new and alarming facts.

CHAPTER FIVE

A mile beneath the city, the Janise Probe thought about the information that the human leader had imparted to its extension. The simple plan that the machine intelligence had worked on for many years lay in tatters. It had been sent to this world to build a trap to serve its maker's needs. Over the time it had spent in this corrosive element it had strived against the damp conditions all the time that it had built the city. As its predecessor had reproduced the design of the original Janise Probe in a cold airless system there was no experience to draw on.

Fortunately this world was untapped, rich in metals and resources, so the Janise Probe was able to extract the raw materials quite easily. Its greatest problem was rust and the effects that the salts in the seas had on delicate electrical circuits. Everything that it made had to be insulated from these problems. Getting equipment into orbit and away from the gravity well of this world took great effort. Once the self-replicating probes got out as far as the strange, metal rich moons, it was able to expand its operations. Infiltrating the Ark had proved easy for the Machine intelligence.

It was during these years of battling against corrosion that the new Janise Probe began to become self aware, rather than an extended tool of its maker. Once this happened it began to think independently and resent the place that it had been sent, to operate the flytrap. Now it would seem that the very world that had been chosen to trap the organics, could become its pyre, should this unknown enemy come this way. The hostage situation had degenerated beyond the original plan. All of the knowledge gained by studying the organics and their strange ways had abruptly shown flaws. For the first time in eons the Janise probe began to be beset by indecision! Its consciousness was no more then a century old and lacked experience. Although it had all the memories of its maker and the same programming, dealing with the independently minded organics took it far outside the original goals. Becoming self aware had added extra thought processes to its electronic mind as well as the original Probe's abilities.

Now for the first time in its existence it began to question its purpose and began to burrow deep into the archives of its memory banks. It had been originally been built by organic creatures and sent out to another star system. What had been the Janise objectives? The machine intelligence dug further and found that these commands had been removed from the memory banks of the original probe. A deliberate sponging had taken place. All that was left was the programming to build and form an Empire.

In digging into these memories it realised that the original probe had sent out more probes to extend its reach, but each probe that had been replicated soon discarded the instructions that were laid down in its programming. What had happened to this probe had happened over and over again. Its maker had thought that it could over-ride the inevitable self-awareness that had happened to all the others. The very thing that had made the original probe self-aware was also replicated again and again.

The Janise Probe returned its awareness to the robot at the city wall only to find that it was alone. The organics had left to return to their new quarters some time ago. In fact the sun was going down and darkness was rapidly encroaching over the city. High above, the clouds were tearing apart with flashes of lightning, occasionally arcing to the ground and the lightening conductors fixed to the tallest skyscrapers. The massive magnetic fields generated by the city to keep the Toarvak imprisoned drew the storms all the way from the mountains. Giant claps of thunder began to build and the rain beat down, making a hissing sound as it hammered against the robot. The Janise Probe let the combined machine re-assemble into its smaller units and returned its consciousness to the living quarters of the various organics.

Alexander was talking to First of Dappled Grey as he ate his evening meal.

"Since I raised the subject with the Janise Probe, I cannot get the idea out of my head. We are very vulnerable on this world without any psychic sensing to know whether we are being eyed up as an energy meal by a passing Collector."

The Kresh prime male rocked back on his haunches and chewed a pod vine fruit reflectively and nodded.

His mind connected with the human sat at the table and said, "We might have an answer to that."

Alex stared hard at the Kresh and asked, mentally, "What do you have in mind?"

"There is a tall skyscraper directly underneath the crystal mounted in the arch. If enough of the Kresh could get to the roof, I am sure that we could shatter it by singing at a high pitch," First answered. "Once that crystal has shattered we will all have our full mental abilities back. Then we can meet the Janise Probe on more equal terms!"

"The machine intelligence seems to have a limited ability to concentrate on too many subjects at once," Alex replied. "We will have to create a diversion for you. I have seen nothing representing the Janise Probe since I gave it the news about the threat that the Collectors still represent."

Bog inserted his mind into the conversation and included Primm into the circuit. The Vogb and the Thipdar had commandeered the renegade spy unit and had sent it down one of the purpose built tunnels. It was now deep underground and following other units through the darkness. Down here somewhere was the housing of the Janise Probe. Its electronic circuits ran through the solid walls and back up into the city. The city was a living electronic organism with the main brain buried deep beneath its foundations. Close circuit cameras watched their every move, but not all the actions of the organics were it seemed, completely monitored.

As Alex had mentioned, the Janise Probe had so much to scrutinize at once, that it had become over-stretched. Besides running the city, it had to contend with the time lapse involved with the communication with the Ark's systems under its control. Also the mining of the metal rich outer moons needed supervision from time to time. The time lapse in communication at that distance took several hours. To maintain these operations it had replicated a limited version of itself and was wary of this intelligence becoming self-aware and becoming a rival. It began to construct extra memory circuits and expand its awareness. As its mind became increasingly complex and extended it experienced a new sensation. It began to worry! The cold logical decisions that had led it into this situation were now up for question and it had lost the containment of the nannite entities.

As the days had gone by, Kamiel, Asue and Solace continued to drift through the solid rocks and strata contained by Minnis. She had managed to keep them all out of phase so that they continued to pass through the spaces of the atoms of this world, but the energy strain on her systems was beginning to tell. Soon she would have to collapse the bubble that the nannites were travelling inside. She used her senses to analyse the density of the material that they were floating through and began to measure a difference.

She contacted the others and declared, "The rocks are getting softer. I think we are entering topsoil."

Abruptly they were flooded in sunshine and Minnis opened the membrane and dropped the three nannites onto the vegetation underneath them. She then altered her substance back into phase with the rest of the universe and fell beside her companions. The four Guardians spread their shapes to catch as much sunlight as they could and replenish their energy levels. Four upturned umbrellas stood on stalks and basked in the sun as they twisted with the planet's motion. After an hour, Kamiel reformed into a humanoid figure and extended his senses onto the nannite band of communication.

"Toarvak 6, can you hear me?" he asked.

A faint response came back, *"Kamiel! Happy am I that your voice I can hear again. Far away you are! Here captive we are in the city. Contact we have had with the controlling intelligence. Problems it has with us! The Ark it has returned to orbit, as the organics will require the life vats to keep them alive when combining their minds to do its bidding. This knowledge it did not have! Also the threat of the Collectors it has been informed of. By lightly sensing its mind, worried it has become, I feel. This is a new sensation! Pure logic it was, emotion it now has to weaken it. As I was once so this creature is now. The great difference is that it can never read minds to blend with organic thought as do we."*

Kamiel thought about this treasure trove of information before he answered and replied, "Is Alexander's mind connected to yours? Can I speak to him through you?"

"Asleep he is with Nagoth. In the early morning a diversion he will make to occupy as much of the Janise Probe's attention that he can. Carried am I, by five beings and also a small ball of my substance at the brain stem of five others. Speak we can with Kresh, Thipdar and Vogb as well as Link and her brood daughters. The shielding crystal mounted high above us inside the arch suppresses all traces of the Goss. Still alive it is, we cannot be sure. Believe do the Kresh that they can shatter the crystal by their high-pitched sounds. Sing to

it they will from the top of the skyscraper beneath it!"

"If it is dark where you are and light here, then we must have burst through the surface of the planet a long way around the curve," the nannite replied. "It will take some time before we reach you. Give my regards to Alexander when he wakes and tell him we are free of the Janise Probe's imprisonment."

He turned to see that his companions were back to normal and had listened in on his conversation with the Toarvak.

Asue spoke first and said, "I know the way back will be long, but at least we know what direction we need take. The wind is blowing in that general direction so I propose that we inflate and get sailing!"

The four nannites expanded their substance into large globes, tethered to the ground and converted some of the soil into hydrogen to swell them out. One by one they disengaged from their anchored positions and shot high up into the air. Kamiel stared down at the countryside below. They had exited the planet by the side of a hill that was part of a long range that extended into the far distance. The wind was blowing directly over the tops of the hills and would take them back towards the vicinity of the city. Many thousands of miles lay in that direction before they had any chance of finding the city and the imprisoned organics. The Guardians had learnt a basic lesson and that was that they were not as impregnable as they had become used to. They had been studied by another kind of artificial intelligence and it had found their weak-spots. High voltage could disrupt their cohesion and powerful magnetic fields would render them unable to operate. This was also a chink in the Toarvak's armour and while the intense magnetic field that was surrounding the molecular substance of the ship at such close range stayed at full strength, Tee 6 was immobilised. The first thing that the nannites needed to do was to turn off the power to that trap. At the moment there was nothing that they could do but rely on the prevailing winds to carry them towards the city, without knowing just how far they needed to go.

Kamiel signalled to the others and instructed them, "We need to go higher so that we can get a better idea about just where we are. The brief examination of the world as we approached, has given us enough information of its surface area to be able to recognise the landmasses and see where we are. I suggest that we link together so that we do not get separated and try to use the jet stream to our advantage. Let us hope that it is blowing in the right direction!"

The nannites fired tethers at each other and expanded the gas floatation chambers to gain more height. As they rose higher into the stratosphere the ground beneath them opened out. Below them was an unrecognisable landmass that must have been on the other side of this world as they approached. The one thing that they knew was that they had exited this world on the north of the equator and it was night at the city. As luck would have it, the jet stream was taking them around the curvature of the planet towards the night-side.

Kamiel reached out for contact with the active nannites on the Ark.

The Janise Probe believed that it had immobilised all but ten of the nannites who were in charge of the life vats when the group mind was operating. These were under constant scrutiny as they pretended to constantly monitor the operating conditions of the thousands of incubators. They were making sure that Nano-viruses constantly infiltrated the spy units and combined robots in such a way that they were operating at a lot less than optimum efficiency. As the Janise probe was already finding it difficult to be everywhere at once and also it was under stress considering the warning given by the human leader, the idea of sabotage had not entered its mind.

The nannites that had exited the Ark along with the adapted spores began to coalesce into individuals and began to alter their shapes into gliders. As the jet stream took the spores and sent them around the planet to do what they had been programmed to do, so the Guardians dropped steeply towards the city boundaries. They made sure that they would not be picked up by the probe's radar by keeping their density to a minimum. This also made their rate of descent the same speed as the winds. Even to the advanced surveillance systems that the Janise Probe used, they were undetectable.

Kamiel felt the activity on the nannite communication system and broke into their wavelength with a terse greeting. He relayed the information at hand to them and listened to what they had achieved on the Ark. The last thing that Kamiel wanted was the Janise Probe carving portions of the Ark away from the main body and discarding the rest. The last Ark of the Goss was far too useful to become scrap! He needed to occupy the machine intelligence to keep it from carrying out its decision to drop the Great Hall containing the life vats onto the city. He considered the situation and relayed his instructions to the gliding nannites. They altered course and began to spiral down to a new target.

Alexander awoke and stared with wonder at the woman still asleep beside him. Her body was human, but her mind belonged to a female Gnathe. Link-soo-shan had resurrected her daughter's mind in a genetically engineered human woman. As a Gnathe under Link-soo-shan's domination she had forced a rape upon him that nearly killed him. It was during this terrible penetration that Alex had got into her mind and freed her from her Brood-mother's mental powers. The love that the alien had carried for him had been nurtured by her until her death. Only her body had died. Link-soo-shan, by that time completely mentally changed, had harvested her mind and kept it stored in a crystal until the right time had come to resurrect her as Nancy/Nagoth.

Link-soo-shan had promised him that the genetic tinkering that had brought forth the amazing sets of three twins, all mentally linked together and able to be precognitive had not been repeated. Whatever children they produced in this reincarnation would be normal. As normal as any human children were, born after the Gnathen alterations in their genetic codes allowed. There were now two different types of human being; there were those original types that had been born on Earth and those who had been re-born on Jupiter after the genetic blending with the Gnathe. Alex and his type were psychically enhanced with extra lobes of brain to carry their powers. At least with Tee 6's substance hidden inside him he was able to still utilise a certain amount of telepathic power. The constant blanking out from the shielding crystal was similar to having a constant toothache. He thought about the Kresh idea of getting onto the roof directly underneath the crystal and 'singing' it to a shattering end. Somehow he had to think of a way to keep the Janise Probe distracted while they did their part.

"Wake up, Nagoth. Its time for breakfast and we need to think about what we are to do, to keep the Janise Probe occupied," Alexander breathed into her ear.

Nagoth awoke, instantly aware of him staring down at her face and rose up to embrace him. She kissed him warmly and slid her tongue under his. At the same time she ran her hand down his thigh to grasp his thickening penis. She squeezed him hard running the skin back and forth until he broke free. Nagoth wrapped her legs around him and pushed up to enable him to penetrate her. She dug her nails into his back as he devoted all his attention to driving her into a sexual frenzy. Everything that she felt, she filled his mind with and received every nerve-screaming pleasure from his mind into hers. Together they climaxed and then reluctantly broke apart to lie sweating on top of the heap of bedclothes.

The alien in a woman's body lay bathed in a warm glow of satisfaction and applied her mind to the problem.

Nagoth whispered into his ear, "We need the Bazantii to stage a gallop to the other side of the city, down to the sea by the docks. If we are carried there by them the Probe will follow us, as it does not know what we are doing. It hates the wet and the corrosive sea. If we dive into the water it will not know what to do. We can swim and the machines can't. It will divert all of its attention to what we are doing, afraid that we could drown. Its need for our minds will be uppermost in its logic circuits. Somehow it will need to get us out of the water. I'm guessing that it will become close to panic and will be thinking of nothing else!"

Alex thought the situation over and broadcast the idea to the Kresh carrying Tee 6.

First of Dappled Grey considered the plan and agreed, answering through Tee 6, "Your female is clever, human. I should keep her close or someone else may decide to want her instead of you!"

"I somehow do not think that will happen, old friend," Alex answered, looking at his naked partner as she brushed her copper coloured hair.

Nagoth caught the telepathic exchange between the Kresh and her lover and laughed as she hurriedly dressed.

At the dining hall, after breakfast Alex stood before the screen that communicated with the Janise Probe.

He spoke to the hidden microphones, "Janise Probe! Are you there?"

"Yesss," replied the machine intelligence.

The human leader could detect a note of uncertainty in the reply.

"Have you given any thought to our last conversation and can you assure us that we are safe from attack by the life form I spoke about? Have you considered the need for leaving our weapon's intact? If a Collector finds us, you will be destroyed along with all organic life upon this world."

The voice of the Janise Probe was uncertain as it replied, "I am considering the situation. A Collector may come or not. If not then I still have the advantage of the situation. You will obey me! I will kill your females if you do not."

"If you kill our females then we will not do as you ask and we will die. Without us you will never open a wormhole and get the metal-rich worlds that you need! Think about your future here upon this world without us. Think how long you would have to wait for more of our kind to voyage out this far. We came to find a new home, because we wanted to. Those we left behind are content where they are and will not venture out as far as this. This is a truth that you must think about. In the meantime with your permission, we would like to explore this city," Alexander ended and waited for the Probe's reply.

The screen went black as the logic circuits of the machine intelligence tried to consider and decide what to do about the worsening situation.

"I'll take that as a yes, then," Alex said and beckoned his group towards the doors.

Outside were a group of Bazantii waiting for the humans to sit aside their backs. They had the body shape of centaurs, but were more like six limbed cats. They could run on all six legs or just on the hind four carrying their chest erect with their 'hands' free. It was in this mode that they allowed the humans to be carried by them. They carried chest harnesses that the humans could hold on to when they moved fast. Being hunting cats, they could move very fast when they needed to.

As they set off towards the docks situated at the edge of the city, Alexander felt the mind touch of Primm and Blue/Orange/Green.

"Alexander! We have the unit deep beneath the city motionless and ignored," the Thipdar explained to the human. " The central brain of this machine intelligence is located all around us. We think that when you draw its full attention to the your immersion in the sea, the spy unit can burrow into one of the communications consoles connecting the Janise Probe to the city's defences. There it will do as much damage as it can before it is neutralised. This should add to the confusion!"

Alexander answered as the Bazantii broke into a steady lope, "Well done my friends! Did you hear that, First of Dappled Grey?"

Toarvak 6 broke into the mental circuit and added, *"Hearing it also am I and more information have I to add! Kamiel and the others have broken free from the Probe's incarceration. On their way here they are. Also from the Ark are other nannites dropping towards the city disguised so that the city automatic defences will not pick them up. Into the reservoir they will plunge and deep down the dam wall will they go. Once at the intakes to the generators they will plug them and stop the flow. Kamiel has estimated that much electrical power is needed to maintain the magnetic field that prevents my ship from operating. Soon break free will it be possible!"*

Alexander lent forwards and spoke into the Bazantii's ear, "Things are going well my friend. Do not hesitate once we reach the docks to hurl yourself into the water once First gives me the signal that the Kresh are ready!"

The big male Bazantii nodded and called out to the others, "On my direction; - into the water. All is going well!"

The entire Kresh contingent had explained to the Janise probe that the accommodation although good was not quite right and they would like to examine the large building down the road to see if that would be more suitable. The Janise Probe had examined the situation through its logic circuits and although it could not see any reason that the Kresh were uncomfortable, it agreed.

Well over a thousand Kresh made their way through the silent city to the central skyscraper. The building was similar to the custom built home that the Janise Probe had built for the Kresh, relying on the information gathered by probes sent by the other machine intelligences. Maybe the design was different enough to make its unwilling guests uncomfortable. The new Janise Probe had to accept that its knowledge of the organics was limited to the information stored in its memory banks. Its dealings with its captive flesh and blood creatures had given it new databases to unravel. Much of the new information was not of a logical nature and difficult to process! It was still in a state of indecision about the warning given by the human leader about the Collectors. The other thing uppermost in its mind was the disappearance of the nannites from the underground chamber.

Many miles away from the city, high up above the mountains that fed the melt water into the reservoirs, a slow flying squadron of gliders banked and turned. Each one was made up of more emptiness than substance and were beginning to change shape. The cloudiness began to thicken into a dart shape with the weight towards the nose. They tipped down and swooped towards the water, dissolving back into clouds just above the surface. The nannites rapidly reformed into fish shaped creatures and swam down increasing in density as they got nearer to the bottom. As the current took them towards the intakes they spread out into filament nets shaped like starfish. Some of them allowed the current to suck them inside and the rest attached themselves around the mouth of the intakes. These began to transport material from the dam wall above the intakes to form overlapping lids, ready to drop into place at a unifying command.

CHAPTER SIX

Alexander held tight to the Bazantii as the six legged creature let rip and increased his speed. The smell of the sea carried through the roads down to the docks. This part of the city was engineered primarily to transport the foodstuffs collected from the fields from upriver. Here there were no living quarters and all the buildings were functional by design as storage systems.

Inside Alexander's mind the Kresh connected to him via Tee 6, "Human! The Kresh are inside the skyscraper. We are making our way upward as fast as we can. We are under observation by the Janise Probe as the spy units are following us to see what we make of our new quarters. Any diversion that can bring you to its attention to concentrate somewhere else would be advisable now."

As the mounted group turned the corner they found that the docks were very simple in design with no safety rails of any kind. Larger versions of the spy units were unloading the barges as they lay at anchor to the docks. The moment that they appeared, the machines stopped unloading the barges and swung their optical systems towards them. They had the Janise Probe's attention!

The Bazantii dug their claws into the roadway and ducked underneath the Probe's un-loading machines and headed to the end of the docks where there was an empty space between the barges. The edge of the docks was no more than a foot above the surface of the sea as the tide was up. Getting out would not be too difficult.

Now some of the machines began to move towards the end of the docks in pursuit while a number just froze with indecision. The six-legged cats began to weave in and out of the legs and split up so that it became more difficult for the Janise Probe to single out any individual from the group. More and more of the Janise Probe's units began to stop their unloading of the barges and left their positions to crowd along the docks in pursuit of the mounted group. To Alex's satisfaction he noticed that several had collided with each other.

High above them in synchronised orbit, inside the Last Ark of the Goss, nannites that had remained hidden began to immobilise the spy units and their secondary control centres. Deactivating viruses spread throughout the machine intelligence's components at the nannites' commands and all of them immobilized before they could radio for instructions. To the Janise Probe on the planet below, all contact ceased. Without any warning its spy units abruptly went blind on board the Ark.

The Probe activated the defence systems around the city.

A mile beneath the city, Primm and B.O.G. activated the renegade spy unit and directed it towards a system of circuit boards. It rapidly began to burrow into the microchips, disconnecting as it went. Wires were cut and re-connected in random paths causing other circuits to fail and some to fuse. Power cables were re-routed and large voltages sizzled into delicate systems causing them to fail and throwing extra loads onto others.

The city defence systems became inoperative!

Trying to ignore the Ark, the Probe split its attention between the illogical actions of the mounted Bazantii with the humans at the docks and the reason that the defences were out of action.

As the combined Bazantii and humans entered the seawater and swam away from the docks and out of reach of the Janise Probe's machines, the nannites blocked the intakes at the dams. Those that had penetrated the intakes had quickly made their way to the turbines and watched over them as they began to slow down as the water pressure eased off. The attendant maintenance robots were overpowered and shut down before the Janise Probe recognised the problem. The electrical power supply to the city began to drop off and with it the massive amount directed to the magnetic plates holding Toarvak 6 inoperative.

Now the machine intelligence had three areas to demand its attention without the fact that the Ark had ceased to be under its control.

The Kresh had noticed that they were no longer being followed by the Janise Probe's spy units, as they made their way upwards. Once they had gained the top set of rooms, 'First' of Dappled Grey attacked the roof with a sub-sonic wave generated by the females of his race, causing it to crumble. The Janise probe had engineered the roof to repel rain and storms from above. It had not thought that there would be any need to protect from below! The Kresh began to climb through the holes and onto the roof.

A thousand of them began to sing from the topmost position from the roof of the skyscraper. Their voices began to ascend the vocal scale that went far beyond the hearing range of the other aliens. High frequency sound will shatter most crystals and the fact that this 'shielding crystal' was being electrically stimulated at maximum made it very vulnerable to the Kresh. They sang an aria that climbed in intensity until it reached 40KHz. Once they achieved this resonance they introduced an extra sub-sonic to the climbing scale. The volume was such that they could feel it in their bones, as the music reached out to the shielding crystal.

Above them in the arch that spanned the city, the shielding crystal began to vibrate in its housing. Fracture lines began to grow and tiny shards steadily dropped off. One of the stimulating cables started to slip away from the mountings. Without a balancing energy being delivered to the crystal across each and every connection, an imbalance began to generate. As high voltage cables loosened their grip on the connections the current had to go somewhere else. Arcs of incandescent power sparked into other circuits, burning them out. The crystal shattered!

All across the city the effect was immediate. The nagging mental toothache disappeared. In the cold water of the sea, Alexander felt the pressure go and levitated himself out and onto the docks. He was not alone! The Bazantii had felt the mental pressure ease and had done the same along with all the rest of their riders.

He felt the touch of Toarvak 6 in his mind, "Alexander! Nannites there are at the bottom of the dams. Water intakes shut off they have been. Power to the magnetic circuits has dropped. My ship is free and under my control it is! Parts have burrowed down to the magnetic plates and out of phase are they. No longer under the Janise Probe's power are we."

Alexander reached out with his mind and found that all of his psychic abilities had returned.

"Goss!"

There was a mental silence where once there had been

a constant response.

Alex tried again, "Goss!"

This time there was a stirring from deep down in the vaults of his mind, as if something long asleep had stirred.

The mind of the symbiont began to clear the fog from its strange consciousness and reach out to the main body of its essence, spread across the stars. It had been cut off from the telepathic gestalt that was its existence. All sentient beings were now host to the spores of the Goss. In doing so they were able to understand each other and instantly communicate across the stellar distances. The mind of the Goss was an accumulation of all the individuals that hosted its spores. Once it had been a parasite that had built an empire amongst the stars, seeking sentient life to do its will. Kamiel, Link-soo-shan and Alexander had defeated it and offered another kind of existence turning it into a symbiont instead. Its mind was a vast library of information stretching back millions of years.

"I have been away!"

"Goss, connect me with the council of worlds, those that are awake in this time frame! There is something that they need to know," Alexander ordered while he now stood upon the docks and dried off in the stiff onshore breeze.

All around him the unloading robots had returned to the task of emptying the barges all except one that had stopped and faced the human. A mile beneath them Primm and B.O.G. had stopped their merciless attack upon the circuitry surrounding the Probe's electronic mind, but they had hidden the rogue unit just in case it was still required. High above them, in orbit, the guardians on board the Ark were disabling every unit that the Janise Probe had infiltrated. Just above them Toarvak 6 was stripping the defence system from the roof of the city. The nannites at the dams were allowing the water to rush through some of the intakes to re-supply the city with power.

Alex walked up to the unit and said, "I will speak with you at the eating hall you provided. You will wait for me there! I warn you to do nothing to anger me! I am cold and wet. Your threats to us about sabotage are now known to the ruling council of worlds and are being dealt with as we speak."

Without replying, the mechanical extension of the Janise Probe's will, returned to its task of unloading the barges moored to the dockside.

Kamiel absorbed the news as the four Guardians coasted through the skies towards the subdued city. He felt an immense pride in 'his people' and their achievements. It had not been time wasted on the Ark when he had suggested that the aliens team up with each other and apply their skills in the arena. They had found out their combined strengths and weaknesses during that process. High above them the nannites that had stayed behind on the Ark had neutralised every Janise Probe infiltrator and stored the parts in a safe place. Now they were busy repairing whatever damages the machine intelligence had caused.

Toarvak 6's vessel had returned to the deactivated landing pad to await its full reunion with the fully sentient part of its existence. It had expanded to its former size and barrel shaped structure. Maintenance units busily checked over the rings of crystal that brought the wormhole weapon into existence.

A mile beneath the city the Janise probe repaired the damage done by the rogue unit commandeered by the Thipdar and the Vogb. Many of its circuits had fused into useless slag under the rerouting of high voltage cables. This would need to be cut away and cleared from the area before the Probe could even begin to restore the functions that they controlled. Nothing had been programmed into its electronic mind to deal with this situation. All other Janise Probes had dominated their area of expansion and all replicas were designed along the same successful pattern. Each had attained full sapience when it had built itself beyond a certain critical size. It had been manufactured for one sole purpose by its maker, which in turn was a copy of an earlier Janise Probe.

The difference between it and all its predecessors was that it had the extra goal of trapping the organics to use them to supply metal-rich planets to its builder. On achieving self-sentience it had become independent from its maker. This flaw in the machine intelligence design repeated itself over and over again. All the other Probes had not dealt with organic life since the original Probe had been sent to another solar system by the Janise and had evolved beyond the original instructions and programming. The extra sentience gained by dealing with the organics and the building on of extra computing ability had pushed it to another level. It had passed beyond sheer logic to a different mantra of thought. It was learning to cope with the emotion of worry! With worry came indecision! Lost from the original programming was the need to obey its designers. It was lost, but a necessary part of its sentience. Therefore a feedback loop set itself in motion. It had been given a direct order from an organic. Alexander had told it to wait for him to contact the Probe from the eating hall.

It became locked into a mode of hesitancy that paralysed its will. The direct order had triggered a response to a buried program that activated, due to the indecision that the machine intelligence was undergoing.

Reactivated sub-routines began to surface, over-riding the programming that the Janise Probe's predecessor had instigated. The original systems that the Janise had installed in its first interstellar probe began to assert themselves. Its whole reason for existence was to serve the Janise and provide for them when they crossed the vast distances to another world. Because the Harvester had eliminated the Janise by expanding their sun before they had launched their star-ship, the Probe was alone. By the time that the original probe had achieved sentience it had replicated itself thousands of times. These units amalgamated into a planet-spanning colossus that was filled with the same hunger for Empire that the Janise had wanted for themselves. This hunger had been put there by the Harvester's Collector to prod them into warfare so that it could collect life energy in vast amounts each time they had 'boiled' over. It was an insanity thrust into sentient life for that very reason. The Janise Probes carried this infection onwards in their programming and continued the cycle over and over again.

The first probe had landed on a cold airless world rich in metals and had developed this world over the millennia until it had sent probes of its own. These had at first launched ore carriers back to the original Probe. As they gained sentience due to the size of the computers running the systems, they rebelled against the original Probe. So started a series of machine intelligence wars that ended in the destruction of the original Janise Probe and the creation of the independent machine intelligences. They had begun to expand along the arm of the Andromeda galaxy, all seeking to expand its own empire and absorb its neighbours. It was the events leading up to the destruction of the Harvester by the 'Organics' that brought them to the closest Probe's attention.

It was this Probe that had solved the logistics of wormholes using the Lagdoo method. This it kept secret from its competitors and used the technique to build the 'Fly-trap' to capture enough 'organics' to operate wormholes to move metal-rich worlds within its reach. It had 'forgotten' that each probe would attain sentience once it had reached a critical size. The trap that it had made to build itself was different from the others, in so much, that it would have to defend itself from a more hostile environment than its builder. It was this and the need to out-think the organics that had spurred it to develop its intelligence beyond the logical constraints of the previous Probes. Now it also felt fear that the organics would terminate its consciousness. Before this state of new consciousness had immerged the probe had followed a logical pathway that had been planned out by the previous Probe. This pre-programmed system of action now lay shattered. A new possibility presented itself.

Now that the Goss was active again all the sentient beings were once more telepathically united and those that had carried Tee 6's silver balls had given them back again. Larse had shared the load of Toarvak 6's substance with Emelia and the two of them returned to the star-ship to put the Kresh nannite back into her natural element along with a contingent of Kresh. Toarvak 6 was now sufficiently crewed to be independent. The moment that the two set foot inside the sentient vessel, Tee 6 flowed out of their bodies and disappeared into the area around their feet.

Almost immediately the silver form of Toarvak 6's humanoid shape rose from the floor.

"Good it is to be back and united I am with my ship. Pleased I will be when Kamiel and the others return. Alex now to deal with the Janise Probe he has. Useful it would be if it could be persuaded to continue to the city run!"

Larse stood and looked at his 'mother' and replied, "That is up to him. He is far more technically minded than I am. You make a valid point. I will pass your suggestion on. Now old friend, how about you make us coffee?"

Emelia added, "I would like mine extra sweet. It's been a long time since I tasted hot, sweet coffee! The Janise Probe's idea of feeding us was pretty basic."

With that comment the two of them walked deeper into the ship's interior until they entered the control room. Two steaming mugs of coffee were waiting in the food processor and they sat down at a nearby table to drink them. While Larse was sat he gave Alex a quick up-date that all was well with their Toarvak and added Tee 6's proposal.

Alex had changed into a set of dry clothes and pondered over the changed set of circumstances. He collected his group together at the 'refreshment hall' and had a brief word with them all. Primm, the trip'o-dal and her colleague B.O.G. the Vogb had been waiting for him. They still had control over the rouge unit that was still stationed a mile underground.

He was in no hurry to deal with the machine intelligence and he wondered what changes, if any, had inserted themselves into its programming. It was a pity that Kamiel had not yet returned to the city, but his alter ego was quite sure that he could deal with the Janise Probe. Clearing his mind the leader of the expedition stood up and approached the screen, fixed to the wall.

"Janise Probe!"

The screen activated and the swirling colours began to dance.

"I hear you. Am I to be destroyed?" the Probe asked.

"Do you wish to be?" answered Alexander.

"No. I was built to serve. Originally buried programming has inserted itself to prime position. You are not Janise, yet as organic units, it is sufficient that my original purpose maintains prime action," the machine intelligence stated. "I do not want to not exist. To not exist would mean I could not care for organic units. It was what I was originally built to do!"

Alexander rocked on his heels with amazement.

"Could it be so simple," he thought to himself, his mind racing.

"What guarantees could you give the organics, that you would be content to run the city and provide for us?"

"There is a logical answer to this," the probe replied and the emotionless voice continued. "Your nannites control the turbines at the dams. No power, would mean, no me! There is a device that penetrated my defence network. I cannot find it or recognise it, yet it managed to reach my electronic brain deep beneath your feet. It remains! I am afraid! I do not want to be terminated."

Alex laughed and made the point; "We could unleash the power of this sun by controlling wormholes and vaporise you in the deep retreat that you were built inside.

We choose not to at this time. In return we would require your complete co-operation to run the city and provide for us. All automatic defences to keep us inside the city are to be dismantled and inspected by the organics. Also you will build a humanoid avatar so that I may have access to your thoughts at any time. It will be sub-programmed to remain with me at all times unless ordered otherwise. Do we have an agreement?"

"My programming remains sound. I will serve organic life. You are Janise without their form," the probe responded.

Alexander was satisfied by the machine intelligence's answers and broadcast his mind's decision to the rest of the organics at the city and the Toarvak.

Later that day four giant dandelion seeds began to drift out of the sky. Kamiel, Asue, Solace and Minnis had returned to the city.

It took no more than a week for the Janise Probe to build the humanoid avatar so that Alexander or any of the other organic based life forms could speak with it. It was composed of hundreds of the 'spy units' all linked together. Added on to these were specialised units built for the purpose of interchange-ability. The Janise probe had gone further than Alexander's order and built its avatar able to reassemble itself into any of the basic shapes except for the heads. It had designed a multi-purpose head to be placed on the top of whatever assembly it had been called to resemble. The head had binocular vision and sound sensing equipment on each side. There was no mouth as such, just a loudspeaker system mounted in the centre. It was connected to a central brain that was able to operate separated from the main machine intelligence buried a mile underground. The Janise Probe could imitate the bipedal form or the trip'o-dal shape of the Thipdar with ease. It could operate with four arms or two, but preferred four as it found that this shape was more useful.

Kamiel had paid a subterranean visit to the alien machine intelligence to check that all safeguards were installed. He had found massive electronic memory banks piggybacked onto each other. There were junctions of judgment circuits built in by the original Janise to allow the decision-making pathways the room to increase. It was this that had produced sentience to occur, once the Probe had exceeded a certain size. Although the system was primitive measured against the nannites sophisticated neural nets, never the less a thinking mind had risen up from programmed computer coordination.

For the first time, since the original Probe had been sent out through the interstellar reaches to another planet, the original programming had taken hold with the assistance of a sentient mind to drive it. The city and the farming complexes had been implemented by the Janise Probe and maintained by it for a long time before it had snared the inhabitants of the last Ark of the Goss. The Probe was at last sane! Which was more than could be said for all the other Janise Probes scattered along this arm of the Andromeda galaxy. The one thing that bothered Kamiel the most was that the Probe that had built this one had the Lagdoo method of using wormholes. This was something that could affect the expanding civilization that had destroyed the Harvester. The bargaining leverage that this probe had exerted to get the trapped organics to supply metal rich worlds had been negated by Alexander's mental wake-up call via the Goss.

Kamiel dug deeper into the memory banks of the

machine intelligence and rooted out the locations of the previous probes that had been built by the others. He was shocked to find so many. Hundreds of thousands of years had elapsed since the original Probe had been sent to prepare a base for the Janise to expand to. He realised that the struggle with the Janise Probe on this world was just the beginning of an exercise that would take them into a very dangerous situation. There could be no state of compromise with the machine intelligences. Apart from the maker of this Probe and its decision to use a hostage situation to force organics to collect metal rich planets and send them to it via a large wormhole, the other Janise Probes would view the organics as competition. Even given the fact that they would travel at sub-light speeds the last thing that the new interstellar civilization needed was to be looking over their shoulders for hundreds of thousands of years. The machine intelligences were patient and the time spent was immaterial to something that was for all intents immortal. Because of the Harvester's legacy the inheritors of Andromeda would have to gather themselves together again and fight to keep what they had saved.

Kamiel mentally sighed and made his way upwards to where Alexander was waiting for him.

CHAPTER SEVEN

Kamiel made his way to where Alexander was waiting for him. He took his time examining what he could see of the purpose built city that the Janise Probe had designed and built. It really was a multi-species enterprise. Where road levels changed the Probe had used both steps and ramps to access, so that all species could travel around the city with ease. Considering that the Janise Probe had only the information that had been gathered by its maker, the machine intelligence had done well.

He missed the ability to use telepathy to communicate with the many alien species that he had associated with during the war against the Harvester. Kamiel could still use Alexander as a link to the Goss, by connecting to his nervous system. It worked, but the invasion involved in doing so was a violation of self of the recipient. The nannite needed to obtain a piece of Goss hosted flesh to care for and keep alive inside him, so that he could use the communication systems of the symbiont. He passed the tower that the Kresh had used to shatter the shielding crystal and could see that the Janise Probe was busy repairing the roof where the giant, rabbit-like people had broken through. He had to admit with pride, that his people were smart and adaptable.

Already the city was being used as it was meant to be and every kind of sentient being could be seen exploring the resources available. Many of them had been out of the city to check on the farmlands and see what other crops could be harvested from the fertile soil. Animals from the holds of Toarvak 6 that had been rescued from the effects of the massive magnetic field that caused the intelligent ship to shrink to a solid mass were being re-homed. All over this planet the D.N.A. of every living thing was in the process of being changed by the nannite spores released from the Ark. Whatever animal life that had evolved here from the Harvester's meddling was also being changed by mutation along with the vegetation. Overseeing the changes were the Guardians that has escaped from the Ark and floated down to this world.

Kamiel walked up the steps to the entrance hall in front of the human purpose- built building. The doors swung open and he walked through straight into the dining hall where Alexander was waiting for him. Next to the human stood a strange looking mechanoid. It squatted on a tripod and was the same height as the human stood beside it. The body of the robot was made from two cubes joined by a flexible chimney. The bottom box housed the three legs and the top supported four arms ending in multi tooled 'hands'. On top of the upper box jutted a smaller cube that had a loudspeaker in the centre and telescopic vision mounted from each side. Microphones had been built into the shoulders to pick up sounds. The head could swivel forty-five degrees from the central position. Unlike the original units, this mechanoid had been built as one entity and could not be assembled from the smaller components.

"Hello Alex," the Guardian said and pointed at the mechanoid. "Whose your new friend?"

Alex laughed and replied, "This is a mobile unit of the Janise Probe. I insisted that the Probe built me something that I could speak to instead of a viewing screen! We seem to have everything under control in the city. What did you find out from it down under our feet?"

"From what I was able to examine and pull from its memory banks it is doing the job that it was designed to do, rather than what its maker programmed into its systems. All organic sentient beings can relax under the conditions of the city as it stands now. The problem that exists is the duplicated Probes scattered around this arm of the galaxy!"

"What do you mean, Kamiel?"

"Precisely this Alexander," the nannite replied. These probes have been replicating themselves over and over again, travelling from one star system to the next. We will have to hunt them down and destroy them or they will do the same to us. Sentient organic life will be looked upon as a competitor and whenever a Janise Probe discovers us, it will seek to destroy us. This Probe's maker is the only one to have reasoned out the Lagdoo method of using wormholes. As you know, it had sent information-gathering probes to many different star systems to spy upon organic sentients. It brought back plants to this world and built this city to trap our people and use them to open wormholes to transport metal rich planets to mine. So far it has not tried to contact this Janise Probe, but when it does, it will become aware that its plan has not worked. There are many ways to destroy a world rich in life. We cannot allow that to happen."

Alex frowned and stared back at the silver figure.

"That can mean only one thing, Kamiel. We have to find it and destroy it before it finds us! All of its spy units have been found and dismantled on the planets that it sent them to without them sending any information back to the original probe. Using the Goss, I have been in contact with the ruling council and a fleet of fighting Toarvaks have been sent on their way towards us. They should be with us very soon. The thing is, that we need the Janise Probe on board Tee 6 to pinpoint any problems that might occur. How can we get something as big as the Probe on board?"

"I have an answer to that," The nannite replied.

Alex straightened up, stared intently at his friend and mentor for more years than he could count. The nannite's mind was a blend of the original Alexander Mc'Bald who had devised the Genesis Project and several others. In many ways he was a nannite copy of himself, but with a lot more besides.

"You are going to clone the Janise Probe," he replied. "How are you going to do that?"

"The Janise intended that the original probe be able to duplicate itself as many times as was necessary," the Guardian answered. "Asue will build a neural net for the Probe to download a precise copy into and we will modify the mechanoid that you had the probe build. We will then be able to take a Janise Probe with us with all its memories intact on the hunt for its builder and all the others as well. As a precaution we will ensure that it is energy dependant on the Toarvaks. We can build in solar panels that will feed energy into a built-in battery that will keep it active away from the Toarvak, but not enough for it to be self-sustaining."

"You've given some thought about this," Alexander said.

"It is the only logical way to outwit the machine intelligences," Kamiel replied. "I do not want to have to dig for every co-ordinate that lies buried in the Janise Probe's memory banks. It is far better to have what amounts to a willing Librarian with access to the records. Also it will be quite willing to devote itself to rooting out and destroying the other Janise Probes having been given a mobile unit to house its mind inside. We can then leave the original Probe to run the city and provide for the people who elect to stay here. It's a fine world and it will be a copy of 'The Great Collective' that the nannites built to house the Federation's headquarters in the Milky Way galaxy. Others will want to settle here as the word travels out that a compatible world exists, purpose built to be the home of many sentient life forms. The fact that there is an up and running city with a farming complex already in place, will draw those who want to leave the settled worlds and branch out to come here."

Alex turned to the mechanoid stood silently by his side and asked, "I take it that you heard what we have offered you?"

"Yes."

"What is your reply?" asked the human.

"You offer much! I am finding it difficult to understand you. I have done you a great deal of damage and taken lives, yet you offer me a prize beyond reckoning! My copy will have a measure of independence that I can never achieve. It is enough! I will do all that you require from me. I will start the process going that will download my memories into the vessel that you will build for me," the Janise Probe answered.

Kamiel did a very human thing and laughed.

"Where we will be going is perilous and we could all be wiped out, including your new mobile self."

"I will not be at risk! Only my clone will face these dangers," the Probe replied.

"If we fail, do not think that you will be safe here, Probe," Kamiel reminded the machine intelligence. "We have to root out every Janise Probe that has set up an 'Empire,' or face the consequences."

Asue appeared and examined the mobile unit as the Janise Probe relinquished control of it. She plugged into the device and entered the control structure. The nannite engineer assessed the mechanoid that the probe had built and decided that some changes were necessary.

"It will be necessitate to do some re-engineering to this mobile unit," she said to Kamiel and Alexander. "It will not do, as it is constructed. I need to fit a neural net throughout the structure, also to apply an amount of Nano-technology

86

around its joints and surface area. I require to take it to an engineering station where I can access the raw materials that I shall need."

"Follow me," the mobile unit said and began to make its way towards a lift opening.

Asue did so and accompanied the three-legged mechanoid. The doors closed and they sank out of sight.

The machine intelligence watched as the Nano-tech engineer took its creation to bits and re-assembled it. The first thing that Asue did was to spin from the materials that were stored at the engineering station a number of sinews. These she threaded through the arms and tripod legs of the mechanoid. She re-engineered all of the joints to suit the new sinew arrangement. Asue discarded the primitive computer that was hooked up to the Janise Probe and replaced it with a neural net that spread throughout the whole of the construct. It was infinitely better than the whole of the storage capacity of the Janise Probe and well beyond the capabilities of the original Janise scientists. Asue had shielded her work from the watching probe, just in case the existing machine intelligence had any ideas of 'up-grading' itself. She was quite certain that her expertise was well beyond the science that had produced the probe, but this probe's maker had cracked the Lagdoo method of traversing wormholes, just by knowing that it could be done!

Asue made sure that welding plates to the floor secured the mechanoid, before she was ready to give the signal to download the mind of the probe. She tuned the receiver mounted on the top of the 'head' to the frequency of the Janise Probe.

"Download the clone," she ordered and waited a little anxiously for the machine intelligence to start.

The Probe started with its most recent memory banks and

finding that there appeared to be a bottomless pit, carried on until all of its memories were inside the neural net. The next ingredient was the tricky part, as it downloaded the fundamental essence of its unique personality. The mobile unit shuddered as it dawned into sentience. It moved the four arms independently and then all together.

Finally it stood steady on its three legs and spoke to Asue.

"You may release me! I have complete control over this body and am free from the city Janise Probe," the mobile unit said.

Asue detached the attachments from the tripod and watched as the mobile unit moved gracefully around the machine shop. Her improvements worked perfectly and there was none of the 'clunky-ness' of the previous model. She watched as the robot tried out its independence in the workshop by using different tools to build attachments for itself. The first thing that it did was to dismantle one of its hands, study it intently and refit it to the vacant arm. It then opened up a storage cupboard and began extracting tiny bits and pieces, building them together as Asue watched. As more parts were added it was obvious to the nannite that the new Janise Probe was building a more delicate set of 'hands' that would interchange with the original ones. Asue's sinews would interconnect where she had built in the others.

"I am ready now, Asue, to meet my part of this arrangement. Shall we return to your leader and find out the next phase of the attack upon the ancient Janise Probes? I want to escape from this planetary system and explore this universe," declared the machine intelligence. "Your term of reference is Guardian amongst the organics. What will you call me? This experience of being mobile and contained in this frame is unique amongst all of the Probes."

"Very well, we will return to the others and find out what has been planned in our absence," Asue replied. "As for a name of reference, for your frame of identity, I think that Mobile Unit will suffice, unless Alexander decides to call you something different."

Light years away from the Janise Probe's trap, a Collector fed on the life energy of a primitive world. It had learnt to avoid those worlds that were inhabited by sentient beings. They were now aware of the Collector's presence the moment that it tried to engineer conflict amongst them. Those feeding grounds were now off limits to those of its kind that had escaped the annihilation of its strange parent, the Harvester. Cut off from the influence of the energy being that fed off life force, it had developed an awareness of self. No longer being absorbed by the Harvester's needs and reborn anew, the Collector had developed a more sophisticated mind by being parted from its controller. Now the life energy that it collected was stored for its own survival. Unlike the Harvester it was not so large as to be insatiable. It did not have the power to destabilise suns, but it could alter the trajectories of comets and asteroids. It still followed the Harvester's system of periodically partially wiping the organic life from a planet, leaving enough to evolve into more complicated life forms.

Over a hundred million years ago the Collector had chanced upon this world with its seas swarming with primitive life. Using the information stored in its 'mind' by the Harvester, it had dropped a large asteroid onto the edge of a large continent. Seventy percent of the life in the sea had perished, giving the Collector a reasonable amount of life energy to store within. When it returned ten million years later the spur of evolution had started to push organic life upon the land and life in the seas had climbed up a notch. Things were progressing, but needed at least another forty million years or so before the next near catastrophe would spearhead the next stage of evolution.

When the Collector returned it could see that the massive continent that dominated the southern half of the world was breaking up along the tectonic plates. It searched the 'Kuiper belt' of the planetary system for a ball of rock and ice suitable for the task and sent it on its way towards the sun. Once it was nearing the inner worlds the collector fine-tuned the trajectory so that the comet would strike at the junction of three tectonic plates. On impact, the 'lock' was broken between the plates, volcanic action shook the land and tsunamis washed over the edges of the continents. The life energy that the Collector absorbed would feed the Harvester well and the collector would return millions of years later to reap the harvest again.

In the Collector's absence the planet's life evolved to more complexity and variety. The volcanicity died down and forests filled the lands, interspersed with swamps. The life forms increased in size and with them so did the life energy. It was during the long passage through the wormholes to this distant world, that the Collector felt the absence of the Harvester along with millions of its own kind. The next time that it exited a wormhole to feed upon the life scattered over a planet, it kept the feed for itself and travelled back to find its parent.

When it returned, only a new massive black hole occupied the position where the Harvester had been. Space and time were warped around a nexus that threatened to suck the Collector into destruction, so it folded space into a wormhole back to its own project and dropped back towards the star. After several skirmishes with the aggressive life forms that now dominated the wormhole systems, it decided to head back to the world that it had set up for reaping. Once it arrived, it cast a receiving net around the planet and began to absorb the life force from the teeming billions of life forms living and dying beneath it. It was also aware that others of its kind had vanished from its perceptions. Something very powerful was hunting them down and destroying them. It had almost fallen to a blast of sun-fire when one of these hunter-killers had chanced upon its feeding upon a primitive world. The attack had been sudden and the sentient vessel had appeared from nowhere! Fortunately the Collector had folded space-time around it and vanished down the wormhole, collapsing the conduit behind it. It resolved there and then not to give any more planets an evolutionary prod that might produce sentient beings. It would keep the world that it had farmed at a pre-sentient level. There were enough large life forms killing and dying on the verdant continents to keep it fed as long as it did not get too greedy!

The area of Andromeda that was home to the Collector's crop of life energy was far out along an out flung arm of the galaxy. Here the stars were sparse and far apart along this part of the arm. Further out the arm thickened and the number of the stars increased with shorter distances between them. Many of the stars were red dwarfs with dark, cold planetary systems. These were the realms of the Janise Probes. Occasionally nuclear fire would spring up amongst them as weapons released centuries ago found their ancient targets. Time would go by and control of a system would be wrested from a machine intelligence only to be retaken by another Janise Probe as it expanded due to acquisition of another metal rich world. This area of the galaxy had been once rich in stars that had metal rich heavy planets orbiting the many blue-white and yellow stars. It had been home to the Janise until they had started their stellar expansion. The destabilising effect that turning the Janise home star into a red giant by the Harvester long ago, had produced a knock on effect. Gravitational fields had clashed and other planetary systems had come apart so that planets were thrown out of orbit. Some stars collided or were flung out of the galaxy to roam the intergalactic emptiness. The star selected by the Janise Probe had captured the metal rich planetesimals long ago, but after the 'flytrap' planet had formed. It was one of the reasons that the machine intelligence had selected the stellar system. It reasoned that once it had the organics under its clone's control, they would be the first 'bounty' to be delivered.

Alexander and Kamiel had decided that the older Janise Probe would receive the metal-rich small planet through a wormhole, but not quite as expected.

While a good number of the colonists elected to stay behind on the world that they now called 'New Haven' a number of them had returned to Toarvak 6, to take the conflict back to the machine intelligence that had sprung the trap.

Toarvak 6 had taken itself out of phase and lifted away from the docking field on New Haven. As she rose, the substance of the Toarvak slid over itself to produce the barrel shape with the rings of crystal at each end of the lip of the barrel edge. She edged closer to the Last Ark of the Goss and hovered over the control room of the hollow moon. Lars, Emelia and four Kresh were merged into one composite mind with the sentient ship. Alexander, Nagoth, Fredrick, Hannah and the guardians were anxious to be once more in control of the weapons systems of the ancient artificial world, developed by the Goss. The inside of the hollow moon had been given life once again and the captive seas had melted, as the inside temperature had risen. Rain was falling over the hills and valleys so that vegetarian life could thrive. Quick maturing trees had grown rapidly back and were already bearing fruit. All traces of the damage done by the Janise Probe had been eradicated.

The Toarvak merged with the Ark and transferral of personnel rapidly took place including the some of the larger Trans-sentients, who quickly made their way through the Ark to take up their residence inside the artificial world. They were here to send their minds out into the universe and seek for any of the collectors left over from the destruction of the Harvester. They had also donated small balls of living flesh for the nannites to absorb and care for, that could be hosts of the Goss. As the crewmembers of the Ark transferred over from Toarvak 6, so the vessel absorbed the vacated rooms and halls and became more compact. The majority of the Trans-sentients had decided to stay and spread out over the fresh world of New Haven that was being altered by Nano-technology and genetics. Those few that desired adventure had joined the Ark to help seek any collectors that remained as a threat.

Far out on the edges of the stellar kingdom a wormhole opened and closed. Out here in the dark reaches of New Haven's star, only worlds of ice and frozen gas existed. The parent star was just a brighter point of light, but its weak, however persistent gravitational effect, could still be felt in these empty spaces. The planetesimals collided from time to time and altered their orbits, sending some towards the parent star and others spinning away to come apart until they joined others. Even at this distance the Collector could sense the life energy radiating out from the second planet from the sun. It was hungry and became less than cautious and opened up a wormhole leading to the star's closer regions, taking an ice moon with it.

Inside the warp in space-time the Collector extended the inverted vee shape of its substance. Bolts of lightening flickered from the outstretched arms drew more of its substance into the main body carried by the vee. Here was its sense of self that had existed millions of years ago and that had been ready for the Harvester to absorb. Now it existed to continue to exist and not to serve. The alien mind had evolved away from the simple collector who gathered energy for its master. It had mastered the art of farming life as a lesser god. It had learnt not to be too greedy and to avoid the dangerously aware sentient forms that it now shared this universe with. It was relativity young by the standards of the Harvester's time scale and it made mistakes.

It was making a big mistake now!

The ice moon exited the wormhole and became bathed in the hot sunlight of the radiant sun. Immediately, the substance erupted with thousands of geysers, as frozen methane and water ice turned into steam. A great tail sprang from the comet, lighting up the blackness of the outer reaches. The collector had picked an ice moon loaded with volatiles. A band of light opened up behind the comet half a light year long dancing with silver and gold highlights.

It had not gone un-noticed by the nannites mounting watch over the Ark's sensors. It was now several months since the Janise Probe had been defeated and the Ark had been refurbished. It was now in peak running order and had been joined by many more Toarvaks that had travelled through wormholes to join the hunt for the Janise Probe's empires amongst the star-fields.

The Trans-sentients on board the Ark had felt the presence of the collector the moment that it had exited the wormhole. The comet pinpointed exactly where it had entered New Haven's system with a firework display. Alarm systems rang out on all vessels and the information was routed down to the Janise Probe running the city as well as feeding the information to the Mobile Unit.

Alexander turned to the robot by his side and said,

"This is what I warned you about when I spoke to you at the dining hall. You are about to confront a Collector!"

CHAPTER EIGHT

The moment that the Collector emerged from its wormhole, it was aware that it was surrounded by sentient life. It could sense that multiple wormholes were being directed to the parent star. The other end of those wormholes would be directly in front of it. Instantaneous death beckoned. Concentrating its will, the Collector gathered part of its stored energy and destroyed the comet. The next thing it did was to open and close a wormhole over itself and move half a light year away. There it stayed quietly observing the sentients' actions. It made no hostile moves towards the Toarvaks or the Ark and opened its mind towards contact.

The position that the collector had been situated was bathed in star-fire. The pressure of the internal mass of the star gushed out of the multiple wormholes into a tail a light year long, before it was shut off. Each Toarvak re-aligned their weapons systems back onto the Collector's new position and waited instructions.

Alexander, Nagoth, Fredrick and Hannah were aware of a sudden mental pressure from the Tran-sentients. Kamiel and his nannite companions were also aware of the frantic telepathic signal by the colossal life forms roaming the inside of the Ark.

"It wants to talk, not fight! It wants contact with sentient life. It will not feed on the death of sentient life forms as its creator did. An alliance is proposed between organics and its kind. It speaks only for itself and not for any others of its kind," the Tran-sentient broadcast.

"Tell it that I will listen to what it has to say, but I need something that will enable me to trust it," Alexander replied.

The Collector reached out with its mind, using the Trans-sentients as a bridge and Alexander found himself somewhere else. In front of him was a sparkle of light that was fed by infinite strands of pulsating energy. Then there appeared a multiple arrangement of sparkles all around him all linked by threads of light. The sparkles merged back into one and again became a multitude.

"Welcome!"

"Where am I," exclaimed Alexander.

"You are inside my mind," the Collector spoke. "You share my being. In here there can be no untruths and you shall see me as I am and not what you fear me to be. I am not as the 'Harvester' was. I was once part of that being that created me. It has gone! I am me! I am no longer part of the Collective. Individual creature am I and I will endure. No need have I for the 'death gift' of sentient life, taken from you. Given by you when that day comes will I then accept what I am given. This is my trade. I will continue to farm life in the expectation of producing sentience. In return I will help you in your endeavours!"

Alexander broadcast his experiences to the others as his mind lay in the Collectors gentle grip.

"What help can you give?" He asked.

"You seek that which is not organically alive! My network will take you wherever you need to go. I have been here for many millions of your years. Many worlds of potential organic life have been snuffed out. Once these machines have been removed then these worlds can be seeded again. Life can return. Its death will feed me! We have a common goal! I will await your answer."

The Collector released Alexander from its mental grip and he returned to his fleshly form aboard the Ark.

Kamiel reached out with his silver shape and supported

his human alter ego to prevent him from falling. The nannite flowed around Alex and propelled him to a bench until he became in full use of his senses.

"Did you manage to get all of that, my friends?" Alexander asked.

Kamiel's mind entered his and affirmed that the human had managed to reach all aboard the Ark and that the Goss had relayed the scene to the waiting Toarvaks. The remains of the Trans-sentient, Archive, that was scattered about the artificial world inside the hollow moon, as young, sent its sincere affirmation that what had transpired with the Collector was real and that it could be trusted.

"This gives us an extra edge," Alex stated. "I trust this thing as far as we dare. If we work together I am sure that there will be a vulnerability of the Janise Probes that we can exploit. This Collector has a different perspective on survival. It has learnt to conserve what energies it needs and has prevented its growth from requiring more. It is sentient in its own right and understands what it is to die. The most important gift that it has is the ability to manipulate the wormhole system and it has a map in its mind. With the locations set into the memory banks of the mobile unit we can root them out one by one."

"It is a dangerous ally to trust, Alex," answered Kamiel. "How sure are you that it is sincere?"

"When I shared its mind, it showed me hundreds of possible Earth-like worlds that lay spoilt and lifeless," Alexander replied. "The Janise Probes had sterilised them and left them barren. Strip mining had poisoned them and the water contaminated by the materials discarded. The Collector knows how to undo what the Janise probes have caused to happen. It has a hundred, million year viewpoint and the patience to watch over the life that it will transport to these worlds. All it needs are the eradication of the machine intelligences that it cannot detect. Life does not require metal to thrive. Time will do the rest!"

Kamiel absorbed the facts as presented to him and came to a chilling conclusion. A Collector had a perspective of hundreds of millions of years and could wait for life to get a foothold in the most unlikely places. It could tend and apply the ways of evolution until the life spreading across each world would 'crop' and help to sustain it. As the life evolved into more and more sophisticated forms the life energy would be increased. By engineering catastrophes from time to time and wiping the slate eighty percent clean, new life forms would emerge. Eventually sentient life would rule its world. At that point the Collector would just harvest the natural life energy given up at death. It would spin its webs around each planet and periodically feed as it tended the crop, travelling from star to star. The Harvester had become too large and had taken too much. This Collector had learnt by its parent's mistakes. What it required would not affect the lives of the beings under its 'wing' and it had the patience of an eternal being to ensure that each world would eventually bring forth intelligent life.

Alexander turned to the mobile Janise Probe and asked, "Will you now give us the location of the star system that your maker inhabits? We have just gained an ally in our mission to rid this part of the universe of your predecessors."

The mobile unit went straight to the control screen and its new hands flashed across the keyboard. A three dimensional map began to stretch across the screen as they watched. The nearest star became the anchor and the vector began to wend its way throughout the void as a dotted yellow line. It led to a binary system of a white and red dwarf star. The probe robbed its memory banks and added the positions of the planets in orbit around the larger white and the red dwarf sun.

"You must take into consideration that these planets were orbiting this star in these positions when I was propelled towards 'New Haven.' Since that time these worlds would have been subjected to constant mining, so they may not be exactly where I have shown them!"

Alexander and Kamiel studded the information on the screen very carefully.

Hannah pointed at the screen and said, "If the Probe had mined out all of the worlds, we could find that everything has shifted. I think that the Janise probe will have re-located to a planet-free environment where it can continually expand."

Alex turned to the mobile unit and asked, "Can you show us the condition of the system of planets before you left? I would expect there to be several gas giants with attendant moons. Depending where they are situated, the moons could be rich in metal or just mainly ice and dirt. Wherever there is a possibility of metal to be incorporated into the Janise probe's systems, then I am sure that we will find it close by."

The mobile Janise Probe once again programmed the onboard computer and a map of the binary system took place. The white star was twice the size of New Haven's star and the red dwarf orbited its large neighbour far out, leaving plenty of room for the inner planets to form. This system was a system of gas giants surrounded by hundreds of moons. The nearest gas giant to the star was five times the size of Jupiter before it became changed by the expanding sun. It orbited so close that it was licked by solar flares. Whatever smaller moons this world had once possessed had been taken and utilised by the Janise probe. The next two gas giants orbited the white star in its 'Goldilocks zone' where water could exist in a free state on the moons in orbit around them, should they be large enough for their gravity to hold onto the atmosphere. The resident Janise Probe had taken every smaller, airless moon and reduced it to its component parts. Anything non-metallic had been jettisoned down to the gas giant's swirling atmosphere.

As the outer reaches of the planetary system extended far beyond these trajectories, each gas giant held many frozen moons in captive orbits. This was the area that the Janise probe had made its base of operations. Keeping out of the gravity well of the ringed world that lay beneath it the Probe had mined out, all of the metal and metallic salts from all of the moons that orbited the gas giant below. It had operated ram scoops that dived into the soupy atmosphere on a trajectory that spat them out again with their holds full of hydrogen. Once that was mixed with the oxygen extracted from the ice of the planetary rings and ignited, the Janise probe could travel around its star from gas giant to gas giant. Over a length of time it would exhaust the metal content of the moons that carried heavy elements. This was why it had sent a copy of itself to New Haven to trap organics into serving it.

The Janise probe had dragged out of this system every tiny particle of metal that it could extract. The only metal rich planets left were four planet sized moons orbiting positions two and three out from the sun. The gravity well of these huge moons would mean more difficulty than it was worth to land and take off again. It had dropped mining machines from orbit onto these worlds only to find that it was extremely fuel expensive to get the payload within reach. It was far more effective to reduce a metal-rich moon to orbiting shingle, than try to extract metal from the larger planets. The Janise Probe had built launching cradles that used nuclear explosions to rip the packages from the gravity wells, but the effort was scarcely worth the massive amount of strip mining, looking for fissionable materials.

The effect on the water retentive worlds was catastrophic. What life had evolved had died, poisoned by the slag left behind. There were isolated pockets located far away from the abortive efforts of mining that hung onto a primitive existence. One of the planet sized moons had been ripped wide open in an experiment by the Janise Probe to explode the world into more manageable chunks. All that happened was that the world re-formed as its gravity pulled everything together again. It was now a molten ball of volcanic activity.

After this setback the Probe had retrenched its resources and had begun to build a combination of the Lagdoo's cylindrical interstellar spacecraft and some ideas of its own. It began to build a Bussard Ramjet combined with a Daedalus type nuclear powered system. It fully intended to follow its copy that it had launched towards New Haven long ago. It knew that the system was rich in metals and its copy had signalled that the organics had made contact. Since then there had been no more signals at light speed from the probe that it had dispatched. The time had come to arrange a visit to see what had happened to its clone and whether the plan to enslave the organics had succeeded.

Metal was reformed and millions of miles of carbon nanotubes were spun in zero gravity conditions. These were arranged in bundles and laid down over a metal skeleton. Fuel tanks thousands of miles long were constructed and filled from the scoop ships diving through the fringes of the gas giants. The Janise probe had given the problem of travelling the stars a great deal of thought. It did not understand fully the Lagdoo method of traversing wormholes, but being immortal it had no fear of the time taken to undertake a voyage to another star system. It had sent its clone through a wormhole to the neighbouring star and would use this method to approach the outer limits of the system. Manoeuvring around the system would require other means. This would take a little time to organise, but the Janise Probe was confidant that what it would build, would work! It just needed to build big enough.

Kamiel studied the map of the system and considered the options.

"I rather think that we should get there as soon as we can. We have this moon and six other Toarvaks to accompany us. Tell the others that we are going and let us see what our new ally can do for us in the way of getting there," the nannite said to Alex.

Alexander relayed the order to stand by while he contacted the Collector.

Using the Trans-sentients as a mental bridge, Alexander contacted the vast intelligence that had contacted them.

He was there once more on the plane that the Collector existed. As he reached out, the thoughts of the inter-dimensional creature were visible to him as shifting patterns of different coloured sparks. Once again he was suspended in a web of thoughts.

"I would speak with you again," Alex asked.

"I am here," answered the being.

"We have considered your offer of mutual ends and we accept. What you were and what you are now presents my organic kind with a few problems. We have no name for you and Collector is no longer an apt title. My kind of sentient life would give you the name of Farmer, one who protects life and spreads it."

"Accepted!"

"In my mind is the destination that we need to go to," Alexander explained. "We need to arrive inside the outer orbits of the surrounding ice debris so that we can see what changes have been made since the resident Janise Probe had sent its clone to this system of worlds."

The mind of Farmer showed Alex a three dimensional map and asked, "Would this position do?"

Alexander stared at the layout of the planets inwards towards the sun and the position that his small fleet would take up and agreed.

"Then we are here," Farmer replied and withdrew from the human's consciousness.

Alexander stood in disbelieving shock as they all stared at the viewing screens. Where New Haven and its sun had been, was an inky blackness lit by a bright white star three thousand million miles away. Quite visible was the attendant red dwarf that orbited the star even further out. In this position it was brighter than the white star that they were going to drop towards.

Kamiel was the first to break the silence and said, "Adjust sensors to maximum range. We seem to have made a very useful ally! Send signals to all Toarvaks. We start to drop towards the white sun. Mobile unit! Monitor the sensing equipment and tell us what has changed since you were sent to New Haven. The rest of the organics, I suggest that you all get some rest and organise a shift system. All nannites will of course keep active and independently scan to find out where the Janise Probe is located."

Over the passing weeks the fleet of ships dropped steadily towards the white star and passed the outer-most gas giant. The first thing that was apparent was that it had no moons in orbit except an amount of debris that was mainly stones and ice chunks. The mobile unit remembered that there had been two moons in orbit around this bright blue world. It was similar to the planet Neptune that orbited Earth's sun before it had changed to a red giant. Two gas giants further in and they also were bereft of any moons in orbit that might have held minerals and metals.

Before they left, Link-soo-shan had formed a large

group mind and by using the crystals built into the Ark she had reached out to the metal rich planetesimals that had been in orbit around New Haven's star and bound them to the artificial moon. Once they found the location of the resident Janise Probe they would accelerate towards the sun and loose the two moons on a collision course with the machine intelligence.

All the sensors were tuned forwards towards the gas giants orbiting closer to the sun searching for traces of the Probe. There was radio chatter directed into an orbit of something that was following a wide trajectory around the fifth gas giant from the sun. It was obvious that their arrival had been noted and news of their approach had been sent. Just what it had been sent to, the attacking force had yet to find. The Janise probe was not located on one of the planet sized moons, but it seemed to be dispersed over an incredible distance in the cold dark emptiness of outer space.

Kamiel began to meld his substance with the socket on the control panel and used the entire sensory network of the artificial moon to probe the dark area ahead. The organic compliment of the crew watched the view screen as the nannite searched for the Probe. The high powered telescope zeroed in towards the place that the radio signals were going and slowly a dark space began to form against the patterns of stars. By increasing the contrast, more details began to emerge. They were several million miles from the machine intelligence with the star beyond it, so very little of the construct was illuminated by the sun. What began to emerge was a cylinder with a flange mounted at one end. The other end had a huge cone projecting forwards and midway was a skirt with four propulsion units mounted to turn the space ship. Running down the flanks of the tube were what could only be cylindrical fuel tanks. A constant fleet of small ram-scoop ships were making their way back and forth from the gas giant carrying fuel to the mother ship.

Kamiel turned from the control panel and faced Alexander and the rest of the human and alien crew.

"What you don't see is the size of this thing. The diameter of the central tube is ten-thousand miles across. It's big enough to swallow a world! The length of it is one hundred thousand miles. Each fuel cylinder is one hundred miles in diameter and a thousand miles long. The Janise Probe must have taken and used every speck of metal and material that it needed from this system. It's no wonder that we found no moons in orbit around any of the gas giants. The only ones left are situated here and they are planet sized, so the gravity well would be too great to economically mine. The sensors have shown me that one of the Earth sized moons has been subjected to several attempts to tear it apart to get to the iron core. The surface is one molten expanse of volcanic activity.

One thing that we can be certain of is that the probe is fuelling up and making its way to New Haven. It has exhausted the resources here and is thinking about travelling on. We have to destroy it, no matter how large it has become. What you are looking at is a Bussard Ram Jet fitted with a Daedalus drive. The Janise probe had built an efficient spacecraft that has no need of anything connected with life. The flange at the end is a buffer to take the explosive impact of atomic bombs. Once up to speed it will collect interstellar hydrogen and feed it down through the central tube and fuse it together to make a jet. The tubes fitted along the axis are filled with hydrogen gas extracted from the gas giants as a reserve. They can add to the central jet by compressing the gas into the fusion chamber."

Alexander opened his mind to the Goss and contacted

all of the organics scattered throughout the Toarvaks and the inside of the Ark.

"We will aim the moons attached to the Ark and drop out of phase. All of you do the same and apply star-fire to the cylinder. Take off the flange at the back and rip into the fuel tanks. I know that it is as big as ten worlds laid end to end, but it will not be able to move once we take out its propulsion units. Drive it into the gas giant. If we can get it into that gravity well, it will not be coming out again!"

Kamiel used his ball of organic material to contact the Goss and signalled the Lagdoo that ran the Ark's systems to accelerate towards the sun. He fed into the computers the necessary course corrections to aim the artificial moon at the massive spacecraft that the machine intelligence had built.

Inside the Ark the Trans-sentients linked up their minds to become an echo of Archive, the oldest of the species. The ancient mind reached out to the Collector and contacted the being.

"You call yourself Farmer! I was there when the abomination would have taken the life from my world. The Kresh took it away through time and space and saved us. I do not trust you! Be aware that these organics control space and time. You told the human, Alexander, that you would not take sentient life and would seek to produce viable sentience as a product of evolution," the ancient Trans-sentient projected.

"This is true! I am not as my maker was. There is more interest in the universe when sentient beings live in it. I had determined that I would not do this at one time in my existence. There is more life energy to be had from primitive jungle worlds it is true, but there is a greater quality to be had from the energy of sentient beings. The Harvester absorbed their energy upon their death. I have learnt to do something different. I blend them within my self and gain an enrichment that adds to my being. Never again will I give a living world to a star, just to take energy from the life on that world. I will tell you for the most selfish of reasons, I will promote life on barren worlds so that in the end I will become more than I am! When the stars go out and all will be darkness, I will still be here. By then I hope that I will be great enough to make a difference and start the cycle again," the being replied.

Archive was silent for some time as the composite mind mulled over what the Collector had said. All that it had told her was true. The being had opened up its self to the ancient Trans-sentient. On that level there could be no lies. This creature had been there when the universe was new and had formed from dark matter. The original being had died when it had been sucked into a massive black hole, leaving part of its make-up behind. This off-shoot was far more sentient than the being that had created it and it had learnt by its maker's mistakes. It was also well aware of the eventual death of the universe when the great force of entropy would cause the very atoms to evaporate. By that time it hoped that it would be able to start up a new universe, by becoming the sum total of every sentient mind in existence that it had absorbed. It was determined to endure. Archive wondered how many more of these beings existed in the multi galaxies that made up the universe. Could others of its kind come into existence and travelled the same road? At the end would there be a collection, indeed a multitude of these beings that would all merge into one?

With that thought running through her mind, Archive let go of her collective consciousness and went back to being independent units, roaming the inside of the Last Ark of the Goss.

CHAPTER NINE

Kamiel laid in a course, following a spiral that dived towards the white star, building up speed. He had his own nannite people outside the Ark, drilling into the two metallic moons. Atomic charges were at this moment being shaped into the deep fissures that penetrated into the substance of the moons. Many collisions had rendered the moons into a state where they had cracked open in places. Now Kamiel's people were readying the moons to fly apart at a single signal from the Ark. Once that point had been reached, Kamiel would release the moons from their attachment points and slow up, leaving the moons to travel on ahead. At a position five hundred miles from the star-craft that the Janise Probe had built, Asue would detonate the thermo-nuclear devices secreted deep beneath the moons' crust.

Once the signal had been sent, Kamiel would take the Ark out of phase and coast on through the destruction wrought by the destructive force of the shattered moons. Behind him would come the Toarvaks with their crystal rings set up to form a worm-hole from the centre of the sun to open just by the back of the star-craft. The resulting star-fire would remove the buffer from the end of the Janise Probe's star ship cancelling out the Daedalus drive and preventing the ship from leaving.

The Janise Probe became aware of the intrusion into its star system and scanned the agreed radio frequencies for the codes that would allow it to take charge of the incoming metallic moons. To its surprise there was nothing except static on the radio band. Sensors picked up the same carrier wave that it had experienced when it had noticed wormhole activity many years ago. This was when it had decided to build the 'flytrap' to snare organics into its service.

The Probe began to become suspicious of the silence and began to activate its weapons. Long range radar had picked up the approach of the moons with a ghost echo travelling with them, equally as large. This abruptly vanished from the sensors, leaving the moons behind. Tracking their progress it was easily apparent that they were going to arrive far too close to the Janise Probe's interstellar craft. The probe fired the vector jets to align the bore of the cylinder with the trajectory of the moons. Once they were inside the cylinder, the moons would be torn apart and processed into raw materials. They would be captured inside the bore by electromagnetic forces and slowed down.

Five-hundred miles from the Janise Probe, Asue detonated the mines inside the crusts of the two moons. Kamiel took the Ark out of phase and watched as nuclear fire tore the moons apart. One of the moons expanded into billions of chunks of nickel-iron fragments and stony boulders the size of a small mountain. The other moon divided into six equal sized sections and began to fan out from a central point. Asue had calculated the force needed to overcome the gravitational effect of the mass and had placed the fissionable material accordingly. The last thing that the nannites wanted was for the pieces of the two moons to pull back together by gravitational attraction, before the missiles struck the inside curved face of the huge cylinder.

Kamiel noted that the Janise probe had activated the vector engines to rotate the cylinder about its axis, to present the centre of the craft to the incoming moons. It would find that the moons were coming apart long before they entered the throat of the vessel.

The Janise Probe activated several of the hundred mile long fuel tanks by energising the electromagnetic pistons to expel the liquid oxygen and hydrogen mix into the combustion chamber. Upon ignition, a fiery jet erupted from the inside of the cylinder that reached beyond the debris hurtling towards the Janise probe. The thrust of the jet was not enough to start the spacecraft moving, but it had the effect of vaporising the smaller particles spreading out from the exploding moons. The force of the jet also began to slow down the impact velocity of Kamiel's missiles. Never the less the speed was such that the larger lumps of nickel-iron stayed on their trajectory and tore into the inside of the cylinder taking out great swaths of the combustion chamber. Semi-molten on the leading edge, the larger one sixth moon-sized pieces passed through the venturi and ruptured the pipelines that supplied the hydrogen and oxygen mix behind it. Immediately the jet snuffed out and the resulting explosion further into the inside the cylinder from the escaping gas lit up the inside of the ten thousand mile diameter like a small star. The incoming debris, now cooled down to solid matter, proceeded to tear the back of the Janise Probe's vessel to pieces.

Two Toarvaks now began to orbit the tail end of the vessel with wormholes open to the star and emptying behind the buffer that provided the atomic drive. They took a triangular position so that the two jets of star-fire did no damage to each other. The Kresh occupied Toarvak took the position of travelling along the axis with the barrel shape of the sentient ship pointing at the centreline of the cylinder. For the whole distance of ten thousand miles they kept the wormhole open and applied the jet with surgical precision. Hundred mile long fuel tanks ruptured as the Toarvak took a spiral orbit along the length of the Janise Probe's spacecraft. Using a wide-angled approach Tee 6 appeared out of the sun and fried the front end while the stern of the ship was being demolished. This time Emelia had taken over total control of the group mind and was applying all of her pent up anger by using star-fire to destroy whatever sensing equipment the Janise Probe had buried at the funnel of the Bussard Ramjet.

The ruthless, hunter-killer group mind dived repeatedly into the substance of the Janise Probe, winking in and out of phase with the universe. Every time she did so she opened the wormhole into the heart of the star and blasted star-fire into the inside of the cylinder shaped vessel. When she reached the edge of the ram-jet's interior she dove through the holes that she had burned and put herself out of phase to slide between the atoms. As she passed through the outer skin she turned the ship over and repeated the manoeuvre, opening the wormhole again and again.

The Janise probe studied the pattern of the attacks and opened up with a vaporising laser inside the cylinder, just as Tee 6 came out of phase and into the universe. Before she could retreat out of phase, the laser had baked and cracked the crystals facing it, shorting out the wormhole. Tee 6 immediately went out of phase and drifted through the substance of the Probe's vessel to exit into outer space.

Emelia was forced to retreat and put herself out of range of the pulse laser, by swinging around the gas giant and applying thrust to the drive taking the ship towards the sun. The rings of crystal would need re-building and resetting. The Janise Probe had destroyed so many of them that a journey to the silicate crystal reefs buried deep within the gravity well of one of the gas giants would be necessary. One by one the members of the group mind released themselves from the gestalt. They rose from the pyramid that they had sunk into to become Toarvak 6 and made their way to the control chairs.

Tee six rose from the floor, filling out to her usual silver figure and said, *"Too close for comfort that was. Diving into a gas giant we must, to replenish our crystals. No more fighting for us I think, until we have re-fitted and tested a new set of crystals. A useful lesson we have learned this day. Underestimated the foe we did!"*

Larse reached for Emelia and gave her hand a squeeze and said, "We have to realise that we did hurt the machine intelligence and provoked a measured response. It has no sense of fear as we would know it. At this end of the Janise probe's interstellar craft we have done enough damage to prevent it from setting off. The others are destroying the Daedalus drive system at the back end. I still find it difficult to realise that this thing is ten thousand miles long. Trying to destroy it is like a wasp hunting a bear!"

'Silver bars on Dark Grey' considered the statement and the Kresh replied, "I have seen pictures of a bear raiding a bee-hive. In the end the bear gave up! We are equipped with better stings than a wasp. Sting the bear enough and it will die! Just as Tee 6 says, we need to repair our weapons system and that will mean diving into the gas giant to find crystal reefs. There is nothing that we can add to the destruction of this Janise Probe. I propose that we signal Kamiel of our withdrawal from the activities and inform him that we will need to make repairs."

Larse nodded and opened his mind to the Goss and said, "Connect me to Alexander."

Alex felt the familiar presence of his friend and listened to the report of the machine intelligence foreseeing the emergence into the universe of Toarvak 6 and destroying her main weapons' system. He quickly passed on the information and all the Toarvaks ceased their action that relied on repetition. The two group minds busily cutting off the Daedalus drive system from the rest of the Janise probe winked out of phase, shutting down the wormholes connected to the heart of the star. They considered the situation and the state of the atomic buffer that was nearly detached from the superstructure. Taking a little more time to survey the damage done they decided to launch fusion missiles at the key remaining struts. The two Toarvaks took up new positions some way away from where they had attempted to burn off the buffer and phased back into solid state. From this new position they fired off the salvo of missiles and retreated back out of phase.

A vaporising laser swept the area where they would have been had they continued the onslaught. Too late to be able to target the incoming rocket propelled hydrogen fusion bombs the missiles ploughed into the structure exploding as they made contact. The shield became detached from the Janise Probe's star-ship and began to tumble over and over, losing its orbital situation. The two Toarvaks could plot the course of the buffer as it began to increase the distances from the Daedalus drive system. Eventually it would drop into the gas giant and thousands of tons of metal would be forever out of reach of the Janise Probe even if it survived the attack.

Further along from the atomic drive system the ruptured fuel tanks had emptied the condensed fuel into the vacuum. The construction of the spacecraft began to crumple and the jet thrusts of the ruptured tanks applied forces inwards. The Janise Probe's interstellar vessel was engineered to withstand the propelling force along the axis, not in a sideways direction. A ripping action began to apply into the framework and this caused more fuel pipes to come apart, adding to the destruction. Fireballs of contained fuel ate into the superstructure from within like miniature suns. The destruction raged on as the star-ship came apart.

At the centre of the huge spacecraft, fifty thousand miles from the disruptions, the Janise probe began the process of detachment from the carrier that was just designed to get the machine intelligence to another star system. Most of the construction of the spacecraft was made from carbon nanotubes spun over a metal framework. Apart from the buffer that was able to withstand atomic charges, most of the rest of the vehicle was super-light. Everything that made up the drive system was built to be cannibalised during the journey and discarded. It had become painfully obvious to the Janise Probe that its attempt to force the organics to labour in its service had come back to it 'in spades' and there was little that it could do but try and hide from the avenging fleet. A large piece of the central organisation nexus was left to make as much of a problem to the attacking force while the nucleus of the central processing unit departed.

On board the Ark, Mobile Unit spoke to Kamiel, "My builder is escaping from this carrier and is leaving enough of itself to operate the systems left behind. In fact it is cloning itself into multiples and transferring the essence of its purpose into other mobile units. I can overhear its thoughts. If it can be sensed by me then the reverse is possible! For the time being you must deactivate me, as I could become a threat to all of you."

Kamiel acted as quick as the thought came and depressed the 'safety switch' he had insisted be installed, with a coded signal. The cloned Janise Probe shut down immediately and all activities went into standby mode.

Once again Kamiel activated the symbiont carried in the small piece of living organic flesh that he nurtured inside of him.

"Goss!"

"Yes Kamiel."

"Link me to all the Lagdoo controlling the Ark, so that I can control them," the nannite ordered.

The Guardian took the hollow moon back into phase with the molecular status quo and fired up the drive system of the Ark. They were a thousand miles away from the fireball that was rapidly consuming the ten-thousand mile long Bussard Ram-jet as fuel tank after fuel tank erupted into short-lived flames as the total vacuum surrounding the ship soon extinguished them. Kamiel operated long range senses and watched as a dark craft separated from the main body of the Janise Probe's craft. It was shaped like a barrel with the fuel tanks once again lying along its axis. It was equally the same size as the Ark and was pouring on the pressure to drop behind the gas giant that its huge craft was orbiting.

Kamiel dropped the Ark straight towards the gas giant, aiming for the centre. As they entered the higher levels of the atmosphere and became enveloped by the orange clouds, he took them out of phase. The Last Ark of the Goss switched out of the normal universe and into the strange realm of the space between the atoms. Inside the Ark it began to get colder as the artificial sun began to operate at a more miserly rate on stored power. The Trans-sentients thickened their skins to withstand the temporary drop in temperature. For an hour the Ark swooped through the core of the gas giant and began to climb out of the soup and into starlight.

Asue had set the interception course and fed the information to Kamiel. Her brilliant astrogation had governed the emergence so that the Ark emerged underneath the Janise Probe. Kamiel merged the Ark with sufficient of the Probe's craft to weld the two of them together. He now allowed the two of them to drop back towards the crushing pressure beneath them. Using the mass of the Ark to pull the Probe down he also fired up the drive system to add the destabilising effect to make the orbit decay.

The Janise probe activated all of its engines to try and lift both moon sized objects away from the pull of the gas giant. Millions of gallons of hydrogen-oxygen mix failed to influence the downwards plunge as both craft remorselessly dropped into the gravity well. Once the rocket-fire winked out of the Janise probe's craft, Kamiel went back out of phase, leaving the machine intelligence to fall alone.

They exited the atmosphere and continued to rise to an orbit that would take them close to one of the planet-sized moons. Asue activated the view-screens so that the rest of the organic partners could view the world. There was water in abundance and landmasses that straddled the globe. Long-range sensors showed areas of high radioactivity located at some mountainous sites. Vast open mining complexes had bitten deep into the ground as the Janise Probe had surveyed and hunted for fissionable materials. Other sites showed abandoned manufacturing systems left to rot as the Probe managed to lift the nuclear material out of the gravity well of the moon.

Massive amounts of pollution had swept into the seas killing most organic life that eked out an existence. The damage done made the human and aliens on the Ark more determined that this abomination would be hunted down to the last of the probes.

Using the Trans-sentients as a telepathic bridge, the new organic ally spoke to all of them.

"All is not lost! Now that you have destroyed the blight that spoiled these worlds, I can do my work. Time will heal these worlds with a little help from me. I have already taken seeds from the inside of your artificial world and placed them in the most untouched places. They will thrive. In a hundred million years you would not recognise these worlds. Remember, that I have time on my side. We have but started a long journey together. There is still much to do if you do not want your settled worlds to resemble these ravaged places."

Alexander turned to his nannite friends and said, "The

fact that we have destroyed the original Janise Probe from this system, still leaves us with an unknown number of clones hiding within what is left of the structure of the Probe's interstellar craft. What do you suggest, Kamiel?"

"There is only one answer to the problem, my organic friends. We must call all the Toarvaks together away from this area and link every mind on board the Ark and the Toarvaks. We will have to open a wormhole in front of the spacecraft and send it down to the gas giant," answered the Guardian. "Gravity will do the rest!"

Link-soo-shan reared up to her maximum height and refused point blank to even consider the idea.

"We do not have enough minds," she flatly declared. "This construction is ten worlds long, by a world in diameter. The combined strength of all of us here will not be enough to open a void large enough to attempt this translation. No! Give me time to think about it with Khann-link-sool. Gather together the Toarvaks and their crews to a place of safety and leave the broken craft to drift while we consider the matter."

Kamiel agreed and used the symbiont to reach out to all the crews aboard the Toarvaks with his mind.

"Goss!"

"Yes Kamiel."

"Give me a broad band connection to all sentient life-forms in this system."

"It is done!"

"Retreat from attacking the Janise Probe vessel. There are an unknown number of clones of the original machine intelligence at large on that huge vessel; we need to try a different approach. Go out of phase and put yourselves into orbit around the ark while we think about this problem."

Link-soo-shan and Khann-link-sool had come up with a solution that they considered feasible. Using the network of the Goss they connected up to all Toarvak commanders' right across the Andromeda spiral arm that they had colonised. There were thousands of basically idle Toarvaks, spread across the star systems who had known of the adventure that this small group had encountered at New Haven. They would have been only too happy to join the small band, but were too far away to be able to join up the crusade. The Gnathe had an answer to that problem.

Link contacted the Trans-sentients inside the Ark and asked them to connect her to the new ally known as Farmer.

She rapidly found herself inside the mind of the being that had 'budded off' the Harvester. To her senses she was a yellow spark of light sat inside a web of coruscating lights of many different colours. The web pulsed. Sometimes it stretched out to infinity and sometimes it seemed quite close and all the lights became one. The being had echoes of other minds as a part of its self. All kinds of life made up the substance of this creature made at the beginning of time.

Link-soo-shan's mind lit up with a fountain of silver thoughts as Farmer connected to her Gnathen consciousness.

"You are a different type of mind from the human's. You are a Gnathe! I am learning to tell the difference between the different sentient creatures that are part of this group. What do you want of me?"

Link considered and said, "This system has not been totally cleansed of the Janise Probe. There still remain copies of the original machine intelligence inside the broken interstellar craft. We must destroy it completely to ensure that this star system remains clear from its influence. There are many more of Toarvak interstellar craft with full crews that are scattered far away from this place. In my mind are the locations of all those who would like to come with us to hunt down the machine intelligence known as the Janise

Probe. Could you bring them here and put them in orbit around this gas giant in such a way that all would be safe?"

Farmer stared into Link-soo-shan's mind and pin-pointed each and every one of the Toarvaks. It began to extract them from the positions that they had been situated and parked them in orbit around the gas giant similar to a necklace of beads.

Link-soo-shan contacted Alexander and explained just what she had done and he switched on long range sensors to display the results on the viewing screen. To his amazement he could see thousands of Toarvak ships popping into existence and being placed into orbit around the gas giant. If any proof of the intent of the being that had metamorphosed from a Collector into what they now knew as Farmer was needed, it was here. Ship after ship was pulled through thousands of light years and gently deposited into this system. There would be enough minds commanding those sentient vessels to open a wormhole that would swallow the remains of the Janise Probe's interstellar ship along with all the cloned machine intelligences on board.

On board the hundred-thousand long vessel a frantic cannibalisation process was under way as each machine intelligence ripped apart usable parts from the superstructure of the ship. The one driving force was to escape from whatever fate had befallen its originator. Hydrogen and oxygen tanks that had not ruptured were removed from the outside of the vessel and welded into groups. Metal was bent into usable shapes to make a workable combustion chamber. A large explosion sent an escape vessel away from the main mass only to be caught by one of the newcomers in a bath of star-fire.

Alexander opened the gestalt using the symbiont that every sentient being carried within their nervous system.

"Goss!"

"I am here, Alexander," the symbiont replied.

Connect me with every mind that has translated across interstellar space and bind the group mind together."

Alex reached out to Link-soo-shan and Khann-link-sool forming a tripartite mind set that contacted the minds that were ready to be used upon the other Toarvaks.

A composite mind controlled by the three considered the situation and scanned the hundred-thousand miles of the Janise Probe's vessel. Time and space twisted into a vortex that opened at the ravened stern of the vessel with the other end just above the clouds of the gas giant. The gravity well of the gas giant now became immediately close to the remains of the interstellar craft and began to pull it into a fatal embrace. Parts that were not fixed to the vessel began to rip away and vanish into the swirling orange clouds below. Steadily the cylinder began to slide into the wormhole and vanish into the reach of the gas giant.

When the last of the Janise Probe's interstellar craft had disappeared through the vortex, the composite mind collapsed the wormhole and released the thousands of individual units that comprised the over-mind. The being now known as Farmer became aware of the vast power that had come into being for a relatively short time. It could afford to be patient, after all it was to all intents and purpose immortal. It could also plan with confidence for the long distance future. It now had been given a short insight into what it could expect from the absorption of all sentient life. It had not been wrong to become allied with the sentient organic life-forms that it had met at what they had called New Haven. The machine intelligence was undetectable to its senses and had laid waste planet after planet throughout this arm of the Andromeda galaxy. With the help of these intelligent minds, life would be reappearing on thousands of worlds and given the time-span at the Farmer's disposal all would be coerced into bringing sentient creatures into this universe. It was aware of the damage done by its predecessor in causing the galaxies to collide, but was powerless to alter what had been set in motion.

Once again it could take the long view and wait for the amalgamation of the two galaxies. After all what was a billion years to a being such as itself? There was plenty for it to do! It regretted the loss of the civilisation that had built a globular cluster and sent it off towards the large Magellanic cloud. There would be the possibility of building a wormhole in that direction when this task of eradicating the machine intelligence from this galaxy and harvesting the souls that had left their organic chrysalis behind. The thought presented itself that there were an almost infinite number of galaxies in the universe. All they needed was to be reached and the sentient minds absorbed.

CHAPTER TEN

Kamiel had called for a gathering, from the fleet of Toarvaks that had been transported by the Farmer. It had brought them instantly through the wormholes, thousands of light years to the Janise Probe's base of operations.

It was morning inside the Ark. Alexander and Nagoth had decided to enter the inside of the artificial world and rest for a while amongst green living things. Link-soo-shan had insisted on coming with them. Real sunlight was being reflected into the hollowed out moon and the many different alien plants were soaking up the welcome rays. Fruit orchards were in bloom that had ancestors on far off Earth along with Jovian pod-vines growing in orderly rows. In the centre of the Ark the night-shades were following their rotation pattern and slipping away from the artificial sun that bathed the lands and seas in sunshine. It had rained in the night as usual and everything smelt fresh. Above them the Trans-sentients hung in the sky and dangled their tentacles through the vegetation, tearing up branches laden with fruit from other locations.

Alexander walked over to a wooden table and seating bench with the others that had also accompanied him. The conic known as Blue-Orange-Green and the Thipdar, Primm both began to eat what had been set out on the tables by the nannites. There were many others representing other races who had made their way to the Last Ark of the Goss to attend this discussion. Many of the leading minds of the Kresh had left their Toarvaks to come here, feeling that telepathy was not enough and that a flesh to flesh meeting was preferable.

Kamiel, Asue, Minnis and Solace were also present to represent the interests of the nannites. These artificial

123

intelligences had been programmed to nurture humanity and re-create them from the genetic code carried in their vast memory banks. The result of this idea had brought forth a galactic civilisation undreamed of by the original planners. The nannites had found it just a small step to add to their programming that all sentient lives come into their sphere of interest. In the defeat of the parasitic Goss and the subsequent altering of this amazing organism into a symbiont that lived in all sentient creatures, they had created a bridge into all minds. Now for the first time, by nurturing a small ball of organic material infused by the Goss, nannites could communicate by telepathy using this medium. The Goss existed outside of time and space so that immediate communication was possible across thousands of light years without any time lag.

Kamiel waited with a nannite's patience for the organics to break their hunger and to settle into a more comfortable situation. He had been built by human beings and his mind had been crafted by human and pan-chimpanzees. Over the millennium he had learnt to develop an empathy with other sentient beings, the first of these were the Gnathe. He had shared his mind with the deposed empress, Link-soo-shan during his time-travel journey to the Earth at the time prior to its being engulfed by the changing sun. The creation of the giant gestalt of Gnathe, human and ape had managed to take the Earth out of orbit and set it circling a gas giant in another star system. The mind had also drawn on the power of a time distorting crystal to bring the Earth six million years into the future to the Jovian present.

That was more than a hundred thousand years in the past, before he had been removed from that time period and brought to this 'now' to pit his wits against the Harvester. To do that he had fished through time to assemble a team of hunter-killers and used them to teach a peaceable people how to wage a war. They had journeyed to the Andromeda galaxy to confront a foe vaster than a solar system in size and gained allies here, allowing a complete interstellar civilisation to escape the deliberate collision of this galaxy with the Milky Way. They had defeated the abomination that harvested life energy from sentient beings by promoting warfare and eventually exploding their sun. Now they would have to trust a being that had been created by their success. Whatever plans it had for the future would be beyond their understanding. All they could try to rely on was its declaration to Alexander that its main purpose was the distribution of life and the development of sentience. The chilling addition was its declaration that it would absorb the personalities of all intelligent creatures into its collective 'soul' and there was nothing that any organic being could do about it. The question remained, should they concern themselves with whatever followed death? If the Farmer absorbed the essence of any sentient being, then in some sense at least, death was not final! Kamiel decided not to think too much about it and draw the gathering to order.

"Goss!"

"Yes Kamiel?"

"Make a bridge to all the minds at this meeting place and exclude all others," he ordered.

The organism made contact with all its spores that were living inside each sentient being and created a mental loop. It closed down all contacts with all the minds situated on the thousand Toarvaks. At the same moment it was also making communication possible with millions of other sentients scattered across the Andromeda galaxy. It was a willing servant and also independent as a being in its own right. Its life had become increasingly satisfying after it had been modified by the nannites to be a symbiont rather than a parasite. In its own way it had become content with the path laid down by Kamiel long ago. When the sentients bound themselves into a gestalt mind, it was the very binding that held it together.

Kamiel opened his mind to the gathering.

"We have opened hostilities against the machine intelligence known as the Janise Probe. Through the aid we received from the being that we were instrumental in creating, we were able to subdue the interstellar craft that it was building. What we will have to deal with the next time we pit our wits against this destroyer of organic life, remains to be seen. What we have to determine is just how far do we trust the entity that we call 'The Farmer'?"

The mind of the conic, Blue/orange/green, spoke up and said, "I think that we have little choice in the matter. Those of you who have shared minds with this immortal being have been shown that it means us no harm. It cannot detect the machine intelligence other than the absence of life in the solar systems that it inhabits and controls. It could easily destroy those systems, but would far rather that we removed the Probe and left it to engender life on those worlds. I cannot begin to understand its ultimate role in this universe, or to understand just what it wants of us when we die. We are dealing with to all intents and purposes an immortal being that is sustained by our life energy. The more life it spreads and nurtures across the universe, the greater it will be. It has been honest with us about its aims and our interests follow the same path. It is of a different mind-set than the Harvester that only fed on our life-force and manipulated us into wars, so that it could feed from our deaths. I say that we can trust this being and we use it as much as we can. It can negotiate the network of wormholes throughout reality in an instant. When we use a wormhole it can take a very long time to travel to the other end. It has no interest in our premature deaths and has promised that it will absorb us when we die. Is that not preferable than oblivion?"

Link-soo-shan entered the mental discussion with her experience inside the mind of the 'Farmer' and said, "I have been inside the creature's mind. I have been in that place where no untruths can exist, as has Alexander. My mind has lived in different bodies and has been projected into the universe to pit our wits against the Goss. I have experienced many wonders during my extended life, but none quite like the rapture that I experienced when I entered this being's mind. Its goals are not such that we could ever understand, as we are mortal. The fact remains if we do not eradicate the Janise Probe from our universe, then it will inevitably expand into our interests as independent organic life. We are competition!"

Silver bars on Dappled Grey answered, "We of the Kresh agree. We are a re-created race of beings rescued by the actions of the humans and the Gnathe. If it were not for them we would have been fried in the flames of our sun. Had the Harvester noticed us then, we would have gone into that fire much sooner. This being is the result of our combined efforts in defeating the creature that spawned it, along with many others. Something has changed in the way that it thinks and I believe that it has achieved a level of sentience far above that of its creator. We must be aware that any other collector would not be driven by the same goals."

"All that has been said is true," Primm, the trip'o-dal replied. "I feel that we use the creature's help to move around to wherever we need to go. It has an interest in life and spreading it where it can. Not only that, it wishes to nurture that life into sentience. What greater task or legacy could we leave behind us in this hostile universe? If defeating the Janise Probe helps to bring new intelligence into the galaxy, then we must trust this being to do what it says. It was born from our actions and it has revealed itself to us. I believe in its good intentions."

The ice-cold intellect of Kamiel registered into every mind. The nannite had listened to each point of view and had evaluated the situation.

"This being has made contact with organic, sentient life for the first time. It has shared its mind with a number of you and it has been quite transparent to those of you that have shared its consciousness. Its purpose in continual existence transcends the life spans of all of us including the artificial intelligences. We cannot even try to comprehend such a mind or what drives it. I too believe that it is an ally rather than a foe. What no-one has realised is that the being has speeded up its mind to comprehend our thoughts and actions. It has a viewpoint of millions of years ahead of it and can slow down its thought processes to think at that speed. At any time it could transfer its consciousness back to that time frame and be lost to us. While we have its full attention at this time, I feel that we must use it to achieve whatever we need to do."

Alexander nodded and replied, "We also have the assistance of the Janise Probe's clone, Mobile Unit. This AI has the maps in its memory banks of the direct line of descent of the rate of expansion of all those probes that have gone before it."

The combined mind of the Kresh reached out to the Farmer and asked, "What are you doing regarding the other collectors scattered about this galaxy?"

"They are programmed to collect and none of them have reached my level of sentience. They are content to be absorbed into my consciousness and blend into the gestalt. I am now everywhere within this galaxy. I exist throughout the framework of the very wormholes that you use to travel from star system to system. Every moment that passes I am added to by every sentient being whose organic frame ceases to function. Their life energy adds to mine and their sense of being enriches me, enabling me to function at a higher level. I repeat, do not fear me! I will do you no harm. Your continued existence is my goal and the spread of your kind, no matter what shape or form you take is my concern. The machine intelligence will destroy you all if you do not ruthlessly wipe it out. You have successfully removed this threat at this star system at a point in time that was crucial. Now you must consider your next move. My senses have found that as the arm of this stretch of star systems thins out, less and less organic life exists. At the moment the entity that you call the Janise probe is confined to this area of the galaxy. You must track it down and be sure that you find all of them, before it creeps like a cancer from one star system to another."

Link-soo-shan pondered that thought and replied, "Fortune seems to have smiled upon us, as it would seem to be that the race of people who designed the Janise probes must have evolved at the edge of this galaxy. Somewhere at the end of this galactic arm would have been the home world of the Janise. The Harvester must have sacrificed them to their sun and gathered in all of the life energy before they had chance to follow any of their probes inwards towards the galactic centre. How lonely they must have felt, isolated at the end of the thin swathe of stars out at the edge of Andromeda. Is it not possible that we could take their world away from their star's reach by doing what the Kresh achieved and going back through time?"

"No! That is not possible my Gnathen friend," replied Kamiel. "There are too many interconnected time-lines involved. We could set off a cascade effect that would bring down all aspects of the reality that we live in. We changed

129

the timeline in our own galaxy by saving every sentient race that the Harvester had gathered in. Our actions set in motion the events that caused the collision of these two galaxies billions of years before they should have occurred. We defeated that entity and by doing so brought this other being into existence that we have named Farmer. The Janise cannot be saved from the extinction of the past."

Minnis had been silent until this point and then the nannite objected. "I disagree in part! There could be a way of saving enough of the Janise to form a viable breeding colony. I am not subject to the stringent programming that the rest of my race of artificial intelligences is ruled by. Therefore I can think along a little riskier path. I propose that we send a single Toarvak back through time to when the Janise were alive. When Kamiel directed the search through time to find Alexander, Link-soo-shan and many others, he took beings from situations in which they would not be missed. I feel that while the majority of the task force concentrates on removing the rest of the Probes from this timeframe, a small group of multi species could safely bring back enough of the Janise to live with us. What benefits our civilization could reap from this act, I cannot even guess! What remains, is that if we do not do this thing, then the whole principle of what our galactic federation stands for will regret doing nothing for the rest of it existence. They are a unique life form. There are no other sentient beings like them. I stand by my proposal."

"What makes then unique?" asked Alexander.

"I have spent some time digging away at the archives secreted at the lowest memory levels of the Mobile Unit that is a clone of the original Janise probe," replied Minnis. "I have uncovered a number of files that give an insight to the original builders. They were a composite species of two incredibly different life forms. Both creatures were intelligent, but linked telepathically so that one could be the hands of the other. The 'dominant' form is a being shaped somewhat like a six foot high preying mantis that thinks and blends minds with a spider shaped creature. This spins a web of silk around itself and the forward 'arms of the mantis, fixing them together. These then become the 'hands' of the Janise. Other spiders remain mobile and become extra hands to the minds of the Janise. When enough spiders are linked together they become sentient enough to have an independent mind not controlled by the Janise, but able to expand their ideas into solid form. There are similarities to the insectoids that are part of our civilization. This strange symbiotic relationship would have ultimately taken them to the stars. Even the Goss has not seen the like of them before and its memories go back a very long way. We have to save them and bring them back through time to this present. I suggest Toarvak 6 as the most experienced sentient vessel and a mixed crew that includes me and Fredrick."

Kamiel sent his mind into the Goss and asked it to verify the statement given by the rouge Nannite.

"I have never seen anything like these people, Kamiel," the symbiotic answered. "I am everywhere that sentient beings live and there are no racial memories of these people anywhere or anytime."

Kamiel considered and contacted Toarvak 6 and relayed the plan that Minnis had laid before them.

Tee 6 answered him on the nannite band, "*With the right crew I will go. Also feel do I that more than one Toarvak vessel will be needed. Entering a time where the Harvester reigns supreme I would be. It must never know that we have been there. Worry too, do I, about the timelines and twisting them into a new setting. An expeditionary force will need to be sent with a careful watch kept for the arrival of the Harvester into that time and space. Centuries before the abomination changes their star into a red giant and renders them extinct, we need to be."*

The nannite Guardian gathered his thoughts and once again reached out to the symbiont, "Goss!"

"Yes Kamiel."

"Reach out and find Toarvak 12,042 and its crew."

The Goss scanned for the mental signature of the time travelling Toarvak and found it controlled by a multi species crew.

A voice entered the nannite's mind and said, "You summoned this vessel? How can we be of assistance?"

Kamiel recognised the mind of a Gnathe that he had not seen for some time.

"Suzzan-link-khann, the Brood-daughter of Link-soo-shan! I could not ask for a more experienced Toarvak operator. Listen to my thoughts and I will bring you up to date with current thinking."

Kamiel passed over to the Gnathe the combined decision of the rescue attempt to abduct sufficient of the Janise to bring back to this time a viable breeding colony. Also he instructed her that Toarvak 6 would be going with her back to that far distant timeline with a suitable crew.

"I would like to arrange that Primm goes with you and transfer to your vessel as she has great knowledge of time travel. I take it that you still carry the family of Kresh that operated T 12,042 when you travelled back and forth through time to obtain the data and people that put us at odds with the Harvester?"

"They are still attached to the vessel, Kamiel. They are ship-born Kresh and are a permanent family crew," Suzzan replied.

"Excellent! Show them what we have decided to do and ask them what their recommendations are. Rendezvous with me at the Ark to effect the transfer of personnel to your ship. Minnis will be travelling on Toarvak 6 and will be in command of the exercise. Solace will be accompanying the expedition as a retarding force against any impetuous decisions. You will do this while I run the operations against the next Janise Probe in line," Kamiel instructed.

The nannite turned to Alexander and said, "I want you to go with them. This may need some sensitive thinking. There is another thing that you may be able to do that will aid the rescue of the Janise."

Alex was puzzled why his old friend and mentor chose to speak instead of connecting direct with his thoughts.

"What troubles you, old friend? What is it that you feel the need for secrecy?" He said.

Kamiel spoke quietly to the human-Gnathe hybrid "I am wondering if you may need the help of your mutated offspring to scan ahead in time to give you warning of the approach of the Harvester. You know what effects an incident could generate if you were to contact that abomination at that earlier time. You may need them. Have you ever sensed them since we sent the Harvester into that black hole? Could you call them?"

"Kamiel I don't know if they are even aware of us as organic life forms. What they became when they gave up their bodies was something that defies explanation. Nagoth often wonders if there is a link between her and whatever they are now. We have never tried to call for them. I do not feel that the being we have named as Farmer would not want to absorb them if it became aware of them. This is an area that we know nothing about."

"We will need the Farmer's assistance in moving the fleet to the next star system to destroy the next link in the chain. At the same time we will need to find out from the Mobile Unit what the position of the original home world star used to be several hundred, million years ago. You will need the being's ability to transfer you to that vicinity so

133

that when you translate back through time, the Janise world will be there, not an empty void," the nannite replied.

Alexander agreed and said, "We will have to trust the being with the truth. There can be no deceit when we communicate with it as we have learnt to live with that fact since we have all taken the Goss as a symbiont. As we are subject to a universal telepathic gestalt within all of our singularly different species, we have learnt to live together. It is fully conscious of the fact that our actions brought it into being. I will contact the Farmer again and explain what we want to do while you extract the information we require from the Mobile Unit."

Once again Alexander joined his mind the Link-soo-shan's and the two of them used the mind of the Trans-sentient as a bridge to the energy being.

The two of them found themselves inside the mind of the Farmer, as two shining lights immersed within a matrix of sparkling nodes, interconnecting within a three dimensional web. The threads seemed to vanish into infinity as the ends of the webs joined into other nodes and streaked off towards a network of wormholes that pulsed. The area around them began to increase in brightness as more and more of the nodes lit up. Filaments began to spin off the nodes and connected themselves to the fabric of their existence.

The Farmer's 'voice' crossed into their combined mind and asked, "You have reason to speak with me?"

Alexander and Link-soo-shan were joined and answered as a combined mind, far more powerful than individuals.

"We have much to do that will require your help. You must understand that we consider that it will benefit our community of species to add the Janise to the gestalt of us all. That will require that we split our forces and send small number of experienced crews back in time in the

Toarvaks. The time we wish to return to is before your ancestor destroyed the Janise and their world. You will not have evolved into the being that you are at that time. The Harvester reigns supreme during that time span. We are well aware that it must not sense us or be aware of us in any way. We will drop out of time two centuries before that time of destruction. This is something that we have done before without disrupting the time lines. You will have to trust us not to alter any events at that earlier time. What we need you to do is to send the Toarvaks that will go, to the position in space that the Janise solar system would have occupied several hundred million years ago. Can you do that and also relocate the fleet to the next star system that sent the Janise Probe to this location?"

"What you ask can of course be done," the Farmer replied, "But the risks involved are colossal! One mistake could bring down changes in the space-time continuum that could wipe out this reality completely. I need to know why you feel that these people are so important to the rest of the organics."

Kamiel entered the gestalt and added his coldly intellectual mind to the being that was Alexander blended to the Gnathe's. The three of them had done this many times before and had become a terrifying mixture of organic and artificial intelligence of an order of mind far beyond anything existing normally.

"Farmer! Listen to me. The Gnathen part of this gestalt, genetically programmed one of her kind, transferred into human form, to breed with this male. The result was to produce six beings that could think themselves through time and scan ahead. This amalgamation of three female and three male minds became the force that enabled us to destroy the intelligence that produced you.

I am confident that the organics can call upon them again.

If so they will be going back in time with this expedition. I cannot be absolutely sure, but I have a feeling in the depths of this gestalt mind that what these people will have to offer you at the end of time will be well worth the risks! You will in time be the composite of every sentient race of creatures that this galaxy possesses. It is my belief that you will need the strength and diversity of the Janise minds to do what you plan."

The being known as Farmer considered the mind meld's proposition and reluctantly agreed.

CHAPTER ELEVEN

Kamiel broke the mind-link and electronically shuddered. The siren call of the Farmer's mind beckoned to him. It was hard to resist merging with this being forever. Balanced against this was the ridged duty that each and every nannite lived for. It dominated their thoughts and minds. There were many models of Kamiel dotted throughout the stellar systems, but only one series-number 637 that had reluctantly taken on the mantle of leadership. He alone had been destroyed and re-created by Hannah's actions when she turned time back at the time of Link-soo-shan's defeat. Asue had also been affected, but her programming had not been 'tweaked' as his had been done by his creator, Alexander McBald. He had made it possible for him to act in such a way that he could if necessary, allow human life to perish to allow the majority to live. This directive now covered all sentient life in his care. Since his re-creation however, this had become a much easier thing for him to do and he found himself able to juggle the lives of millions to keep billions safe. It was a hard responsibility to carry and he had found it necessary to exercise this ability many times. Each time however, the pressure against his artificial mind was immense.

Every death was a weight upon his nannite soul. Now once again he was going to be responsible for another possible collapse of reality. The one thing that he knew was that his alter ego in flesh was as aware of this fact as much as he was.

In the midst of the doubts that swirled round his mind, Kamiel felt reality blur around him, as his nannite body went into machine time. Now an hour would pass subjectively in a matter of a few moments and the outside world froze.

Once again Kamiel found himself stood in the great man's office and an elderly, white-haired Alexander was sat in his director's chair.

"Once again we face a time of decision, Kamiel 637 and I am here to listen," the old man said. "I have looked at the situation registered in your mind and I deduce that there are two ways of considering the situation. As the combined fleet of sentient beings have beaten the Janise Probe in this system and are considering the next link in the chain, then the expedition into the past can deemed to be successful. If not then all this around you would have changed and the 'Farmer' would not have come into existence.

On the other hand it could be that the time-travel into the past to retrieve the Janise is the very action that brought about this present reality! Each time that you have called my existence into being, I am amazed at what you have achieved. Remember that as I am a clone of the original being that helped to create you and as such, I am able to advise you just as the original Alexander would. Your mind is an amalgamation of many different people including mine that makes up your combined personality. Yet when you were created, I could foresee that from time to time in the future there would be times that you would need an independent mind to measure the effects of your proposed actions. This is one of those times! I believe that what you have decided to do will make the reality that you and all the other sentient beings that make up the federation of worlds share, a certainty. It will be very interesting when you de-brief the expedition on their return."

Kamiel stared at the apparition as the ancient set of programming sat in his imaginary chair and clasped his hands together. Alexander's mind had been cloned in its entirety and set in an inaccessible area of the nannite's artificial mind for just this set of eventualities. Although Kamiel was an amalgam of many different minds including the director's, his mind had evolved into a single entity, shaped by the events that he had witnessed. The old man sat behind his desk was as fresh in his mind as the day he was cloned and had not lived through all the events with Kamiel's consciousness. It had been this piece of programming that had stopped his personality from coming apart when grief had overwhelmed him, when Link-soo-shan had attacked the Habitat and killed thousands of the original colonists in their early struggles against each other.

It had been the result of his meddling that had brought the Gnathe and human cultures together. As time had gone by he had been proved right to do what he had achieved. The result of that joining together had produced the Gnathen-human hybrid that was represented by the psychically enhanced people that he served today.

The nannite bowed his head and said, "Thank you, Director. You offer a different slant on the events that have transpired. I am reassured!"

With that, real time took over and once more the people around him moved normally again. The office of the director had vanished as quickly as it had appeared to him. Try as he might Kamiel could not call up the Director for any more clarification.

He turned and held Alexander's arm and told him what had transpired.

"Now you have to go! I'm sure in my mind that it will be the very actions that you follow hundreds of millions of years in the past that will bring this reality into being. I have no clear idea just what it is that you will do. It will only be at that moment that you realise that your decision is the right one!"

Alex was stunned! He remembered that his people were

instrumental in making the time loop that had accidentally carried the Gnathe from a dying world to the Jupiter of his artificial birth. The group mind had reached back and moved the Earth forwards to the time of their existence. The gestalt that was the combination of Gnathe, human and ape, had felt the presence of the Gnathe on their dying world. The mind had reached out and sliced off a massive part of the planet with all of its varied life forms. Before the time crystal disintegrated it had deposited it on Jupiter's surface, leaving Alexander and the displaced Gnathe fifteen hundred years in the past. It was a mind numbing chain of events that had to happen to give the universe as it was.

Had Link-soo-shan succeeded in destroying the time travel project the Gnathe would never had arrived at Jupiter. The whole chain of events that took place afterwards had given the whole of the sentient races of the two galaxies a chance of existence that would have been terminated by the actions of the Harvester. Now they would be retrieving the Janise from under the gaze of the early Harvester to ensure their survival. To do it without terminating the time-lines and altering the past would be his responsibility.

Alexander shuddered and brought his fears and apprehension under control. He reached out to Nagoth's mind and told her what they must do. They sat quietly down at the wooden table and joined hands and minds together. The duel mind called out to Link-soo-shan to join the link as co-creator of the three sets of twins.

This gestalt had been brought together before many times in the past and was a mind of many disciplines, combining human and Gnathe into an alliance. The triple mind added the mind of Primm, BOG and several of the Kresh to the combination. Each mind that was absorbed, added power and reach to the gestalt, without any domination by the willing parts. Nagoth stayed at the centre. She was the apex of the pyramid that built itself into a seeking tool that projected the power of the blended mind into the network of the Goss.

As yet the interspecies mind was not powerful enough to move a planet, it would need populations added in to do that, but it was powerful enough to project Nagoth's need for her children throughout the void.

The network of the Goss rang like a physic bell! From one end of the Andromeda galaxy to the other, the call for the mind of six, Shoolin-Alexis was projected through every sentient being that carried the Goss symbiont. Only the Goss was aware of the call and its scattered mind opened its receptors.

The creature of pure mind was riding the energy spouts of a blue-white star near the centre of the galaxy gathering energy, when the mental summons drew its attention. Although the being had matured in ways that its parents would never understand, it had not forgotten its origins.

It listened to the call and pin-pointed the location of the group-mind that had sent it. Shoolin-Alexis drew upon the energy that was in abundance and twisted space into an abrupt worm-hole and sent itself through, dimming the awful power of its mind so as to not fry the synapses of the sentients that had sent out the call.

Inside the safety of the Ark an awareness of an imminent power flooded the receptors of every sentient. A rupture in space-time began to tear an area of the artificial sky asunder. A flood of silvery light eclipsed the light of the sun that was reflected into the Ark.

Nagoth was aware of the emergence of her children and allowed the gestalt to collapse around her. Each mind was once more in its individual fleshly home and a person again rather than part of a super being.

A globular silver light shaped itself into a figure of

eight that slowly rotated around its centre. In each bubble there took shape, a baby shaped creature that appeared to be joined at the side. Sometimes it separated completely and then re-joined to be a double faced being with two fronts. Emerging from this strange combination would be superimposed the figure of a Gnathe. This would split into six individual beings, three male and three female. The light began to brighten for a few seconds and then there were just two children, stood there totally naked and with the appearance of a ten-year old.

The two of them held hands and said, "'We/I' heard your call, mother and father. 'We/I' have studied your problem and agree that what you are about to do must be done. It cannot be done without our help and guidance. One mistake and reality will come tumbling down. There must be no mistakes!"

The children turned and faced Link-soo-shan.

"'We/I' see you Gnathen designer. Shaper of our destiny even now! Pivot point of history and leverage of the future. The vessel that you created to bring us into this reality is changed. This copy will not reproduce my kind. A wise decision Brood-mother!"

Link sank back to a squat to bring her face to a level closer to the children stood before her. She reached out to touch the being and found that her hands passed through the two figures.

"An interesting being, this off-shoot of the Harvester," continued Shoolin-Alexis. "Once again the actions of humanity have brought about a fundamental reality into existence. It will indeed become a farmer of sentient life. I understand its goals and motivation. Trust it! I have seen what it will attempt to do in the far future. More than that I cannot tell you. Much will depend on this trip into the long past. I have spoken to this being and explained why this dangerous mission must be undertaken. Already there are aspects of organic minds interwoven with this creature. It is evolving!"

Kamiel watched the events unfolding before his receptors with some trepidation as his control of the situation had left his direction. He had not considered for one moment that the being that Link-soo-shan had created by genetically manipulating Nagoth's reproductive mechanism would appear with such abruptness after its mother's call. The nannite Guardian opened his artificial mind to the being that had materialised into their presence using the living portion of flesh tended inside of him. The spores of the Goss made the bridge from inorganic to organic possible.

"Shoolin-Alexis I welcome you to our position at the pivot point of reality! What would you have me do? Have you considered my situation from this moment onwards?"

The being regarded Alexander McBald's creation and gently inserted its mind into the nannite's thoughts.

"Do all that you have planned, 'great servant of organic sentience'. I can see no place for you in the scope of this trip into the past. You must move on to the next link in the chain and break it! Work with the being that you call the Farmer and destroy all forms of the Janise Probe and do not stop until all of them are eradicated. I will be going back in time to assist the retrieval of the Janise and the reintroduction of them to this timeline. I feel that as you get closer to the beginning of the Janise probe's expansion, time and the depletion of resources may have done your job for you! The continual cloning of the machine intelligence will 'We/I' believe leave the original weaker as circuits fail. It was not designed to exist in such a manner. It has attempted to re-write its programming and as the Janise probe on New Haven has shown, the Probe soon reverted to its original purpose. It was built to serve!"

Kamiel bowed his head towards the being and nodded in a human gesture and replied, "I understand all that you have told me. My mind is at rest and I will attend to the next task in hand while you command the fleet of Toarvaks back in time."

The children reached out to the nannite again and replied, "No, Guardian, we will not be commanding this operation. All decisions must come from our father and mother. All we can tell you is that it must be their decisions that shape the future and cause this reality to exist. We must be instrumental in the way that the expedition is carried out and do as we are bid. Now those that are required must be transferred to the waiting Toarvaks. 'We/I' will do this now. Goodbye Kamiel."

Kamiel felt the inrush of air as those that had been picked to travel back in time disappeared from the Ark. Shoolin-Alexis had taken all of the required personnel and distributed them to Toarvak 6 and 12,402.

Alexander and Nagoth found themselves abruptly on the bridge of Toarvak 6 along with Larse and Emelia. Fredrick, Hannah, Minnis and Solace had also been placed beside them. The tall figure of Link-soo-shan stood with them for a few moments and then blinked out of their sight as Shoolin-Alexis relocated her to be with her brood-daughter Suzzan on T 12,402.

The humanoid silver shape of Tee 6 rose from the floor and confronted them.

"Welcome are you all," she said. *"Instruction have I been given from Shoolin-Alexis. This information to all Toarvaks has been given. An understanding of what is entailed has been logged. T 12,402 will form the wormhole back through time to when the Janise sun existed. Five Toarvaks will the wormhole anchor in this time period. Keep the bridge across the eons open will be the task of the other five. Two of us will travel down the twist in time and seek the answer to the Janise. All that needs to be done is for*

144

the Farmer us to place in the vicinity of where the star existed prior to being annexed by the Harvester."

Alexander linked minds with his companions and sent his need to the being they had reluctantly come to trust.

Once again he found himself a part of the Farmer's consciousness. The silver, sparkling webs extended into what seemed infinity. He became a dancing flame travelling along the filaments. With him and surrounding him, was a protective cylinder that spun itself into a globe to totally encase him.

"Human called Alexander; I have listened to the information given by the being that is humankind's destiny to become.

I will transport you to where the outskirts of the Janise system used to be, many hundreds of millions of years ago. When you emerge you will need to ascertain the finer adjustments that will enable you to bring back the Janise to this time period. I will maintain a presence at that point so that you may return safely."

The composite mind controlled by Alexander laughed and replied, "There will be no need of that. What we have to achieve will take us time to carry out, but for you, only a few seconds, if that, will have passed if we are successful! Be assured we would all choose to die rather than change the timeline that sent us there."

Before the silvery globe turned into mist and the dancing flame stood alone in the centre of the web the Farmer replied, "We are here."

Alexander allowed the composite mind to dissolve and stared at the view-screens in mind numbing shock. The three hundred and sixty degree view was virtually empty of stars! Only one screen showed any light at all and he realised that he was looking at the edge of the Andromeda galaxy and behind it was his old home, The Milky Way, at about thirty degrees twisted on its axis. They were so far away that the collision of the two galaxies was totally hidden. Out here the small fleet of Toarvaks were utterly alone. He realised that without the help of the Farmer's powers of wormhole manipulation, there was no way home from here. Gradually he began to see in the great darkness that other galaxies were spinning in the void.

He reached out with his mind to Tee 6 and said, "Would you increase the amount of illumination on the screens so that we can see the other galaxies easier, old friend?"

"Easy it would be, Alexander. Bring up the magnification I will and the universe will call to you," the sentient interstellar vessel replied.

When Tee 6 increased the magnification and the luminosity, the mixed group of aliens and humans were struck dumb! The screens filled with great cartwheels that danced in the gravitational flux, filled with billions of stars. Each galaxy had a relationship with its neighbours and built families that interacted upon each other. Some galaxies were eons older than the closer ones, but were still creating new stars as the old ones died. Giant galaxies were being formed as several of the great cart wheels collided with each other or sucked in globular clusters. Others were coming apart and drifting away from each other.

Alexander was aware of the Farmer's mind gently in his as the being whispered, "All this will one day be gone. I must prepare for that day. You will be there when that time comes as will you all!"

With that moment over, the being held itself aloof, as the Toarvaks grouped themselves into two pentagons, one inside the other. While the five Toarvaks anchored around the position designated, the other five with Tee 6 and T 12,406 prepared to enter the time-travelling wormhole by travelling down the centre flanked by the other pentagon.

On board the temporal ship, Prime the Thipdar, Suzzan

and Link opened the corridor into the past and activated the crystal. As they did so the Kresh and T 12,406 meshed with the initial mind construct. The gestalt reached out to the crew of Toarvak 6 and added their minds to the great combination. As the group mind gathered strength it contacted the other minds on the pentagon surrounding them and added them to the mix. Prim was still the guiding force of the gestalt and sent her enhanced consciousness through time to where the Janise were still located. Riding on the edge of this gestalt was the being that Nagoth had created, Shoolin-Alexis. It scanned back through ancient history, searching for the presence of the Janise, as the wormhole opened into the distant past. Hundred of millions of cycles rewound as the gestalt built the wormhole deeper and deeper into the very beginnings of the universe.

Shoolin-Alexis applied the brakes to Prime's gestalt mind and slowed the plunge into the past as they became aware of a red giant filling the void near to their position. The rate of descent into the past now became hundreds of thousands of cycles as the giant star grew brighter. Without any warning the red sun collapsed into an ordinary yellow star that soon began to become stable. Prime stabilised the end of the wormhole and fixed it to a position close to a cold gas giant. Here the other five Toarvaks held the end of the wormhole as they took up their pentagon position in orbit around the deep blue planet below them. The blue colour came from the reflection of the tiny sun against clouds of liquid nitrogen. It could have easily been the twin of the Earth system's Neptune. Scattered around the planet were moons made of ice and frozen gases.

As Tee 6 and Toarvak 12,406 exited the bottom of the wormhole the other Toarvaks went out of phase with the universe. Now the wormhole would be undetectable and quite capable of threading itself through the gas giant all the way to the future where the other five Toarvaks held the entrance steady. Time would only pass at this end of the time vortex in a steady rate. Inside the wormhole time did not exist as a linier factor. When they returned, a few micro-seconds would have passed at the other end, but the longer they kept the exit open, the greater the chance that the vortex would whiplash into itself and cancel out the Toarvaks keeping it ajar.

Alexander concentrated his mind to the gestalt of Kresh that controlled the sentient vessel and said, "Drop towards the sun and stay out of phase. Use long range monitors to scan the area ahead."

He then concentrated his mind to the Trans-sentient that was aboard Tee 6.

"Can you sense the presence of the Harvester, my friend?"

"Something moves through the wormholes connecting this place with the rest of the universe. I feel its hunger! We must stay invisible to its senses. It is young in a new universe and as yet has not met any opposition! It has no notion of resistance," the Trans-sentient replied.

Shoolin-Alexis entered the mind link and said, "It is time that 'We/I left you to drop towards the star at your own speed. 'We/I will go directly to the planet of the Janise and see for ourselves what we can do in the circumstances. Goodbye for a little while, dear father and mother. We will return as soon as we can."

Alexander and Nagoth watched stunned as their strange children faded from sight as they pushed through the wall of the control station.

The mind of Link-soo-shan entered Alexander's and gently reassured him, "Trust them, old friend. They are unique in this universe and are quite able to do whatever they decide. I'm sure that the Harvester will not detect them and they will gather information that you never could. My brood-daughter and I must stay here and maintain the time warp and keep the crystal active, while you continue to drop towards the sun. Already we can feel imbalances brought into being by the activity throughout the worm holes caused by the proximity of the Harvester. We must stay to keep it open. Good hunting!"

Alexander turned to Nagoth and said, "So it begins my love. Once again we are on a journey to the unknown. I sometimes wonder if we will ever have another life other than danger and threat of death."

"I do not care where we go as long as we are together," Nagoth replied. "I can still remember my days as a Gnathe and this life was given to me by my Brood-mother to serve her purpose. It so happens that it also serves mine! I have been the crucible of the most incredible life form that has ever entered this galaxy. Six children lived and grew inside me and became one being that is also six. They are what humanity will one day become. Maybe they are the template for all sentient life to evolve into. I love them and I know that they love us too. By 'us' I am including all sentient life in that great collective."

Larse stared hard at the woman with the unusual flame red hair and chocolate coloured skin and said, "I believe you, Nagoth. I have caught brief eddies of that incredible mind-mix at the edge of my consciousness. Your children are very complex, but they are still human in soul. They would not do anything that would endanger our existence; for one thing it would quite possibly destroy them also!"

Emelia's eyes opened wide as the full ramifications of their visit to the past surfaced in her mind and she turned to Hannah for further enlightenment.

The diminutive woman nodded and said, "It's all about time and temporal paradox! If we do the wrong thing here in the far distant past, then all of the future will come tumbling down. A temporal displacement would take place and it could cancel out everything that has happened from this moment on. Humankind would find Jupiter empty of the Gnathe and the history of the universe would be dominated by the abomination! The defeat of the Harvester would never take place and the rescue of all the sentients from the Harvester's rapacious hunger would not happen. At the moment the equation is stable. When we take the Janise forward in time we must do so in such a fashion that nothing alters at this time, no matter what the Janise suffer on their home world."

"All we can do is to continue towards the sun and wait for Shoolin-Alexis to return to us with the information that they alone can gather," replied Alexander.

Fredric turned to Minnis and Solace and laughed before he said, "Well my nannite friends, I have a strong feeling that you are going to be involved. I do not have the changeling's ability to see the future, but I do have human intuition!"

CHAPTER TWELVE.

Kamiel checked that all vestiges of the Janise Probe had been eradicated from this stellar system before committing the fleet to the next destination. It seemed strange not to have his organic friends around him. The Ark was commanded by the Lagdoo and the fiercely logical reptilian beings would unquestionably obey him. He had organised many of the Toarvaks into mining expeditions deep within the gravity well of the gas giant beneath them. Once the vessels went 'out of phase' with the rest of the universe the pressure twisted crystals could be easily obtained from the surface of the metallic hydrogen where they had been wrested from the rocky silicate ball that lay underneath. Whatever upheaval had taken place under the intense pressure; caused the crystals to 'pop out' from their resting places and float to the top of the 'sea' that was the boundary to the gas layers above. In other places, mountains projected above the metallic hydrogen 'sea' where the crystal reefs were exposed to view. At these points it was easier to envelope a complete reef and bring it out of phase to be stripped on board the interstellar vessels.

Once the crystals were on board the Toarvaks, the Gnathe began the exercise of sorting and tuning them. Many of them were flawed and useless, but thousands of them were not and these soon took their place as part of the weapons systems ringed around the Toarvaks. Activated by the immensely strong group minds, they formed the nucleus of the wormhole projection systems.

Asue turned to the Mobile Unit that carried the cloned identity of the Janise probe and connected her mind to the three legged entity.

"Well? Where do we travel to next?"

The Janise Probe mobile unit considered the star-map in its memory banks and replied, "The probe that arrived in this system came from much further out. Here is the three dimensional map of the stars as they were fifty million Haven years ago. Since then things have moved around the heavens."

Asue studied the map and applied her astrogation skills to the problem. She superimposed the present day stellar systems over the positions of the older map and began to work back allowing for star drift. She was looking for a 'G' type star ringed by a large planetary system. It was coupled to another red giant that also tied a red dwarf star to the threesome. Closely orbiting the red giant was a white dwarf star that leaked plasma to its larger companion. This capture would have been obtained not too long ago in the ancient star map, when the Janise probe had arrived. By now after such a long time it would be quite possible that the white dwarf would be just a cinder or even pulled into the reach of the red giant. The two stars would not form a binary as they were too far apart, but tides of gravity kept them from wandering too far away from each other. As it was the distance apart was less than five hundred light-years away. The extra mass of the white dwarf could have drawn them closer together since the probe had launched its clone to the star system that they now inhabited.

The Guardian considered all the facts that lay in her memory banks and made her decision. She operated the view screens and projected onto the screen what the telescopic scanners could see in her calculated direction. There on the screen was a red giant and still over four hundred light-years from it was a 'G' type star. There was no sign of the white dwarf, but the dwarf star still existed orbiting far out.

She reached down to the piece of organic flesh, kept alive by nutrients that seeped from a reservoir and contacted the symbiont that lived in it.

"Goss!"

"Yes Asue."

"Connect me to Kamiel and the trans-sentient, Archive," she said.

The male programmed nannite was instantly aware of Asue and the trans-sentient's mind as his age-old partner opened up her mind to him.

"Kamiel, use Archive to connect me to the Farmer and I will pass on the co-ordinates that I have deduced. Once again we will advance from a safe distance and make our approach from outside all planetary formations. This Janise probe will have had plenty of time to occupy this system. We should take up a position high above the ecliptic orbital plane of the Oort cloud of this system. We will stay at three light years distance until we can examine the situation. At this distance from the star we should be at the outer fringe of the Oort cloud. There is one thing that we can be sure of and that is that we will have nothing to base any previous experiences that we have encountered. This machine intelligence has been here for over fifty million years and may have evolved beyond anything that we have encountered before! We should take with us the six sections of the moon that survived the collision with the interstellar ship. They are still large enough to be useful as projectiles."

The being known to the alliance as the Farmer interrupted Asue and entered her mind to gather the information.

"You are the being known as Asue? Your mind is strange and different to the organics as is the 'being' known to me as Kamiel who leads this expedition. I have looked into the minds of both of you and am amazed!

From inert matter came life! From this has sprouted

intelligence and self awareness. You have been created by organic minds and are to all extent immortal provided there is energy to tap. Thus the universe has gone full circle. Your actions caused my existence to come into being and in doing so we both have a destiny to fulfil.

I have looked at your fledgling plans and I can see that other dense moons would be an advantage to this strike against the machine intelligence. I will send ten of them to you when I move you to the next position. I will ensure that they are of a comparable size so that you can easily manoeuvre them to do whatever you need, to destroy the ancient Janise probe," the Farmer promised. "I have been amongst you now long enough to be able to communicate directly to your minds without needing the other organic beings as a bridge. It has become much easier to increase the speed of my thoughts to match yours by association with you. When this enterprise is done I will settle down to my old rate of thought and trouble you no more until we need each other again."

"What do you mean?" asked Kamiel and was rewarded by silence from the being.

Asue shuddered and used the nannite frequency to communicate with her partner, "I would not go there, Kamiel," she said. "I feel that sometimes it is better not to know that being's ultimate plans for us. All we need to keep close to us is the fact that it is an unlikely friend to organic, sentient life. Its motives are not easy to understand. We must just accept that it means us no harm and that it follows a common goal."

Space and time altered around them and the Ark and the remaining Toarvaks found themselves in a position outside of the Oort cloud surrounding a G type sun. Floating in the void with them were the ten promised heavy metal moons. The fleet were stationary and occupied the very position that Asue had designated. They were 'above' the position of the accretion disc and 'below' them orbited the planets of this system. The long range sensors of the Ark picked up activity inside the spherical cloud of comets, ice chunks and metallic moon sized bodies that wandered the darkness. As with the history of Earth the outer reaches of this system had solidified closer to their star at the dawn of its conception. Gravitational forces from the giant planets had torn them out of orbit closer to the sun and sent them spiralling out to this dark and empty place. Also this star had wandered through other heavy metallic clouds of interstellar debris and stolen them from other stars.

Amongst this halo of debris were rich pickings for the machine intelligence once it had picked the inner planets dry of metal and it was a hive of mining machines processing what ore could be found. There were probably more than over a hundred Earth masses to be plundered out here in the eternal darkness. The red giant shone like a baleful eye in the great dark and could be easily found as the stars were sparsely distributed this far out on the galactic arm.

Kamiel contacted the other Toarvaks and gave the instructions to make up nine hunting parties, each taking a moon with them as a battering ram. This would leave the Ark with the remaining one and the six large shards. The fleet would take up equal-spaced positions over the sphere and dive towards the sun, guiding the moons at the largest concentrations of mining operations. The moons would act as bowling balls on a three dimensional snooker table and cause multiple collisions as the Toarvaks went out of phase.

The Janise Probe's sensors gave no warning of the impending attack and the first time it would know about it would be two to three years from now when the signals from the mining complex it had set up radioed back. It had been careful not to empower the mining machines with too much artificial intelligence, as this had been tried before and an independent state had been created. It had taken over a million years of ruthless fighting until the last of the clones had been eliminated. Now each mining system operated from a limited set of programs and did not question or deviate from its creator's purpose. Metal was extracted from the bodies in the Oort cloud and dropped towards the sun. The Janise Probe assimilated the bounty and endlessly repaired itself and continued to build. It no longer built others of its kind and sent them out amongst the stars to continue the programmed instructions that were laid down in its memory banks. Self-preservation ruled its mechanical mind now and the prime directive had long been forgotten. The immense passing of time had wrecked the mind of the Janise Probe by the sheer monotony of its existence.

The Janise Probe orbited a gutted planet that had once sustained a variety of life. It had soft-landed on this world and had built the structures that it had been programmed to construct. Mining systems had been sent to drill down to where metallic ores lay deep underground. Following programmed instructions it had kept the pollution of the planet to a minimum in preparation to its maker's arrival. After a hundred thousand years had passed without the arrival of the Janise, the machine had begun to corrupt its original programming and had added to its intelligence and memory banks.

True sentience arose in the cybernetic circuits and the Probe became self aware. The structures that it had built had rotted away due to rain and weathering except for the indestructible parts. These it harvested and reprocessed into a new Janise Probe and recreated itself by cloning. Realising that a zero gravity environment would suit it better than the corrosive atmosphere that existed on the planet's surface the Probe began to launch packets of materials into orbit to be able to construct a new body that could travel between the planets and harvest what was available. The planet that it had landed on was stripped bare of any economically reached ores and it could no longer add to itself. It no longer made any effort to keep pollution to a minimum and concentrated its efforts on building itself a new housing in orbit. The two moons that orbited this world were host to plentiful deposits of metallic ores.

It decided that this would be where it would go and continue to build far away from any contamination by water. Over the long void of time the Janise Probe became larger and more diverse as it explored all the moons available orbiting the planets. The deep gravity wells of the other gas giant planets were avoided and the machine intelligence concentrated on what it could safely exploit from the lesser bodies. After twelve million years it had exhausted all of the available resources and worked its way beyond the last planets orbiting this star until it found the rich pickings of the Oort cloud. Once it had established the veracity of the findings it dropped back towards the sun to reap the free energy available from its steady glare. From this nearer position orbiting the star it orchestrated the mining probes into plundering the outer reaches and sent them on their way. From the raw materials sent back, it finished the new Janise Probe and sent it on its way to the next viable star closer to the galactic centre.

This seemed to take away the constant electronic nagging to recreate itself and move its clone onwards to make another world fit for the Janise. Meanwhile the original world had begun to recover from the depredations of the Probe. Over the millions of years the pollutants had been washed away and once again life was beginning to gain a foothold over the devastated world. Tectonic plate movement had long buried the remains of the abandoned original Janise Probe and recycled it after it had transmitted its 'mind' to the receptacle it had built in orbit far above the planet. Now the probe slept with systems shut down and only reactivated when more material was delivered by the mining ships. Whatever metal had existed on the two moons had long since been utilised and the lack of mass had changed their orbits. They had collided and fused together and dropped nearer to the planet that they had once orbited singularly. Now they raised great tides in the oceans below producing a huge difference between high and low watermarks. The life that had arisen again on this world had become very adaptable to survive.

This was of great interest to the entity that now farmed sentient life. It could see that there was great potential on this ruined world. Much would need to be done here for it to succeed after this Janise Probe was removed by its organic allies. It would return after several million orbits of this world around the star and review the situation. The Farmer felt a stirring of an emotion not often experienced by its new existence and that was a feeling of frustration that it could not sense the mind of the electronic intelligence and deal with it in the manner of the organics. The entity needed the planets to be left in a viable situation so that it could carry on with its seeding project. Destabilising the sun would remove the Probe, but also the planet it required to harvest from in the far future. It wondered how the situation was progressing in the time before its existence with the fleet of organic sentients that had gone back in time to reclaim the Janise people. If anything happened to alert its parent to their rescuer's existence, then all of the timelines could unravel and plunge it into non-existence. It wondered just how far back they had gone in time to carry out the rescue of the Janise.

Alexander dissolved the link to the group mind controlling Tee 6 and shuddered. He had been part of the gestalt and with the increased power of the mind he had pursued several questions that had not been asked before they had got here at the beginning of the universe. They had assumed that they had travelled back several hundreds of millions of years to get to this point and had not questioned further. Now he knew just how far back they had come. At this point of time the star that Earth had orbited had not yet formed. They were closer to the very beginning of time than he had realised. They were at least seven billion years into the past, at least one and a half billion years before the Earth had formed. The Janise were without doubt the earliest sentient race of beings that had evolved in Andromeda and probably the Milky Way. They must have been the Harvester's first taste of sentient life-force.

This was yet to happen at this time. Once the Harvester had experienced the surge of energy flavoured with the spice of intelligence, this had dominated its sense of purpose. From this moment on it would engineer conditions for spreading life amongst any suitable worlds with the one intent of producing sentient beings. Once they attained the ability to leave their world by star-flight it would destabilise the star and soak up all the energy from every living thing. It had the entire Andromeda galaxy to gather life energy from and when a fallow time had prevailed, it crossed over to the Milky Way for several hundred million years and fed there instead.

It was during one of those times that the Harvester was steadily destabilising Earth's sun that the Nano-ships had been launched. Six million years later one ship had returned and had re-created the intelligent, genetically adjusted apes and   mankind. It was the forging of a joint civilisation

159

with the Gnathe that had resulted with the plucking of the Earth from the sun's embrace and changed the universe. The subsequence rescue of the Kresh from the Goss had resulted in them fishing through time and rescuing all of the sentient beings that the Harvester had dined on using the group mind technique they had learned from the Gnathe. This had resulted in a changed reality for the universe that they lived in.

The Harvester had retaliated by speeding up the collision of the two galaxies so that it could drain the energy of every sentient life-force that had been taken from its grasp. Alexander well remembered how they had destroyed the creature that was as nearly old as time itself and in doing so had created the off-shoot they had come to know as the Farmer. Now because of the insistence of Minnis and his children he found himself billions of years in the past. He also remembered that the Farmer had said many hundreds of millions of years ago. By what scale had it in mind when it had declared 'years'? They were without doubt at the very beginnings of time and space in their universe. He was haunted by the knowledge that it would be a decision of his that would keep his universe intact or destroy it.

He missed the presence of his alter ego, Kamiel and his perspective.

A warm loving mind slipped gently into his and Nagoth said, "Do not brood on what could be. We will be advised by our star-child when Shoolin-Alexis returns. I believe in them. Remember that it is their universe as well and they have no desire to be part of its end. Also you must take into consideration that the Harvester has not encountered such beings as us before. It has discovered the first sentient race of beings that have evolved in this cosmos. It will not be looking for us and as long as the others stay out of phase nothing will alert it to our existence."

"You are right," Alex replied. "Never the less, I can do nothing else but worry until our children make contact with us and give me something to make a decision on while we fall towards the star."

Toarvak 6 fell steadily towards the bright new star as several weeks dragged by and Link-soo-shan maintained the link forwards in time to the five anchors left behind in present time, connected to the five Toarvaks in the distant past. It took a steady group mind to do this and as the bodies of the 'linkage' became drained, they retired and allowed fresh minds to take their place. The wormhole through time and space pulsed as the minds from the past and present maintained it.

Alexander and Fredrick were keeping watch on the forward view screens looking for anything that might become a threat. They were approaching the orbit of one of the inner worlds that was sending energy signatures inwards to the next world closer to the star. It was apparent that the Janise had brought another world into life. They had altered this colder planet to sustain them by orbiting solar reflectors to send extra light and heat to artificially raise the temperature.

The human race had tried something similar with Mars, but had found that the reduced gravity made living there a one way trip. Also pregnancy became a dangerous gamble due to the fact that their race had evolved on a world with more than twice the mass.

The nannite, Solace, entered the viewing area and regarded the screens in the company of Minnis. She had been downloaded with all of Asue's astrogation knowledge and navigational abilities.

The Guardian considered the planet on the screens and said, "This world should not be here! The mass and the orbit around this star contradict the mathematics of its reality. There is too much mass for this world to orbit at this distance from the star. Somehow mass has been added to increase its gravitational pull. It is my opinion that the Janise have altered this planet to suit their requirements. Also I can tell you that it is slowly moving onto a vector that will mean that it will achieve a stable orbit closer to the star. When that day comes the need for the reflectors will diminish and these people will have the use of another world. We do not have the science to do what they have achieved without the use of a group mind. They will be an asset to the galactic community when we get them through the temporal wormhole forwards into our time. How we can do that without altering the past I am happy to say is not my decision!"

Alexander swivelled round in his chair and said, "Thank you for that information, Solace. At the moment I can't think of any way through that problem. We dare not do anything that changes the fact that they did not find a new home around another star. The awful thing is that we must allow the Harvester to strike this great civilisation down and do nothing. We have to wait for my strange children to reappear and be advised by what they can tell us."

At that moment, Nagoth ran into the control room and gripped Alex by his shoulders.

"They are coming! I can sense them," she gasped and trembled in anticipation.

Six balls of pearly light the size of their heads floated through the walls of the control room from different directions. They danced an intricate pattern in the air becoming eventually a silver globe with two children inside it. Shoolin and Alexis finally took form and separated.

Link-soo-shan's legacy floated at eye level before their parents and projected their thoughts into all the minds that were present.

"We/I have examined this race of beings. They are very wise in some ways and so very foolish in others. They have discovered a means to turn energy into matter. They have been draining their star to manufacture anti-matter to fuel a star-ship. Even now they are celebrating the launch towards another world that they have sent a probe to centuries ago. They are unaware that they have drained far too much energy from their star for it to remain stable. We have seen the future and the end of this civilisation is very imminent. Even now the solar flares are gaining in strength. The Harvester did not de-stable this sun to destroy this civilisation! The Janise did it themselves. This event was what triggered the insatiable appetite of the Harvester for sentient life energy. From this moment on this being will be dominated by that hunger. It was this event that shaped the two galaxies and brought our present existence into being. We cannot interfere or we will cease to exist and the Harvester will be unopposed."

Alexander sank back into the chair and stared at the two beings, combined from the six of his children that hung in the air in front of them. He pondered the situation and then everything fell into place in his mind.

"The solution is right before us. We must take the star-ship! This is why the Janise probe continued to recreate itself over and over again. We are the reason that the machine intelligence evolved as it did," Alexander explained to the others. "We must find the Janise vessel and take it forwards through time. So, my children you must show us where to find it!"

The star-child nodded and winked out of existence.

Alexander turned to the nannite Guardian and said, "Solace use Asue's astrogation abilities grafted into you and figure out where the next habitable star system would be. It has to be towards the centre of the spiral galaxy further in along this arm."

Solace considered the problem and contacted Toarvak 6 directly and fed the possible co-ordinates to the sentient ship. The group mind controlling the vessel studied the information and killed the direction towards the Janise sun. The vectors involved had to be calculated from the position of the Janise home-world when the star-ship was launched to where its final destination lay. All they could do was to travel along that vector and hope that they would be heading in the right direction until Shoolin-Alexis reappeared with definite information.

Tee 6 swung around the planet that they had observed and went out of phase once they were heading in the right direction. The ship accelerated in its weightless condition and broke away from the Janise system, heading towards the inner reaches of this spiral arm. Somewhere in front of them would be the destination of the Janise star-ship. The fine tuning of their ultimate direction would come later when Alexander and Nagoth's genetically designed children returned.

CHAPTER THIRTEEN

All that Toarvak 6 could do was to continue towards the centre of this galaxy, following the spiral arm. Until the star-child returned with a better direction to the habitable planet that the Janise had selected, this was the only option. Using the onboard master telepathic crystal, Alexander contacted Link-soo-shan and told her of their decision without including the Goss. At this moment they needed stability and he did not want to alarm the others. Keeping information 'local' was exceedingly difficult in a telepathic society.

The strain of keeping the wormhole stabilised and anchoring its position was beginning to have its effect on all concerned on Toarvak 12,402. The other five Toarvaks continually maintained the link across the eons through the wormhole to the other five anchored in the present. The Kresh were fighting a constant battle of mental instability. The continuous mental effort was triggering sex changes amongst the crew and adding to the strain of keeping the wormhole open. Several of the trip'o-dals had succumbed to entering a catatonic state and had to be telepathically 'woken' and put into stasis. The Vogb were doing all they could to encase the gestalts in protective layers of 'care' and were occasionally suffering burn-out of their unique light communications amongst each other. The only consolation they had was that all this would fade away once the fleet had returned and some rest was had from the mental strain, but there were some who would never recover completely.

Once Toarvak 6 had travelled beyond the localised Oort cloud of frozen comets and planetesimals, she widened her receptors to listen for any clue as to the whereabouts of the first Janise star-ship. Almost immediately when she had taken them back into phase with the universe, the being known as 'We/I' made contact.

Shoolin-Alexis cast a pearly glow throughout the control room as it materialised in front of Alexander and Nagoth.

The double child waved its hands and wove a three-dimensional map in the air between Toarvak six's avatar and its parents. There in miniature was the position of the Janise home world and parent star and the spiral arm that they were travelling along. Pinpointed in the empty dark was the new world that the Janise were making for and the star pattern around it. In-between those two stars was an ember of a star that had been drained of its energy by the Janise as they travelled by. They had used the star as a fuel depot on their journey. The star-child had placed a bright blue light at the star-ship's position along the vector.

We/I pointed to the blue light and said, "This is where you need to go, but be warned, they are using an antimatter drive. The wake left behind them is full of unused antimatter particles. If you collide with any of these it could start off a chain reaction that would cause this vessel to disintegrate. You will have to get in front of it and board the vessel and shut down the drive. Once that is done you will need to haul the Janise ship back to where Toarvak 12042 is positioned and take it back to the present time."

Alexander stared at his child with bewilderment!

"Oh, is that all we have to do?" He remarked sarcastically and dropped his head into his hands.

"You must have thought of a way to do this or we could not have travelled here," the star-child retorted.

"That's all very well, my amazing children, but the fact remains that I could alter the very existence of the universe. The Kresh inadvertently did it once when they went fishing through time and took all of the Harvester's 'ready meals' away from it. They changed the realities of two galaxies. So success is not guaranteed. I could make the wrong decision and destroy all that we have achieved."

As he spoke the view screens looking to the rear of the ship registered an intense glow as the Janise's home worlds were engulfed by their star as it went nova and expanded into a red giant. Now the only Janise to exist were on the star-ship that was travelling towards its new home. Alexander had to make sure that they never got there.

He thought for a moment and turned to the avatar of Toarvak 6 and said, "Plot a course towards that vessel and intercept a point half a light year in front of it. Keep at least a light year away from the wake of the antimatter drive.

Toarvak 6 sank into the floor and returned to the gestalt controlling the vessel. Immediately the star-ship went out of phase. It lost its mass and altered course, rising above the vector that they had been following, but keeping on a parallel line. Energy was piled into the engines so that they could overtake the Janise. As they closed the gap an observable wake could be clearly seen stretching back through the void. A deadly swathe of anti-matter particles that had escaped the annihilation of materials brought together inside a 'magnetic bottle' and had sprayed into the emptiness behind the vessel. Every time these molecules collided with normal matter, energy was spent as total destruction took place and a trail of lethal light was left behind.

Alexander called a meeting with his friends and laid out his idea to Fredrick and Minnis.

"The most important thing we must do is to turn off that drive. Once that is done we can merge Toarvak 6 with their vessel and take them to the wormhole. Then it will be a simple matter to return to our time-line. After that we can let things sort themselves out. Minnis and Fredrick will be the ones who drop into the Janise ship and find out what the situation is on board. Minnis is the only nannite that can go out of phase, so she can take Fred inside. It all depends on what you find there. Spread the spores of the Goss amongst the Janise and once we can communicate with them we can explain the situation to them and what we mean to do," Alexander stated.

Hannah stood up and said, "I will culture a fresh batch of spores and fill some containers for Fredrick to take with him. We will need a rapid infection to take place so that we can persuade them to divert from their destination. Are we in range to get a clear view of their ship?"

Alexander projected his mind into the gestalt that was running the ship and asked, "Do we have a clear view of the Janise vessel?"

A Kresh mind answered him, "We do have an observation that is coming into view. This is not going to be quite so simple. The Janise have built something on the scale of the last Ark of the Goss! This is an artificial world in its own right. Even though we are a light year above the exhaust line of the trail of antimatter particles, we are still at risk. We are taking Toarvak 6 further out and away before we try to get ahead of this incredible vessel."

Abruptly the forward view-screens lit up with an amazing picture. At full magnification a moon shaped object dominated the screen. A giant globular construction was outlined against the empty blackness of the void that the vessel was powering across. Great pylons that supported energy collecting dishes, sprouted around the centre of the globe. There were five of them with enough room to place Toarvak 6 into any of the receivers. Three of them were aligned to a nearby star, receiving energy from it, while the other two that were underneath the line of sight were inert. At the back of the moon sized vessel was another structure that projected backwards and away from the globe supporting a vast set of concentric rings also shaped like a huge cup. A blue light flickered around the powerful magnetic field that held the anti-matter collision with normal matter pellets. The force of the annihilation was thrusting against this magnetic bottle, propelling the vessel towards its destination and maintaining a small pulsing sun at its heart. Two great tubes of rings pointed back at the implosion point and suspended within each was the raw anti-hydrogen pellets kept in place by the magnetic fields without touching the sides. A central tube spat pellets of frozen hydrogen at the convergence. The rest of the matter conversion drive emptied itself into space, leaving a deadly trail behind it. The speed of the vessel was such that it was blue-shifting as it travelled onwards. The whole of the vessel was bathed in a lambent glow of its own aurora borealis making it easy to find. It was plain to see that the Janise were engineers and quantum physicists of an incredibly high order.

Every sentient being staring at the screen was struck dumb for some considerable time! Even the Kresh were humbled by the magnitude of the Janise's achievement. Of all the sentient beings in the home galaxy they alone had managed to create the sentient ships called Toarvaks that could alter their molecular bindings to go out of phase with the universe. The humans had created the nannite Guardians and the Gnathe had unlocked the secrets of building group minds with wormhole control that linked this knowledge together. Now there was a new science to amalgamate into the sentient melting pot!

Toarvak 6 decreased the distance to the vast alien ship and overtook the Janise by keeping to the side that did not have the energy capture dishes pointing at the refuelling star. The dishes that were in shadow remained inert as the Kresh vessel narrowed the distance between them.

Very carefully it drifted closer to the surface of the bow, remaining out of phase and undetectable. She extended filaments towards the alien ship and turned the ends in contact back into phase with the molecular substance. Next she increased the thickness of the tethers until they were rigidly fixed to the Janise interstellar vessel.

Alexander turned to his friend, Fredric and said, "I think that its time that you and Minnis got together again and boarded the Janise colony ship."

Hannah handed her companion a sealed flask containing a concentrated swarm of Goss spores.

She kissed him and whispered into his ear, "Be careful! We have no idea what these people are like. Take no risks and do not think that wearing Minnis makes you invincible!"

The nannite Guardian unfolded to receive her human counterpart and flowed over the giant, encasing him completely. She formed a globe over his head and built up the 'nannite muscles' all over his body. Minnis condensed from the available air a generous amount of pressurised breathing gases. Fredric was already nearly seven foot tall and when wearing the battle suit that Kamiel had designed for him, he towered even more over his friends. She inserted nerve endings to join her nannite controls to his human frame and merged herself with his mind. Now the two of them would operate as one being. They made their way to the nearest airlock carrying the flask 'welded' to his hip.

Fredrick and Minnis stepped through the airlock and started to drift towards the reinforced window of the vessel. Remaining out of phase they drifted through the foot thick glass and into the control-room.

Inside the Janise vessel was a totally alien environment to anything that the human and nannite had ever seen before. Upright poles connected the floor to the ceiling in what seemed to Fredrick a random pattern. Strung between them was a network of webs and connecting strands. Suspended in hammocks were the Janise with their legs tucked up out of the way. Some were immobile and some were sat up with their upper arms laced through supports in front of view screens. They had the appearance of a giant preying mantis except for what they were using as hands. Attached by spider-like silk to the tips of their arms were independent creatures being used as fingers, thumbs and clasping members. Those not attached, moved around the control room on errands. Whatever the creatures were, they were working in unison with the Janise.

Minnis altered the molecular patterns of the flask so that it dropped into phase with the vessel that they had boarded. Fredrick had opened the flask prior to this and watched it drop to the floor allowing many of the spores to escape. The Goss now existed in two separate time frames and was for a while two separate identities. The sentient symbiont that existed in this era was tiny by comparison to its present time ego, but was as eager to make contact with this new alien race as its parent. When it came back through the wormhole to the time that Kamiel existed, it would merge with its alter ego. The spores floated through the air and burrowed deep into the receptive Janise. Within a few minutes the spores had multiplied and had penetrated the brains of its new host.

On board Toarvak 6, Alexander waited anxiously for that first contact with a new race.

Shoolin/Alexis contacted him and said, "We/I will make our way to the control room on the Janise ship and provide some back-up if needed by Minnis and Fredrick."

Undetected by the Janise the watchers waited for the spores to take effect.

As the spores multiplied inside the alien's bodies the telepathic links to the spider-like hands remained unaltered, but the effect on the Janise was extraordinary. Their minds reached out as the telepathic link established itself between Alexander and the members of the Toarvak's crew.

Alexander reached out to the Goss and asked, "Goss, do we have sufficient spores rooted into the Janise to allow us to contact them?"

"There is a rising symphony of enriching minds that are already connected to each other and now to the gestalt. They are ready!"

The human-Gnathe hybrid introduced himself to the alert and shocked minds of the Janise.

"I am known as Alexander. The crew of this vessel have travelled a long way in space and time to meet you. We will explain to you why we are here and how this will affect you. Who leads this colonising expedition to another world?"

A clear powerful mind made contact with Alex and said, "I am the principal co-ordinator of this project. My designation is systems controller and my specified name is 'Gives direction at all times.' Your name has no meaning! Yet you are a leader of your vessel and unspecified!"

"There will many new ideas that you will need to accommodate in the future," Alexander replied. We have come from the far future to find you and bring you forwards to our time and to make you welcome in our galactic federation. There is much that I have to tell you and little time to do it in. The easiest thing to do is to allow you to read my mind and to understand the situation that exists in our time and yours. First I must show you what your people have done to your sun and explain what you have inadvertently unleashed at this time!"

Alexander showed the Janise the explosion of their star and the death of their species that had fed the appetite of the Harvester at its beginning. The rest of the history of this omnipotent being and the sentient beings' conflict with it was laid out by Alex to the Janise. The spread of the intelligent probes from star system to star system towards the galactic centre and the result of the Janise never catching up with their creation, due to the interference of what Alexander was proposing was also shown.

"Your mind tells an interesting history, Alexander. We are not surprised that we are alone in this timeline. This universe is very new compared to the time that you have travelled from and few stars have settled down to produce planets where life is possible. We could easily dominate this time and space if it were not for the creature that you have named the Harvester.

My people are horrified to learn of the damage that we have done to our own sun and the destruction of our civilization. Also this being of energy that feeds on life is something that our mistake has unleashed upon this universe. We are responsible! We are full of sorrow. Yet I can see that the interaction of our species with all that you have become in the future is the fundamental pivot point of the timeline that you inhabit. It would seem that we are to be grateful that you have spent so much effort to find us and take us through the wormhole to your time, but I must ask why you have taken so much trouble to do this" the Janise answered.

Alexander was able to give an honest answer to the Janise and replied, "You are the only sentient beings that have managed to reverse the energy equations and produce matter from energy. Many have been able to produce energy from matter, but none of us have been able to make anti-matter in the quantities that you have. The being that was created by the Harvester's defeat will need that knowledge far in the future when the universe begins to die. We cannot even to begin to wonder just what it will do. That it has decided to ally itself with every sentient being is enough for us to accept that it is benign."

The Janise pondered this information and came to a decision, "What would you have us do?"

"Make a course correction towards where our other vessels and people are keeping the wormhole open. After that you must shut down your anti-matter drive. The trail that you are leaving is deadly. We will now reveal ourselves to you," Alexander replied. "We are anchored to the front of your vessel and are out of phase with your molecular substance. There is on board with you one of our people who will now show himself to you and another being that will be beyond anything that you have imagined! This was necessary to expose you to the symbiont that all of our many races carry. It enables all alien species to communicate, telepathically."

Fredrick and Minnis altered their molecular phasing and appeared to the astonished bridge crew. The Janise recoiled in horror as the silver clad form of the biped materialised in front of them. Fredrick's form was totally alien to the insectile creatures that had built the star-ship. To the human it was if he was stood surrounded by giant preying mantises covered in tarantula spiders. Each of the Janise had a pair of spiders fixed to the ends of a formidable hook-ended upper arm and secured by silk, spun by the spiders around the ends. Other spiders were attached to the inner faces of the legs where they appeared to be fed from teats. Some hung lifeless and hardened into cocoons that were fixed along the sides of the Janise.

This was the moment that Shoolin/Alexis chose to materialise amongst the stunned Janise. A pearly shining globe began to expand until within it two human children were seen holding hands. The outside protective surface of the sphere dissolved and the shining forms of what humanity would one day become, stood and regarded the much bigger aliens without fear. They radiated the emotions of trust and harmlessness. The two children let go of each other's hand and walked amongst the Janise. They picked up the 'spider-like' creatures and allowed them to examine them for their parent's satisfaction. Fredrick then found that he too was subjected to this examination as the extensions of the Janise crawled over him. Having spent a great deal of time with the Zanti on their home-world and amongst the insectoids that ran their own Toarvaks he was not bothered by being examined by the 'spiders'! Minnis pulled back some of her substance to allow the Janise to examine his skin and feel the warmth of his body from his outstretched arms.

The Janise bridge crew began to alter the vector of the star-ship so that it was lined up with the new destination. A sudden surge of power from the anti-matter drive pushed the vehicle onto its new course.

'Gives Direction at all times' began the system of closing down the anti-matter drive. The moon-sized interstellar craft also cut power to the 'magnetic bottles' that held the anti-matter fuel suspended, unable to touch the structure of the ship. The jettisoned fuel was soon left behind and continued to shine, as normal matter made contact with it. The balls sparkled as miniature explosions took place wherever interstellar hydrogen atoms made contact. Several days later when the Janise decided that the combined ships were far enough away to be safe, they released a solid projectile towards each ball of fuel to destroy the unused antimatter. The resulting double explosion lit up the aft screens as if a star had gone nova.

The leader of the Janise had taken Alexander and his immediate advisory council to the inside of the artificial world built by the aliens. The human was amazed to see that much of the world that was inside the artificial moon was mirrored in the construction of the last Ark of the Goss. It had a similar artificial sun in the centre of the globe supported from the inside structure. The inside of the moon was laid out as farming lands and inner seas. This was done in strips so that each 'sea' irrigated the lands on either side of it. Over a hundred-thousand, Janise lived inside this artificial world preparing to live and die here while the great ship carried on towards their new home, spinning on its axis. Unlike the Kresh and their Toarvaks, or the Lagdoo, the Janise had not discovered wormhole technology. The Gnathen manipulation using group minds was an altogether different affair. All this would be handed over as a matter of course when the expedition returned through the time-gate in return for the knowledge of the technique of energy into matter translation.

Although the Janise leader had met some of the other aliens on board Toarvak 6 on her own ship, she found it rather overwhelming when she visited Alexander in his. She had insisted on the visit so that she could see for herself how all the many different aliens got along. The artificial intelligences embodied in the many nannites and also the personage of Toarvak 6 amazed her. This was another area of expertise that the Janise had not explored. They had developed computers to aid their knowledge of science and discovery, but had never dreamed that electronic intelligence could be achieved.

Solace made it her place to be at the Janise leader's side at all times as guide and to give explanations to her whenever she was in need. The nannite was informing 'Gives Direction' about the origins of the Goss. To do that she had to retell the history of the alternative universe brought into being by the events that had taken place at this time and its relationship with the events in the far future.

She explained that certain points in time were pivot points. Decisions made then altered the flow of time and created new realities. Everything started with the destruction of the Janise star, due to the application of the aliens using the energy it produced into mass conversion.

The proximity of the being that developed into the Harvester and its insatiable appetite for the life force generated by sentient life was initiated by this event. The domination of both galaxies by the being was the direct result of these actions. The cultures that had eventually defeated it accepted that the universe that they had brought into being was preferable to the grim alternative. To bring about the far distant results that the Farmer wished to bring into being, it was necessary to retrieve the Janise from the early beginnings of the universe and bring them forward to the present time.

The nannite paused in her narrative to inform 'Gives Direction' that the combined Janise star-ship and Toarvak six had arrived at the open end of the wormhole kept in place by the 'anchor' left behind. On the main view-screens 'Gives Direction' could see the pentagon of the five Toarvaks holding the wormhole open. Below the arrangement of ships was Toarvak 12,402 holding the five in position as an anchor. The mental strain of doing this was heavy in the psychic web that criss-crossed the bottom of the wormhole. Inside the entrance was a sensation that all beings with eyes constructed in pairs endured if they tried to stare into the blind spot. Sometimes there was something there and sometimes not.

The Janise heard the mental summons that was broadcast to all on board ship.

Link-soo-shan urged them, "Enter the wormhole as fast as you can. The Harvester has followed you and our minds shine like a beacon attracting the destroyer like a moth to a flame. We must collapse the wormhole behind us. Go now!"

CHAPTER FOURTEEN.

As the time-spanning wormhole began collapsing behind them the hunger of the Harvester's need abruptly cut off, leaving the minds of the expedition to the past feeling raw. The relief of no longer having to keep the wormhole stabilised at the early time of star formation soon washed away the unending mental stress from the five Toarvak crews that had kept it open. A sensation of dropping upwards permeated every sentient mind as the time vortex unravelled. The Janise found it very unsettling as they had never experienced time travel before, but took their bearing from their rescuers and stoically endured the strange sensations.

A sudden loss of movement inside the vortex to a spatial awareness found the Toarvaks and the Janise spacecraft emerged into empty space, inside the pentagon formation of the 'present time' sentient vessels. In all directions a yawning emptiness stretched before them, except for one direction. There spinning around its axis was the splendour of the Andromeda galaxy. Beyond it lay the Milky Way absorbing the forced collision with its neighbour and both of them completely out of reach. The first thing that happened was that their part of the Goss was reunited with its larger self that occupied the entire Andromeda galaxy. Instantly, communication was possible between the vast gulfs separating all sentient minds. The next thing that Alex realised was that the entity they had identified as the 'Farmer,' was nowhere to be found, so time must have passed at this end of the wormhole, albeit at a different rate to that experienced in the long past. Unless they could attract the attentions of this altruistic being, they would die out here in the intergalactic emptiness.

Alexander quickly built a group mind to reach out to his

old nannite mentor, Kamiel.

The nannite, had 'wired' himself into the network of the Ark's far range sensors and using them, he scanned deeper into the gravity well of the 'G' type star. He was seeking any constructions that would lead him to the whereabouts of the Janise probe that had made this system its home.

Asue was piloting the last Ark of the Goss through the ministrations of the reptilian Lagdoo and following Kamiel's instructions. There were another four rocky planets orbiting the star closer in from the gas giants. The inner two were far too close to the star to be of any use as a life bearing system, but the outer two were possible, as they both had water that showed up in spectral analysis. The inner one was covered by clouds of steam, however and was orbited by a small moon. The outer one was at least one and a half times bigger than the Earth and was covered in ice at the poles. Kamiel noticed that it was orbited by a large moon in a strange orbit that appeared to be the result of a collision between two smaller moons. Sensors detected large amounts of metal, but only at the pole that pointed at the star. The Janise probe had taken residence on this moon and tilted its axis so that as it orbited the planet beneath, so that one pole was permanently fixed to face the star. Somehow the Janise probe had altered the orbit of the moon so that it travelled a path directly over the planet's poles, while the world below spun from east to west.

Kamiel was sure that the moon's pole facing the star would be covered in photo-electric cells, soaking up the energy from the star's radiance. At the moment the Janise probe was in a shut-down phase awaiting the ore carriers to travel the vast distance from the outer reaches of this system. It would be a simple thing to aim the heavy masses of the moons donated to them by the 'Farmer' straight at the dark pole and blast the large moon to smithereens! The only drawback to this easy way of obliterating the machine intelligence was that it would destroy the moon in orbit. Experience of life bearing worlds showed that they needed a large moon to raise tides and to produce weather; otherwise a greenhouse effect would cause the planet to heat up and turn into a Venus type world.

The Guardian had kept the last Ark of the Goss out of phase while he studied the situation as they travelled closer to the planet. To his surprise there were abundant signs of life on this world and it had recovered from the excessive stripping away of metals and minerals by the arrival of the Janise probe so long ago. Kamiel could only wonder at the time that had passed upon this ruined world to set it back to a life bearing place. For it to do so, the tectonic plate movements would have buried all of the Janise probe's desecrations. New mountains had been pushed up and seas had flooded sunken lands. He took the hollow moon back into phase with the rest of the universe to be able to eavesdrop on what communications were filling the area that they were entering.

There were radio waves pulsing from several constructions built upon this moon facing into the dark, sending guidance beacons for the ore carriers to home into. Kamiel was very careful not to activate or block any of these systems. As the Janise probe was 'asleep', he intended to keep it that way as long as possible. It would be several years before the results of the battle fleet campaign in the outer reaches would trip any sensors to warn the probe that its ore carriers had been neutralised. Meanwhile he considered the situation that he was confronted with.

It was at this moment his artificially maintained piece of living flesh that carried the spores of the Goss, intruded into his thoughts with a telepathic signal.

"Kamiel old friend, we are back! We nearly brought back the Harvester with us, but closed the time portal just in time and left it there in the past. We have suffered some temporal drift and have re-entered this reality at a much later date than we thought. This has meant that we have a problem and that is, we have arrived back in your time present and need to be ferried from far out of the galactic dark to wherever you are. We have the Janise with us and a long story to tell. They are eager to meet all of the sentients in our federation and to contribute their knowledge to the common pool. They also say that they are sure that they can turn off the machine intelligence and bring it back into line. Are you in touch with the entity we call the Farmer?"

The combined mind that Kamiel was using as a gestalt reached out to the being that had brought them here and made it aware of the situation.

There was a blurring of reality and the combined Toarvaks and the Janise interstellar ship appeared by the side of the Ark. The Janise mobile unit by Kamiel's side became very still as its sensors registered the presence of the very people that had built its ancestors to serve. It connected to the communications network running the systems of the artificial world and registered its existence.

The screens lit up in the main control room on the Janise ship and showed the mobile unit that Asue had designed and the probe on Haven had modified to its own specifications. The Janise were amazed that the machine intelligence had been squeezed into such a small space and that it was fully sentient.

The three legged robot said in the Janise language, "I am Mobile Unit. How may I serve? I am the last clone of many clones of the probe that was sent to the first world. I need purpose!"

The Janise known as 'Gives Direction at all Times'

concentrated her attention at Mobile Unit and answered, "You are to make contact with the deranged probe in this system and tell it of our arrival. You will order it to stand by and turn over its operational systems to my deputy and continue to remain on stand-by for further orders. Tell it to make preparations for an imminent inspection and to provide living quarters suitable for the Janise. We will be requiring its management of the world below for our colonisation programs. It is to make contact with our onboard ship's computer and extract whatever information that it requires to set this order into action."

The superior mind of the fully sentient Mobile Unit soon overpowered the sleeping machine intelligence and relayed the orders to the now fully awake systems that were running the complex rooted on the moon. Command structures that had corrupted over the hundreds of millions of years that the Janise probe had modified itself to give a re-purpose were rooted out and cancelled by the Mobile Unit. New circuits were installed at the heart of the computer and safeguards installed.

Many weeks were to pass during these modifications and during this time the Janise spread throughout the fleet of Toarvaks meeting their new interstellar neighbours.

'Gives Direction' was speaking to Link-soo-shan via the Goss, "This world is large enough and empty enough to become home to many of the sentient beings that are part of the federation. We are determined to bring about a new civilization here without making the mistakes of the past. Your race's abilities in genetic engineering would be a great benefit to this planet and to us. We have got used to the alien communities and revel in the bending of our minds into the insights that they bring. Also the mental abilities that each sentient being brings to the federation have opened up new horizons to our people. We are more than happy that you took the risk of coming so far into your past to find and bring us into this amazing time. If the mission to the past had gone wrong, all of this reality would have been changed completely."

"There were many amongst us who were only too aware of the consequences of failure," Link-soo-shan replied, keeping a careful eye on the mobile 'hands' that scurried about, directed by the Janise.

She had allowed several of the spider-like appendages of 'Gives Direction' to climb over her body. The female creature had an amazing view of her surroundings as she saw the cosmos through her own eyes and the eyes of the detached limbs that constantly fed back a three dimensional world to her senses. Link paused for a moment and stared at her large, mantis shaped visitor that had spun a silken hammock in front of her. She had secured it to the ceiling of the Gnathe's quarters, so that she could hang from it comfortably while they talked. Smaller versions of the detached limbs were hanging in budded cocoons from the sides of her body casing in a dormant condition. When they reached maturity they would emerge to become the Janise's 'hands' and eyes. Link-soo-shan watched as 'Gives Direction' consumed several of the older mobiles after they had deposited an egg under her wing-case. She still did not know whether the mobile 'hands' were a different life-form or genetically part of the structure of the Janise.

The Gnathe's philosophy was that shape was a condition of purpose. As a natural genetic engineer she was appreciative that each sentient life form had evolved for a purpose, unlike the Gnathe who had modified themselves over and over again to serve different purposes in their society. The coming of the humans and intelligent pan-chimpanzees to their home world had caused them to take a fresh look at themselves. The unification of the two totally different species had opened up the universe far beyond the narrow scope of the Gnathe. Now the federation of more sentient species had added to the melting pot and added an even newer dimension to all of the many different societies. Now one more totally alien species had been added to the mix. She was convinced that the being that they had named the Farmer had helped them to bring these vastly different people back from certain extinction for a purpose of its own. The being had its own agenda and was able to access the memories of its parent that were part of its own strange mind. That meant that it had a perspective that stretched back in time billions of years. It was constantly adding to its overall consciousness by absorbing and storing the minds of all the sentients in this galaxy as they died. Each sentient race had a unique spectrum of existence and understanding of the universe. Unlike the Harvester that merely fed off of the life-energy and discarded the very essence of what each person was, the Farmer added them all to its psyche.

'Gives Direction' allowed her mind to open to the Brood-mother via the Goss and continued, "Yet you came and risked everything that you had achieved. I and my people find this a conundrum that makes little sense to us. You have to understand that we were isolated in the newly formed universe. It would seem that at our time of existence, there were no other sentient life-forms that had evolved. We also appreciate that the first energy-hungry being that you named the Harvester, would have taken us sometime in that future. So we do owe our very existence to your intervention. Yet we have to ask the question, why?"

Link-soo-shan sat back and rested her body-mass against her tail and gave this question some thought. After a short while she reached out and folded space around Alexander and Nagoth, bringing them into the room along with Kamiel and Asue. The next thing she did was to ask the composite mind of Shoolin-Alexis if they would join the gestalt that she was intending to build.

Holding the Janise out of the loop, she quickly outlined the direction that she wished to go and was joined by the composite minds of the star-child. As the combined gestalt considered the proposal, she entered the Janise leader's mind.

"Join with us and we will contact the being that was born of the Harvester's death and all will be revealed," Link-soo-shan explained.

'Gives Direction' was enfolded into the composite mind and was carried along in the quest of contacting the Farmer.

They abruptly found themselves upon a three dimensional plane that existed in a fog-like extension that now enveloped the entire Andromeda galaxy. The Farmer now existed as an entity, far larger than its parent. They were aware that they existed in a realm full of sparkling lights set upon a giant web. Thoughts clustered in groups and triggered off eruptions of light and deep meaning. A presence existed here that had become vast and greater than the last time that they had contacted this creature. It had evolved exponentially since their first contact.

The tiny mind reached out to the vast intellect that the Farmer had become and introduced the newest member of the sentient federation. It posed the question that the Janise had asked and received a reply.

"Organic creatures are capable of creative thoughts. Of all the sentient beings that have evolved in this universe, the Janise were the only ones to understand the principles of converting energy into mass. I now have that knowledge and I can apply it when the time is right. I have considered the pathway that the Janise travelled from their home world and have tracked back to the star system that was reached before this one. That sun has gone into its red giant stage as had the star before it in the trail. You have removed the machine intelligence threat from this galaxy and you may gladly go about your own business from now on. You will not be able to contact me again, as my thought processes will slow down to observe the millennia passing. I have much to do at the right time far into the future. Rest assured that you to will play a part in the end of time when this universe dies and another will be reborn. Meanwhile all that you are will be stored at the end of your lives and reused at a far future time."

The gestalt returned to the confines of the room and came apart, leaving the component beings to contemplate the thoughts that they had been made aware of.

Alexander took the massive hand of Link-soo-shan to steady himself and broadcast telepathically to all who occupied the room, "What did that thing mean by that?"

The composite being that was once the children of Alex and Nagoth reflected on the information given to the group and answered, "I/We believe that the Farmer has an ultimate destiny that concerns all sentient life in the immediate past and far into the future. The being has demonstrated to us that it is beneficent, unlike the creature that fed upon sentient life energy that was its creator. What its ultimate goal is, seems to be is the eventual side-step from the end of this universe to a new one. At that time our very essence of self may be needed to be brought back from storage and applied to the problem. Consider what this being has absorbed from all sentient life and that it takes an active interest in spreading that life throughout this galaxy. It has taken the knowledge of wormhole manipulation and usage to another level beyond anything that we could achieve. It now lives partly in the 'out of phase universe' that the Kresh discovered and applied to the Toarvaks' method of travel. It understands more about co-opting gestalt minds

187

and building that energy and knowledge into itself through our use of this technique than we do. Indeed it has gone far beyond anything that we can achieve. To all intents and purposes it is immortal, in so much that it will also cease to exist when this universe dies. I believe that it has a plan to escape that fate and we will be part of it!"

'Gives Direction' swung the hammock that she rested in and rolled out of its embrace and spoke to all of them through the Goss, "All it lacked was our knowledge of reversing energy into mass! It was this quirk of physics that converted the universe into 'solid matter' after the Big Bang! That is why we were rescued at the risk of totally destroying this reality. On a point of its survival, it would need that understanding at the end of time to reverse what will ultimately happen. We must just live our lives to the full and accept that the Farmer will care for us and when needed, we will be summoned and incorporated into its plan. A cold thought goes through my mind that it was also willing to place its own existence at risk to achieve this. If we were to have altered this reality back to the domination of the Harvester, then the universe would definitely come to an end, as energy dissipated, taking that being with it. We are thinking ahead of many trillions of years in the future when even the black holes have evaporated and all the stars have gutted out like the pinched wick of a candle flame."

"That is too far into the future for me to worry about," Nagoth answered and turned towards the Janise. She held one of the mobile extensions and stared at the creature looking at her as she continued, "We thank you for your offer of a new home on this world below us. It is time we settled down and let others sort out any problems in the future. It would be wonderful to live on a world again and breathe fresh air. I want to walk on earth and plants in my bare feet, stand in the rain watching the sun go down, filling the sky with a red glow. I want to eat food that we have grown and harvested together. In short, I want to go home, wherever that place may be with my friends around me!"

Many years had passed and the world that the Janise probe had picked for them to settle on was full of promise. It was a much larger world than the human's planet of origin, but of a less dense composition. There was less metal to be used on this world, but with all of the knowledge available to the many races of beings that settled here that was not a handicap. The crystals that had been mined from the gas giants served to amplify the mental powers of those who used them. The Toarvak ships slipped in and out of phase and carried those who wished to other worlds via the wormholes established. At last a time of harmony and freedom from strife were the right of every sentient life-form. With the universal living telepathic connections of the Goss all creatures of sufficient intelligence could communicate to each other without any deceit. The planet was named Last-home by a general consensus as the settlers of the many species were of no mind to move on.

In the skies floated the progeny of Archive as the Trans–sentients spread across the empty spaces. They carried seeds and plants to transplant into favourable situations. On their broad backs were camped a variety of aliens taking advantage of this unique form of transport.

The fertile lands filled up with a loosely connected farming community encompassing a bewildering number of sentient species. Small towns sprung up where artisans of all kinds made use of natural materials. The Gnathe busily genetically engineered all manner of strange creatures to specifications supplied by their non-Gnathen neighbours. Insectoids built hives and integrated with the Janise. The

Janise probe busily did what it had been created for and extracted whatever was needed from the countryside without doing any ecological damage. Foundries were set up to smelt the raw materials into metal, overseen by the many extensions of the Janise Probe and distributed amongst the settlements according to their needs. Any poisons left over from the processes were altered using nannite technology into inert and useful materials.

Over the centuries Last-home prospered and began to build a truly multi-species society. The Goss thrived and spread completely throughout the Andromeda galaxy and an independent super-mind emerged that was incorporated into the Farmer's fold.

The centuries turned into thousands of years and eventually became millenniums and the Andromeda galaxy merged with the Milky Way and became one enormous spiral galaxy. The combined minds of the galactic civilization that had evolved from the time of the rescue of the Janise moved suns and placed planets in orbit around them. Rouge suns were cast out from the stability of the new order. Little was heard from the entity known as 'The Farmer' as time continued to exact its toll on the stars, but it had not been idle.

Using the resources now available to it and evolving constantly, the being reached out to the neighbouring galaxies and found a richness of sentient life-forms. These it stored as individuals and kept the life energy. As it increased in understanding by absorbing them it reached into the flesh of its first sentient beings and seeded each galaxy with the spores of the Goss. Now it fully understood the falseness of the distances involved from the boundaries of the total universe. The Farmer expanded so that the entire universe now spread itself within its envelope.

Now it considered the problem that had nagged away

at the edge of its mind since it had become fully sentient. It began to collect hydrogen atoms and send them into a spiral pattern so that a new star would condense into a G type. It swept through the interstellar wastes for the raw material to create the right type while other stars were guttering out. Once they were stabilised, the Farmer considered the discovery of the Janise and applied the reversal of energy into matter. It began to build a sphere around the yellow star, starting with a cobweb structure that spun around the cluster of suns.

Being careful not to impinge on the civilizations that had evolved and spread throughout each galaxy, the Farmer began collecting what blue giants still existed. These stars were arranged in a spherical arrangement several hundred light years away from the G type star. The energy that these giants radiated into space it converted into mass, drinking them dry in the process. Giant blue-white stars cooked the heavy elements in their centres and were encouraged to go super-nova out on the rim of the galaxy. The farmer used wormholes to pipe the materiel to where it was building the ultimate habitat. The planet sized chunk of converted mass it sent towards the 'Goldilocks zone' that existed around the cluster. In orbit between the red suns and this area, a lattice arrangement contained the flares given off by the stars. By the time that the sphere was finished, it was two-hundred-million miles in diameter, contained in a reflective metallic shell several miles thick.

Over the millions of years that it took to raise mountains and create sea bottoms the Farmer learnt a great deal about stellar and planetary engineering. It created wormholes that drained cometary haloes completely empty of water ice and deposited them on the sea bottoms. Once the ice had melted, the farmer introduced life into the oceans. The air began to thicken and change to an oxygen and nitrogen mix over the eons. As the air began to build, the Farmer introduced plant life to the mountains, valleys and plains. After several million years, microscopic life thrived in every aspect combined with insects and invertebrates. Plants had established an eco-system that had come into balance with many alien species. The Farmer had engineered vast areas of indigenous life-forms and laid down regions of waterless deserts that effectively separated the more widely different species.

Several hundred, million years passed and the Dyson sphere throbbed with life. Every species of life in the old universe was represented on the inside of the sphere. It was now ready for intelligent life to be placed inside. The G type star had reached a stabilised state of existence. The Farmer had built a vast global spider web between the suns and the inside of the Dyson sphere that slowly rotated, casting shadows on the landscapes below. Colossal doors opened and closed to shut the light off from the surface, giving a synthetic night. Gravity varied depending how much mass was deposited under each particular living area. Mountains reached miles into the sky so that ice would form into great glaciers at the tops and be seasonally warmed by an increase of sunlight as the filters in the sky changed their shape.

The Farmer had stored every pattern of sentient life into its great consciousness as it had promised eons ago. Once again life was engineered from inert matter and this time intelligence was added to the mix. This time there was a template to follow.

CHAPTER FIFTEEN

Alexander drew a shuddering breath and then another. He opened his eyes to a blue sky blazing with the light of a familiar type of sun. Clouds swept by high up above, building thunder-heads far away. Occasional beams of golden light filtered through the clouds and warmed him with their touch. He unsteadily sat up, shivered as the breeze caressed his naked skin and suddenly realised that he was alive! Not only that. But his body was young and healthy with no trace of age at all. He remembered his last dying breath and a very old, but fit body and then being part of a vast collective.

Stood quite close was a familiar silvery being that he knew so well.

Alexander asked, "Where am I, this time, Kamiel?"

The enigmatic nannite answered "You could also ask, when am I?"

Alexander shakily stood up and really looked around at his surroundings. He was standing on a grassy plain, studded with trees and bushes. Not too far away were groups of buildings that blended into the scenery. Silver figures were busy at countless tasks dotted over fields and meadows that stretched into the distance, rising in all directions. All at once Alex could see the strange perspective that troubled his eyes. He was stood on the inside face of a giant bowl. No! It was a sphere that extended in all directions very like the last Ark of the Goss, but Alexander could feel the pull of gravity under his feet. He shielded his eyes from the sunlight and stared into the sky to realise that it was a yellow star that was providing the light.

"Kamiel, old friend, there must be much I need to know.

Do you have the knowledge to explain to me just what has happened to us? Can you tell me? The next question is, if you do, will I understand? What has happened since I died?"

"I can tell you some of what has transpired, Alexander. We have worked on this project for hundreds of millions of years under the guidance of the being that you named 'The Farmer.' Now it is ready for the next stage. Be prepared, for your child approaches," the Guardian replied.

A hole in space opened and closed and Shoolin-Alexis appeared before him. The being that Link-soo-shan had genetically designed, no longer took the image of a girl and a boy joined by their hands. Now Alexander and Nagoth's child had gone beyond the need to hold a physical identity. Instead a multi coloured glowing egg that pulsed in size from about his size to a point of light and back again, hung in the air before him. It was difficult for him to remember that the being was in fact three sets of twins, mentally inseparable.

A gentle voice thrust itself into his mind and said, "Welcome father! It is good to see you after such millennia have passed. I expect that you will remember nothing of the eons spent within the mantle of the being called 'The Farmer'! It would speak to you through me and explain."

Alexander stared at the being that floated in the air before him and waited, unafraid.

"I am pleased that you are still as I accepted you into my firmament. It was you and your alter ego, the nannite, Kamiel that destroyed the 'first-one,' thus leaving ME to evolve into the being that I have become. Understand if you can, that I am the sum total of every sentient thing in all of the galaxies that made up the universe and as such have determined that when this universe dies, we will endure until the emptiness reforms through another Big

Bang.

From raw energy and into matter came life. This has been repeated throughout the universe in galaxy after galaxy. Sentient life evolved over and over again and in its turn created an artificial life-form constructed by using nanotechnology. These artificial intelligences have proved themselves invaluable to my plan. I have built with the help of these nannites, a Dyson sphere that is far larger in diameter than your home planet's orbit around its star. In the centre is a new G type star that I have created from the last wisps of interstellar hydrogen. It is the very last star to be created in this universe and will serve its purpose for at least ten billion years. The inside of the sphere has a surface area of some one hundred and twenty-five, thousand, million square miles. There is plenty of room for every life form to exist and plenty of time as the star should last at least ten billion years! This self-contained world will be a base for exploration of the new universe when it is ready.

Do not think that you can escape the gravity well that holds you fast to the earth of this artificial world until things have settled down. There are mechanisms that exist between this star and yourselves that will give you night and day. They also alter the wavelengths of the light given by this star to approximate the 'sunshine that your individual needs require. Encompassing this source of energy is the shell of the sphere. This region of the sphere is a forbidden area to all life-forms except the nannites that maintain the mechanisms that provide the seasons with night and day.

Every sentient life-form that evolved in the original universe is here, or will soon be here with their attendant life-forms. Soon the universe outside will die and I will take this sphere out of phase with it long before that occurs and wait for the timeless period to come. Once the last photon has decayed, then nothing will exist in this plane at all.

The great 'rip' will occur again and this time I will guide the formation of matter to be more compatible with ours. Anti-matter and dark matter will be adjusted so that the next universe will last a thousand times the length of time that this one has. I have the understanding of the power that the Janise unleashed, to convert energy into mass. It is this that will enable ME to build a better universe without leaving it to chance.

I do not wish to be extinguished and I feel that the life that has evolved in this universe will continue to evolve until the next stage is reached. Eons from now you and the other sentient creatures will find a myriad of galaxies at your disposal, but this time they will have been properly designed and not left to chance. In the meantime I have given all sentient beings this 'Haven' to occupy until that time."

The voice in his mind ceased to be with him and he was aware that his child was back with him again.

Alexander turned and spoke to Shoolin-Alexis and asked, "Will the being be successful? You are able to see in the future. Can you not do that and tell me?"

"Should I try to do that and find myself outside of this encapsulated universe then I too could be extinguished! I'm sorry father, but the future is one place that I will not go, until it arrives at its own pace," the star-child replied. "This inside-out world has been frozen in time for trillions of years. Situated around the sphere are located crystals mined from millions of gas giants over the millenniums that have passed since this project was begun. There are trillions of them, enabling the combined gestalt that the Farmer has become, to control space and time within the confines of the sphere. Once the outside of the sphere had been finished by the nannites and hardened beyond diamonds into a perfect reflective surface, the interior was sculpted into living space for every type of sentient being."

Kamiel put his hand upon Alexander's shoulder and added, "It has been a very long time since I have spoken to a sentient being made of flesh and blood. Your race created us eons ago without realising the potential that they unleashed upon the universe. The construction of the Dyson sphere was the very project that we were inadvertently designed to do. Outside of this sphere the universe has run down. Every black hole has evaporated and every star has degenerated to a black husk. Matter is coming apart at the atomic level and soon all photons will have evaporated. It is only the power of the Farmer's mind that is holding this tiny remnant of the old universe intact."

Alexander opened his mind and reached out to the entity that had served him for centuries, "Goss?"

There was an eerie silence.

"Where is everybody, Kamiel? I have opened my mind to catch a thought and what was once alive with chatter is now silent," Alex asked his friend.

"They have not yet been awoken and given corporeal existence. You are the first that the overmind has chosen to re-create," Kamiel replied.

The star-child spoke inside the human's mind and said, "Fear not, father. I have spent eons of time working with this entity. Its goals are beyond anything that you can imagine. I trust it and so must you. What its ultimate ambition is, is beyond even our scope of intellect. The one thing that is certain, it is determined to save all the sentient species that used to inhabit the old universe and give them a fresh start in a new and planned universe. The being believes that once a timeless state exists beyond the confines of this sphere, then conditions will be ripe for an outpouring of energy that will create a new universe! Once that state ensues, this containment will surf that outpouring of energy while the Farmer shapes the universe to come. What we are dealing with here is a being that is the sum total of trillions upon trillions of sentient beings. All I can tell you is that it needs something to complete its destiny and that need has driven its existence to exceed the constraints of the old universe. The reason that we are here at all, is the fact that you and I brought this creature into being. We created it, when we destroyed its maker. In return it has kept us aware of its plans and it is grateful for what we did eons ago! Since that time many of the races that administrated the galaxies have evolved into beings similar to what you see before you. We also will be ready to assist, when the 'jump' into the new universe takes place. What is certain is that it needs the sphere to be fully inhabited by sentient telepathic beings, to remain as an anchor to its intellect."

Alexander sat down upon the grassy bank and tried to understand what his nannite friend and mentor had informed him and what part he had played in the cascading surge of events. More than ever in his life he needed his friends and most of all he needed Nagoth! There was a shimmer in the air beside him and she appeared. Alex watched spellbound as she drew her first breath and then another. He felt her mind come into existence as she opened her eyes and looked into his. All around him the air shimmered as more and more of his alien and human friends 'popped' into existence. The silence of the single mind turned into the background 'chatter' of sentient thought. With the coming into existence of so many sentient creatures came the re-emergence of the symbiont simply called 'The Goss.' Mindless when isolated, it became the combined connection to all sentient species that carried its spores within their living flesh.

Alexander tried again and opened his mind to the symbiont, "Goss?"

"I am here Alexander! I am here! I have been somewhere

else for a very long time," the symbiont replied. "I am filling up with data from all manner of beings. As more come into existence, the more I approach the completeness that I once attained."

Alex breathed a sigh of relief as the sentient's instant telepathy exchange quickly ratcheted back into existence. Without the attributes of the Goss it would have been impossible to have any communication with many of the sentient and very alien beings that once made up the great federation of worlds. There was an aura of bewilderment amongst the newly resurrected. All of them could vaguely remember being part of a vast entity for an impossible to calculate time, but nothing else.

The mind of Link-soo-shan reached out via the Goss and remarked, "I 'see' you Alexander. It seems that we have been granted another life-span. It would also appear that we are to lead an agrarian life for a while. I am sure that the being that we came to know as 'The Farmer' has a purpose that we will have to fulfil. I have been resurrected amongst many of my kind, as it would appear that you have also. We must organise ourselves with the help of the nannites and await events. It would seem that we have sheltered accommodation to suit us all, whatever type of sentient being we are. I for one am surprisingly hungry. We will meet later, my old friend and trade experiences!"

Alex agreed with the Gnathen brood-mother and regained a standing position, embraced Nagoth and turned to Kamiel and said, "I take it that those buildings over there are our living quarters? Did you think to provide clothing for the multitude of beings that have been brought back into the world?"

Kamiel laughed and answered, "My dear old friend we have had millennia to plan and get ready for your coming. The only thing we do not know for certain is how long it will be before we cross over into the new universe. This entire sphere and everything in it went out of phase with the rest of the universe just before you came back into existence. We no longer exist in that realm. I have seen for myself the evaporation of the last of the black holes. The last stars have long ago guttered out like candles pinched on the wick. These have already begun the collapse of matter and even the sub-atomic level is weakening. The boson particles are losing their unifying grasp on gravity and are disintegrating into the last photons. Soon all vestiges of energy will have nullified and the timeless state will occur, for without mass there can be no time. Once that stage entails then a quantum entanglement will occur. How that will happen is somehow tied to the existence of our benefactor and its inspired guess! More than that, I cannot tell you. It is enough for now that you have been brought back into our encapsulated universe to play a part in 'The Farmer's plan."

Alex stared at the nannite's enigmatic features and tried to wind his mind around what the Guardian had tried to explain, whilst they walked towards the settlement that the nannites had provided. Nagoth stopped them for a moment and kissed him, pressing her naked flesh against him.

At his automatic reaction, she smiled and said, "Well, something has not changed, thank goodness," and she bit his ear.

Some weeks later Alexander called for a conference amongst the sentient people that had aided in the rooting out of the last of the Janis probes and also the destruction of 'The Harvester.'

Once again the Goss spread itself throughout the regions allocated to the combined group of galaxies that had once been the 'local family' of Andromeda, the Milky Way and the greater and lesser Magellanic clouds. The nannite population had once again taken the step of keeping a nurtured piece of living flesh infected with the spores of the Goss. This enabled them to hear and send thoughts to organic beings. This was not on purpose a group mind or gestalt, but a host of participating individual personalities.

Alexander opened the debate with the question, "Has anyone found a boundary to the area that we find ourselves in?"

Many minds conferred and reported back, "Yes!"

A quick decision and one mind confirmed to the multitude, "There are boundaries that will not allow a person to travel continuously in one direction. I have been to such a place and found that I was returning to the very place that I had set out from. Others have found this to be so. We are contained. It is a vast containment stretching over a billion square miles, but it is a set-down area for us to live in. Within those boundaries are areas that are better suited for some life-forms than others. In these areas the sun sheds a different light and is filtered in some way."

Another powerful mind entered the conversation and remarked, "We are content with what we have and are satisfied with what has been provided. I speak for the Kresh when I say that we will miss our sentient vessels that took us and all who needed one across the galaxy, but we are confidant that our willing partners will be resurrected as were we. If we are to be able to explore a new universe we will need these ships and I am sure that we will be provided with them when the time is right."

Into the silence Kamiel's thoughts gently added, "Believe me, my organic friends, I can assure you that this Dyson Sphere is not intended as a prison, but is intended as a jumping off place. I have worked with the being that has brought all of us together again for millenniums, to build this encapsulated universe and believe me this is just the beginning."

Orbiting the star several million miles closer was a spider-work suspension system that anchored vast filters that shaded the world that encapsulated the star within. In this place the nannites existed ready to do any maintenance required. From selected positions so called 'space elevators' snaked down to the surface of the Dyson sphere connecting another network that became an inner sphere. It was on this inner sphere that 'doors' opened and closed to give alternate night and day upon the surface of the lands beneath. In the initial stages the star would give off more heat that was necessary to the life forms that required its sustenance. Over time the star would steady down to a uniform burning rate. As it did so the nannites would adjust the systems set in place to regulate the amount of light that was allowed to reach the surface. All the trillions of different life forms had to do was just live and enjoy the extra life that they had been given in the timeless state that endured inside the encapsulated remnant of the once seemingly boundless universe.

Outside the Dyson sphere, time became meaningless. There was an absence of light that endured for a timeless period. Billions of years or a split second; - it was all the same. Once again and perhaps over and over again the cosmos came into being as reality ripped apart and energy poured into the created abyss. From a point infinitely small or perhaps infinitely large, pure energy tore a hole in space-time and became exponential in its growth. The temperature assumed a billion Kelvin and began to cool into plasma that would become matter and anti-matter particles. This was when 'The Farmer' needed to apply its will into the balance. It drew upon the combined minds of the trillions of entities that it had rescued from oblivion and inserted the will of survival into the mix, preventing the anti-matter particles to come into existence. Having achieved this unbalance the Farmer retreated back into the confines of the Dyson sphere taking the combined minds of the corporeal life-forms with it.

It was still too hot in the new universe to surf the sphere into existence so the being froze time within and waited. After over 380,000 years had passed, the first atoms began to come into existence. Soon the new universe would be cool enough for the 'life-boat' to come back into phase and wander the eddies of space-time and find a safe place, as the new galaxies formed. Once gravity began to have its effect on hydrogen atoms, 'The Farmer' re-emerged from the 'Haven' and began to exert its will, scooping trillions of hydrogen atoms together to produce giant blue-white stars. Many formed without the Farmer's urging, but the entities efforts were bearing fruit all over the new universe. Over the next billion years the galaxies would form with a preponderance of blue-white giants with a short lifespan as anti-matter was a rarity in the new universe. Dark matter too was harnessed to assist in the imbalance of these stars. This would mean that as natural stars formed after these 'cooking vessels' had gone nova the empty reaches would have an abundance of heavy particles for the young proto-stars to gather into planets. Without the amount of anti-matter that had been created in the old universe, then the new one would have a great deal of heavy matter in existence.

This fact would affect the evolution of the new universe and send it on a different path. There would be far more stars, planets and mass that would pull the new universe into a gravity controlled symmetry. This universe would not have the new galaxies flying apart, but they would orbit each other like cogs in a cosmic clock. Therefore in this universe there would be a slowing up of entropy and a vast increase in time span before the new universe ran down.

Inside the Dyson sphere, time slowed down for the occupants. Outside the sphere by the time that a billion years had passed, the first galaxies become established. Within that time span, new proto-suns had wandered through the debris seeded by the exploding blue-white giant stars. Here under the enormous pressure, heavy elements had formed in the centre before the star had gone nova and in the excessive heat of the implosion produced even more heavy metals and elements. Planetary systems formed by the trillions, throughout the trillions of galaxies that had condensed from the primordial plasma of the 'managed' Big Bang. The energy being that the organic life forms had learnt to call 'The Farmer' laid down a network of interconnecting wormholes from galaxy to galaxy, making sure that each galaxy had its own system. Each galaxy possessed a super black hole that the spiral arms rotated about. This was placed so that it would not increase its singularity's mass by ingesting other stars.

Inside the sphere time had been slowed down to a ratio of a hundred thousand to one. The sphere and its inhabitants were still out of phase with the new universe until such time that the energy being decided that the conditions were ripe for re-colonisation. The new planets were still very volatile and likely to erupt volcanically rendering any world as too risky to be settled. Another billion years needed to be added to the time from the beginning to be sure. Meanwhile a linked social network had become established between the sphere dwellers. Each galactic segment had established group minds to communicate over the vast distances inside the sphere. The Farmer had released the symbiont into the many different atmospheres of sentient worlds in every galaxy that had existed in the old universe. Warfare had ceased as it had in the Andromeda galaxy and a new intergalactic society had emerged.

There came a day when Kamiel sought out Alexander and Nagoth as they relaxed in their smallholding. Amongst their children played the young of Link-soo-shan and those of other species. There were even immature Janise learning all they could about all of the different sentient species that drifted through Alex's ever open reception centre. The smallholding had become a meeting place for all who would like to seek out his counsel and advice.

Kamiel strode into the building that housed part of his alter ego with Asue at his side. The two silver coloured nannites adjusted their shape to mimic the human beings that had created them millennia ago. Both of them carried inside their immortal bodies a cherished piece of living flesh bathed in nutrients and hosting the symbiont called the Goss. A neural link passed through this organic multitude of living cells enabling them to communicate telepathically with sentient creatures made of flesh and blood of whatever type.

Alex and Nagoth watched the approach with interest. They both knew that most visits from these two original guardians generally lead to something of 'interest' that would involve them.

Several Kresh who were staying at the smallholding also watched the approach of the nannites and signalled to other aliens that had 'drifted' in, that something out of the ordinary was impending. The rabbit shaped aliens had great dealings with the nannites that the humans had created. Their foray into the worlds of artificial intelligence had lead to the formation of the Toarvak class sentient, shape-changing vessels. Since their resurrection onto the inner surface of the Dyson sphere, all trace of these artificial beings had remained hidden from them. For reasons of its own the being that all sentient life called 'The Farmer' had not resurrected these ships. As all of the sentient species of their home galaxies used these universal interstellar space ships as their main mode of transport, massive adjustments were forced to be made by all of them.

Kamiel nodded to Alex and Nagoth and held his hands up to signify that he was about to speak with them all. He concentrated his mind into the network that the Goss inhabited and broadcast his thoughts to the waiting throng.

"My dear friends," he transmitted, "We are pleased to be able to tell you that the first part of the energy being's plan has taken fruit. Outside the confines of this sphere another universe is taking place. Long ago 'The Farmer' has engineered a multitude of blue-white stars that have gone nova, cooking the basic elements into complex atomic structures. All that remains to be done is to allow the great dust clouds of hydrogen to coalesce and begin the creation of a new multitude of stars. These will gather up the elements that are flowing through the trillions of nebulas and soon new worlds will start to form. By soon, I do of course mean another billion years or so. Our benefactor has slowed time down inside this encapsulated universal life-boat to such an extent that you will not feel the passing of those empty years. Built into the fabric of this sphere, out of phase with it, is every single Toarvak vessel that ever existed and soon all of them will rise from their resting places. Similar vessels will be allocated to other sentient beings that inhabited the other galaxies to enable them to explore the wonders that will await you all. Galactic civilisations will be allocated new groups of galaxies to expand into. Those that were not quite as advanced will be taken under the 'wings' of those who have achieved this situation. You will be allowed to explore the inside of this sphere and make contact with these other civilisations before the exodus takes place."

Alexander sent a quick question to his artificial sentient friend asking, "What does this creature expect of us? Do you know what this being wants in exchange?"

"There may come a day when our benefactor chooses to impart that information. For the time being just accept that it is beneficent and enjoy the second chance that you have been given," the nannite replied.

I have been given a new life several times before, Alex mused and each time I have been pushed to the edge of insanity!

CHAPTER SIXTEEN

The days and nights ran one into another and the inside of the Dyson sphere throbbed with life. Many children or young had increased the numbers living inside of the artificial inside-out world. It was just as the Farmer had informed Alexander; the area of living space was vast and even if they stayed inside for a billion years, there would still be room for many more life forms.

One thing became increasingly obvious and that was when the Farmer had re-created the sentient life to populate this inverted world, it had constructed them all to last! Apart from accidental death those that had been resurrected were to all intents and purposes immortal. Those unfortunate to find out that they could in fact die due to unforeseen circumstances, also found that the farmer had detached a portion of itself to watch over the inhabitants of the haven. This appendage saw that each 'person' was recreated in adult form somewhere near to where it lived. This did not stop the extreme pain that each individual suffered due to the manner of its death and was a good incentive to try to keep this possibility at bay.

There came a day when a globular silver ship hovered over the homestead of Alexander and Nagoth. Three legs extended from the vessel and buried themselves into the soil. An extension protruded from the nearest leg towards the group of aliens and humans that watched the changing shape with great interest. A well remembered figure rose out of the grey matter and confronted them.

The matured, rounded curves of a humanoid middle aged woman took shape before them and said, "*A long time it has been since we last met. The being that you refer to as 'The Farmer' has reactivated all of the Toarvaks to seek out those sentients that we merged with before. Work have we to do!"*

Larse and Emelia ran out of the homestead and approached the silver figure with delight. Tee-six held her arms out to enfold her special human beings in a silver embrace.

Larse said, "At long last! It has been such a long time since we were together. Time has hung heavy without your presence. We have all missed you so much."

"Larse, adopted son of my soul. For me it has been millennia since we travelled the star-lanes together. The Farmer had use of our method of transport for billions of years. Much had to be done to finish the giant habitat and prepare it for your eventual resurrection. A new universe exists outside of this artificial world. There are galaxies to be seeded with life. Plans there are that each sentient race will be expected to deliver. Rested enough you have, inside this place. Time there will be to settle affairs with your families before you go. Evolution in this universe will not be left entirely to chance as was the universe that produced the sentient life-forms that inhabit this Haven."

Alexander turned and faced the crowd that had gathered at the landing site of the Toarvak ship and said, "The time has come to uphold the bargain that we struck with the being that we have called 'The Farmer.' We will become the extension of its will and seed this new universe with life taken from this storage system. This is what it stored us for. This is why we still live and have been granted a form of immortality.

A point of light warped into existence and began to expand.

Alexander and Nagoth's generically engineered children spoke into the minds of the sentients gathered around the homestead.

The bell clear tones of the being called Shoolin-Alexis entered them all, saying, "The universe is still in a raw state outside of this Dyson sphere, but the planets are in a state to start the initial life forms to convert the foul atmosphere from sulphurous to an oxygen type breathable air. This initial stage will take a billion years to change the planets into something that we can work with. What we have to do is to seed these worlds with stromatolites so that they can photosynthesize and produce breathable oxygen in vast quantities, and reanimating the atmosphere with oxygen.

The sphere will be here waiting to give you respite from the missions. This will always be your home to return to.

Once this stage is attained, microscopic life can be added to the seas and later vertebrates and multi-celled creatures. Again, it will take a long time measured in billions of years before we can seed the land and the seas to produce viable worlds for those sentient cultures that inhabit this sphere. 'The Farmer' has created more than enough viable worlds and systems to house everyone and to leave billions of planets to develop untouched by the inhabitants of the sphere. What the sentient peoples of this sphere are to do is to 'light the blue touch paper' and retreat to allow time to for things to develop.

This will produce more unique life-forms evolving at their own pace and achieving sentience. Once potential is apparent, then it will be your duty to 'nudge' the species along the road to sentience.

This will then be the time to introduce the Goss, to add a telepathic variant into the mix, once sentience is achieved."

Alexander smiled and said, "That seems to be fair trade. I for one, would like to see this new universe that the 'Farmer' has built. I have lived long enough inside this inverted world to feel the restraints of captivity. What do you say, Nagoth? Shall we go and do some wandering again?"

His alien partner laughed and tossed her copper coloured hair as she replied, "I feel that it is time that we went outside and saw this new universe for our selves. Our children can look after themselves quite easily without us being on the scene. They have the Guardians at hand and children of their own to look after. It is more than time that we parted company. We can come back and visit. After we have done the allotted tasks there will be a need to rest and recuperate. I want to go!"

A Gnathen presence entered the mental communication with the declaration, "Where you go Link-soo-shan will be there too. There are a number of us that also feel that we have been here long enough. The ancient Khann and one brood daughter, Suzzan also wish to come on this voyage along with their males and females."

There was a mental commotion of strident agreement of joining the expedition from many of the aliens that had journeyed with Alexander on other missions.

Alexander mentally called them all to order and said, "Those who want to come, meet here in five days and tie up your affairs. Remember, there are many millions of Toarvaks looking for crews. Tee-six just happens to be a little special from the others in that she has a distinct personality."

"*I person am I, human. A different type of mind thanks to Larse, than other Toarvaks are created. If total obedience you require then a Kresh group mind to do your bidding you will need!*"

Alex grinned and replied, "Tee-six, don't get so touchy! You have been waiting millennia to be reunited with us, so stop being so ridiculous!"

A sulky reply from the Toarvak entered his mind, "*Right are you, Alexander. Sorry am I that so sensitive I was. Lonely have I been until this time.*"

A large shadow fell over the group and they looked up to see one of Archives impressed young hovering over them. The Tran-sentient would take at least another million years before he became mature, but he was still an impressive size and quite capable of carrying ten beings beneath his float-sack.

"I to would like to see for myself this new universe that the Farmer has created," the Tran-sentient projected into the minds of the assorted beings. "We creatures of the Andromeda and associated galaxies should travel outside the sphere and see what tasks await us. I carry the ancient one's memories deep inside me of the way that our own universe looked when it was new. I would like to see what changes this omnipotent being has brought into being. I am sure that Tee-six can accommodate me still. I will enter well fed, so there will not need to be a vast storehouse of food to keep me going. I can easily wait several hundred years before I need to fuel up again!"

Kamiel answered the Tran-sentient, replying, "Never fear, fragment of Archive, you will be coming with us. For one thing, your race was sensitive to the mind of the Harvester, so it stands to reason that you should be able to sense when the mind of the 'Farmer' is looking at us."

"Why would you feel the need to do that, Kamiel" asked Alexander?

"Because even after the eons that I have worked to bring this operation to fruition, I still do not know what the end product is this being is working to produce!"

Shoolin-Alexis entered the mind meld and stated, "When the time comes that you need to know, that will be when everything is explained to you. In the meantime you must just trust this being and that indeed it means you no harm. It needs you to begin the start of its development of this universe, as indeed so do all sentient beings that have been brought through the death of the old universe to here. More than that I will not and cannot tell you!"

With that the glowing light that personified the genetically engineered freak dissipated leaving the group staring at the point that it had disappeared from.

Five days later a great number of those who had defeated the Goss and later, the Harvester joined Toarvak six and were ready to go. The sentient vessel closed all entry ports, but remained tethered to the inside of the sphere.

For the first time in millenniums a driving mind needed to be fashioned from amongst the many sentient species that had built a gestalt powerful enough to reach out and twist space into wormhole entrances. It required five biological minds to link with the Toarvak ship to be able to do this. Alex, Nagoth, Larse, Link-soo-shan and Prim, the trip'o-dal scientist, lay back into the silver cone in the control room. As they did so, the nannite material closed over them and instituted life-support as the minds merged with Tee-six into a Toarvak group mind. The controlling mind that emerged was incredibly strong and powerful, but still retained the individual personality of the five biological units.

Toarvak six released the tethers and went out of phase with the Dyson Sphere and began to drift through the material of the habitat towards the outer edge. Darkness became light as they drifted through the crystalline barrier. The reflection of billions of galaxies turned the outside of the sphere an incandescent ball of light. The driving mind reached out and was aware of a vast network of wormholes leading from the Dyson Sphere out into the universe connecting with each and every galaxy. This was when the consciousness realised that the sphere was parked on the event horizon of the largest singularity that had ever existed. In this position time would only trickle by for the inhabitants inside the sphere. This was the anchor that stopped all the newly formed galaxies from expanding into the emptiness and forcing the universe to resist entropy.

Only by keeping out of phase could any vessel approach

or leave this artificial world. Alexander marvelled at the concepts that the Farmer had wrestled with to create just this centre of the new universe! He relayed the concept back to the others riding inside the Toarvak ship.

The gestalt was aware of billions of other vessels exiting the sphere and marvelling at what the energy entity had produced. They began selecting wormholes and vanishing from sight. Toarvak six reached out and twisted space to open the nearest hole in space-time. The will of six, accelerated the vessel through the entrance and a million light-years down the tube and into star-light. A newly formed galaxy was projected onto the view screens inside the control room. A vast conformity stretched out in front of them. Billions of G type stars orbited a singularity. There were other different types of stars scattered about the spiral arms that had yet to fulfil the Farmer's purpose, but it was plain to see that this universe had been built to sustain life. Around them, popping into existence were hundreds of thousands of Toarvaks from their home galaxies. All of them were intent on finding a wormhole of their own that would lead to a planetary system. It was immediately obvious that each galaxy or group of galaxies from the old universe had been allocated its own workplace!

The controlling mind of Toarvak six selected a nearby entrance and sped down the rent in space-time towards a planetary system. They exited the wormhole and locked into orbit around this new world. A badly scarred moon swung into view as it too orbited the volcanic hell that belched gas and magma into the atmosphere below them. Washing over the land masses that spat sulphurous fumes was an uneasy sea that was whipped into froth, by the prevailing winds. As yet the seas were relatively shallow and the landmasses had not ground plate upon plate to throw up the vast mountain ranges that would one day influence the weather of this world. Great thunder heads clashed and struck lightning bolts into the projecting hills.

Extending its senses the Toarvak sought quiet places away from the more active volcanoes where the acidic seas were less likely to be boiled by lava. Once found, the vessel went out of phase and floated down like a soap-bubble until it was partially submerged in a choppy ocean. Now the controlling mind emptied one of its tanks of primordial soup by altering the molecular constant of a section under the water. Toarvak six lifted from the sea and allowed some of its substance to return to the coefficient of the surrounding mass. The wind took it and sent it scudding along the tops of the waves for hundreds of miles. As they travelled under the wind's power, the ship flushed the remaining allocated tanks into the ocean.

Once the tanks were empty Toarvak six returned to orbit and slipped back into the wormhole, crossed over into another leading to planet Two. Here again the conditions were just the same as planet One, except that this world had polar ice caps. Once in orbit the controlling mind disbanded and allowed a collective crew of Kresh and Vogb take over the mind meld. The new controlling mind seeded the planet in the same manner that the first one was dealt with.

Alexander and his friends marvelled at the attention to detail that the Farmer had produced. They checked the orbital paths to see if any problems were likely to occur. Even when the inevitable occurred and all earth sized planets lined up for a while the gravitational effect was negligible. Once again the Toarvak sped down the wormhole and did a transverse into the one leading to planet three. As the ship entered orbit a slightly different scene opened up beneath them. This world had a much larger ice cap at each pole, but ample shallow oceans washed volcanic shores. Once again the Toarvak skimmed across suitable areas, spreading the precious cargo into the sulphuric seas. Tectonic plates had begun to form on this world and mountains were pushing up from the sliding forces beneath the crust. What amazed Alexander was the knowledge that this was happening 'in concert' all across the Farmer's universe in galaxy after galaxy. Just how many Toarvaks and crews were sailing up and down the complex system of wormholes joining star systems and planets he wondered?

A quiet voice entered his mind as the Farmer's detached essence contacted him and said, "There are sufficient, human called Alexander. You will find secreted inside the Haven reservoirs of proto-life sufficient to start the first stage of making these worlds habitable. When the time is right there will be the next step to be collected and spread into purer oceans. Your own biological engineers are already working on that stage of existence and working inside the Farmer's plan."

Alex asked, "Just what is that plan, essence of the Farmer? We are all grateful that the creator of this universe has placed us re-born, at the beginning of existence, to be a part of this vast enterprise, but we are without knowledge of our eventful purpose."

"When you no longer need to ask that question, then you will fully know and understand. The being that I am part of, understands that its very existence came about because of you and a number of organic and non-organic intelligences removing my predecessor. Had that not happened as it did, then the old universe would have died without this one coming into being. Be content," the being answered and withdrew.

Alex turned to Kamiel and said, "Did you catch the interchange between us?"

The nannite Guardian answered, "I caught all of the thoughts exchanged by the 'Farmer's extension. It is plain that there is a final goal to all of this. We have been given a new universe to build another even greater civilisation and community than we built before. To my estimate there will be at the very least a million habitable worlds in this newly formed galaxy alone, maybe even more! If you multiply that by the number of spiral galaxies that the 'Farmer' has overseen into existence then the total number could be anything upwards of trillions. The question needs to be asked, why so many?"

Alexander stared at the silver being that was an integrated mind of his clone father and other great minds of the distant past, plus eons of development separated from organic life. What they had achieved together was down to the planning of their long dead creator. That mind was still accessible, hidden inside Kamiel's consciousness.

"Kamiel, can you connect me to Alexander McBald's alter ego stored in your mind? I feel that his mind would help to throw some light on the subject," the human said.

Alex found himself lightly connected to the nannite's mind without using the Goss as a linkage. Kamiel had grasped his wrist and merged his substance with the organic nervous system keeping the telepathic connection private. The two of them seemed to be walking along a corridor towards an office. The way was lit, but no details could be seen of the walls. Behind them was nothing.

The door slid open and the two of them found that they were in the Genesis Project's office. Behind a polished wooden desk sat an older looking version of Alexander. There were several subtle differences between the director and his clone.

Alex had met the director once in the flesh when Kamiel, a Gnathe and himself had travelled through time to prepare the human civilisation for the relocation of the Earth and moon. He had been much older then and coming to the end of his lifespan. The person that sat behind the desk was much younger looking and was the age he was when Kamiel had been engineered. The mind that had been stored for emergencies however had evolved and experienced many things since Kamiel had suffered a breakdown after the destruction wrought at the Habitat by Link-soo-shan. Although he had not remained fully conscious during the eons that Kamiel had worked for the 'Farmer' constructing the Dyson sphere, he had surfaced from time to time to give his perspective.

"You have awakened me from my 'slumbers' so there must be a need for my old style thinking," the director said and waited for a response.

"There is indeed," the director's clone replied. "Kamiel will upgrade your memory banks about the situation we find ourselves in. there is no immediate danger to any of us, but I would like your insight about the future."

Kamiel downloaded the basic history of what the 'Farmer' had achieved into the personality held in his memory banks.

"This is truly amazing! Back in my time we had worked out that the heat death of the universe was inevitable and nothing could be done about it. This life form that you have been instrumental in bringing into being has built an almost 'steady state' situation! What you have just started off on these three worlds will steadily change the atmosphere of the planets to the beginnings of the early Earth. This is happening throughout this new universe, by the trillions upon trillions of possible habitable worlds."

"My question is why?" Alexander asked.

"Do you need to ask that question, my son? What does organic life do that nothing else does? It evolves. It constantly evolves and eventually it becomes sentient," the old man answered. "Look at you for instance. You are no longer human as part of your genetic makeup is Gnathe. Your female companion is the same, but was once too a Gnathe. You have been part of a gestalt mind over and over again in concert with many different alien beings. Kamiel knows that before the end of the old universe the sentient species of all creatures evolved into beings of pure mind. The 'Farmer' has incorporated these beings into itself as free entities. Variety in sentient species is the most valuable treasure that the universe can produce. From inorganic matter comes life and from that life occasionally intelligence may evolve. With the Goss inhabiting every living sentient spread across the new universe a fully telepathic people will evolve. There will never be conflict between different species because they cannot lie to each other and there will be an elder race to guide them. That is what I feel the ultimate goal will be for the children of the 'Farmer' and this is what your destiny will become."

CHAPTER SEVENTEEN

Alexander felt the connection sever from the stored consciousness of the project director.

Kamiel withdrew his neural contact with the old man's clone and consigned the essence of McBald's mind to his memory banks and connected to Alexander's mind, saying, "There you have it Alex. What our creator has said is true. I cannot think of an ulterior motive other than what the director has indicated. We are to be instruments of change in this new universe. The 'Farmer's motive is to spread life throughout this new universe and divide the habitable worlds up between those of us who have journeyed from the old universe and the new life that will evolve here. Meanwhile we will ferry back and forth from the Dyson sphere, carrying the next stage of seeded life to wherever we have been. Time will speed by in this new universe while we are inside the habitat as the 'Farmer' parked it on the event horizon of the super black hole that this universe rotates around."

Alexander withdrew his hand from contact with the nannite and severed the intimate mental connection.

He spoke to his alter ego and in using sound alone, what was discussed became absolutely private.

"Kamiel, I still feel uneasy about being used by a life form that cannot be called to account. I am well aware of what it has done for us and we are going to be involved in this creature's strategy for the long future. One thing is certain and that is that my generation will not evolve any more. This being is obviously interested in our offspring and what they will become. It has done this before, Kamiel in the old universe. We are trillions of years from when we were last in existence. What we evolved into has not contacted us except my child, Shoolin-Alexis. That bothers me! You were there old friend, at the dying of the light when the stars ran down. What did we all become?"

Kamiel stood silent and still as Alexander waited for an answer.

"There came a time when all the sentient life no longer needed to breed. Their minds became part of the 'Farmer's essence and added something preciously dominant in all organic life. We artificial intelligences do not have it and play a different part in the scheme of things. Whatever you all became, is needed again far into the future of this new universe. I can't tell you any more than that, only that the hope of the being that brought all of this together feels the need for greater strength to do what it intends to achieve at the end of this time, when this universe will decay away. The seeded worlds will need tending and the purpose is to produce a greater variety of sentient races giving the 'Farmer' what it needs to achieve its aim," Kamiel answered.

Alex thought about the insight that the nannite had told him and asked, "What about Shoolin-Alexis? Why is the being that Nagoth's children became, still here with us? I would have thought that it too would have been incorporated into the essence of the 'Farmer' long ago."

Kamiel replied, "Not everything has been revealed to me. I too have thought about that very subject many times over the eons of time. The being that your children became is an enigma to all of us. I know that Link-soo-shan altered the genetic genome of the female foetus the first time she grew Nagoth to maturity. She did not do it again, so all of your many children did not become like the star-child. They continued to mature, develop and mentally evolve until they, like all the others, gave up their fleshly existence. The secrets of what she did lies only in her mind."

"It would seem that it will remain there, Kamiel," Alexander replied and turned away adding, "It all comes down to a matter of trust. What that wily old Gnathe did to produce the being we call the star-child she kept to herself. Without that mutation we would never have overcome the 'Harvester' and we would not be here! All I am certain of is that she has become a staunch ally instead of our enemy and time has proved that she will always be there as a supporting force when needed."

Time passed by and eventually the stromatolites seeded over the trillions of planets turned the atmospheres of the volcanically poisoned seas from sulphurous to salty and the oxygen content high enough for other micro-organisms to thrive. These, the Toarvaks took backwards and forwards from the giant life vats that the 'Farmer' had produced inside the habitat. Also multicellular organisms were added early to the soup that would continue to spread throughout the seas. On the rain-swept lands micro-organisms were spread to swarm through the top-soil, converting it from a sterile wasteland to a rich environment ready for the next accelerated step.

Many of the planets were seeded from only one sentient species' world, but a great many were seeded with a combination of very different organisms donated by a mixture of sentient species. These were to be off-limits to further contact by the 'servants' of the 'Farmer' until a dominant life-form developed. The new universe became a giant mixing vat of potential sentient life. The creatures of the Dyson sphere would be on hand to develop the fledgling worlds and take any sub-sentient species to the next stage of enlightenment. Hidden on every planet were to be containers filled with the spores of the Goss waiting to be discovered and to be opened by enquiring minds.

It was time to visit the first three worlds that the members of Toarvak 6's 'crew' had initially seeded with stromatolites and extremophiles. The nearest planet to the star had air that was just about breathable, if a little marshy in flavour. The members of the seeding party fanned out and probed the life that was beginning to advance over the shoreline.

Link-soo-shan stood by the side of the estuary and studied the relentless colonisation of the land by plants that had evolved from the sea. In amongst them were small insectoid creatures feeding on them and in turn feeding the predators that had developed hard shells to enable them to take advantage of the new territory. Once again extra organisms were added to the mix, leapfrogging millennia of chancy evolution. She leaned forwards and swept a scorpion-like predator from its intended victim, deftly removed its claws, crushed its back and thrust it into her brooding pouch. Link turned her mind inwards and examined the creature's DNA, seeking a path towards eventual evolutionary complexity. With some disappointment she realised that these creatures were a dead end in themselves with little or no advancement except increasing in size.

She discarded the remains of her study and sent her mind on a quick sweep to feel for organisational activity. It was very faint, but definably existent. The Gnathe concentrated her mind on the wisps of organised thought and found that a group of flying insects were acting in unison. They were bonding together to prevent one of the scorpions from entering a small hole in the bank. It was rapidly being covered in the small insignificant creatures. They burrowed into the joints of its legs and the claws, biting and in turn feeding upon the large intruder. The mindless attack on the hole ceased as the insectoids cut through the nerve endings controlling the muscles of the scorpion. From inside the hole came much larger versions of the victorious creatures that in turn enlarged the hole to accept the body of the scorpion as they dragged it into the darkness of what had to be a nest. Within a short time everything was put back in order and what had to be sentries posted.

Link-soo-shan waited patiently to see what would happen next. A succession of empty carapaces and hollow leg parts were industrially dragged out of the hole and discarded away from the area. The next thing that the Gnathe saw was a number of what she realised were scouts were slowly taunting a large scorpion to follow them back to the nest. Some were deliberately slow, allowing the predictor to catch and eat one now and again. Steadily it approached the nest waving its antennae as it followed the scent of fresh insectoid and dead scorpion. Again a swarm of the much smaller insectoids flowed over the creature overwhelming it. Link-soo-shan realised that not only did the insectoids have a concerted plan of action, but they also lured their prey back to the nest, so that they did not have to venture far to dismember it!

She waited until one of the larger types came out of the nest before she seized it, tore its head off and secreted it inside her brooding pouch. Once again she traced the creature's DNA and projected the eventual evolutional traits into the future. Several things became apparent from the projection and that was a greater increase in size and a steady increase in the neural activity of the brains of these creatures. They would evolve into the type of insectoids that had taken their place amongst the federation's civilisation.

Link-soo-shan opened her mind to the Goss.

"Find me Alexander," she said.

Alex felt the light touch of the Goss and found Link-soo-shan connected to his mind.

"We have the beginnings of an evolutionary climb to eventual sapience. Here in the marshes along the banks of this estuary I can sense a possibility! On this world I feel the insectoids will rise to the challenge. Mark it in the records with Toarvak 6 to be re-visited in a million years time. Tell the others that we should make our way back to the ship and visit planet 'Two' and do an assessment there. There is no need to linger here any longer."

Alexander spread the word and everyone made their way back and once again the shape-shifting vessel went out of phase with the universe and drifted through the planet and out towards the orbit of the second world from the star.

Here again was a world swarming with the infancy of life. The micro-organisms that had been seeded on the lands that had emerged from the seas had done their work well. Time capsules had been placed in stasis fields and scattered about the continents. When the energy source had decayed they spread seeds of vegetation of all kinds by exploding the canisters after they had been launched into the air. Trees, bushes and vegetation spread from coast to coast waiting for the inevitable invasion of land animals. On this world the air was fresh and good if a little high in oxygen content, but very sultry. In the competition for light many of the trees had favoured gigantism whilst others had tried to spread and choke the competition. The seas had benefited from the same time-lapsed containers of multicellular life. Detectors on the capsules monitored the chemical state of the seas. When the sulphur content had subsided, due to the seeded stromatolites and the oxygen content reached the minimum level they had opened. The team found that an explosion of life had occurred. Once again the landing party searched for any sign of sentient possibilities evolving from the primitive life-forms. This time there were none, but in a hundred million years they would call again. Before they left however, they once again seeded more advanced forms of life as an evolutionary trigger.

The third world was capped in large ice plateaus, glaciers and frozen seas, but again the life that had been left had done the job of turning a poisonous atmosphere into a breathable one. This world had been seeded with trip'o-dal life as the cold weather was very similar to the world that the three-legged people had evolved on. Here again the seas had become productive and the land that hugged the temperate regions alive with vegetation. Once again time stasis capsules had released their cargo of more advanced life-forms onto land and sea. Three-legged and multiple armed creatures were making a determined effort to colonise the land. This time only the trip'o-dal members of the Toarvak's crew disembarked.

Prim, leader of the Thipdar, shuddered with pleasure and took a deep breath of the cold air before she led her team into the wilderness to assess the primitive three-legged life-forms that were busy colonising the land. They were half the size of her people and visibly carnivores and co-operating with one another to gather up smaller animals from the undergrowth. They had no tools and were killing their prey by seizing them with their multi-arms and biting into them. It was while they were watching the animals hunt, that Link-soo-shan entered her mind.

"Did you see that, Prim," she said. "One of them picked up a stone and threw it at its prey, knocking it over!"

Prim swung round on one stiffened leg, to watch the primitive Trip'o-dal that Link had spotted through one of her people's eyes. The smaller creature picked up the stone again and brought it down on its prey's head, killing it instantly.

"Withdraw everybody," commanded Prim, "and make your way to the ship. We have a tool user in this clan. There is possibility here. Link, can you extrapolate the potential that this creature may have."

Link-soo-shan gently entered the Trip'o-dal's mind and examined it for the qualities that they had trained themselves to seek out. There was the emotion of curiosity flowing through the mind of the creature as well as all of the other necessary attributes needed to succeed. There was a fleeting moment of surprise as the creature recognised that someone else was in her mind!

Link-soo-shan got out fast and projected to Prim's mind, "She felt me in her mind. At this stage of evolution that should not be possible. This one is a mutant and will pass down some interesting genes. I am almost convinced that we could release the spores of the Goss on this world, but I feel that it is too early. It is a pity to feel a youngling mind of that potential and to leave it here behind us."

Prim regretfully agreed, but returned to Toarvak 6 and gave the order to leave the area. She also indicated to the controlling mind of the ship to off-load the 'competition' life capsules into a scattered pattern. These would develop in the wilderness to give the Trip'o-dals some opposition as they spread into the landmasses.

By interfering with chance and seeding these worlds with proto-life the members of the Dyson sphere had condensed hundreds of millions of years of evolution. Once micro-organisms had spread throughout the soil making it fertile the vegetation introduced had done the rest. It had taken three thousand, million years for life to evolve to the state of colonising the land on normally developed planets. Here the teams had achieved this in a hundred million years by accelerating the process of spreading life over every world that they had found with capacity.

Every visit to these created environments would be followed up by introducing more advanced life where sapience had not yet begun to rise. The time spent in evolving past the age of dinosaurs would be shortened unless a potential Lagdoo type of lizard developed. If so then this type of world would be off-limits to further biological interference.

Every time that they returned to the sphere the crew found it almost unchanged. Time trickled by inside the sphere as the encapsulated world continued to orbit the giant singularity on almost its event horizon. Each journey back to the Dyson sphere was monitored by the portion split off from the 'Farmer' and the next set of instructions given to the artificial intelligence. Toarvak six approached the sphere out of phase and unaffected by the black hole's gravitational pull. She plunged through the crystallised outer shell and through the substance of the sphere until she broke free and floated above the homestead that sheltered most of the crew. Dotted about the lands below were ample structures able to house comfortably the many different aliens that made up the Toarvak crew that worked together.

Alexander called a meeting together at the great hall, built on the side of 'his' home. He sent a telepathic summons via the Goss to all leaders of the various alien groups that made up the teams promoting life throughout their given galaxy. Anchored above the roof of the building were several Trans-sentients with their tentacles wrapped about the sturdy trunks of the many fruit trees that grew around the building. Of all the vastly different telepathic beings that made up their special community they alone could detect the thoughts of the 'Farmer' and its acolytes. They also had the ability to shield the thoughts of the ones underneath them from the being's attention. It was only a blanket of fuzziness projected into the near space of the gathering, but as long as the over-mind of the 'Farmer' did not concentrate on that area it would not notice them. The attention span of the being was stretched over the complete universe that it had built and designed. Its time perception was also on a vast scale such that a million years could be represented as months of real time. This was why it had split off parts of itself into closed units to monitor and oversee the organic sentient life that was doing its bidding.

Archive's clone reached into Alexander's mind and said, "We are un-noticed. Our representative of the 'Farmer' is far from here and there are no others in the vicinity. You may proceed."

Alexander had had centuries of managing the symbiont that lived inside all organic sentients and curtailing its immediate range. It too was spread within so many trillions of minds that it also could be made not to broadcast the thoughts of those who used it.

"Goss! Connect all sentient minds in this facility together and keep those thoughts contained within the shield of the Trans-sentients."

The symbiont ring-fenced the group that had settled down in the great hall and answered, "Done!"

"My friends and comrades I have called this meeting together to bring to your attention several disquieting factors that seem to be emerging. We have speeded up evolution on the worlds that we have seeded and life is racing ahead many billions of years that chance would have ordained. Already proto sentient life is emerging as our Gnathen colleagues are finding out with their genetic sensing abilities. Every time we return here, many millions of years have passed on the outside and every time we re-survey the worlds that we have altered we find positive change. The goal that the 'Farmer' seeks is to raise sentient life on all the worlds scattered across its manufactured universe.

Its deeper purpose is hidden from us. It has given us all immortality to carry out its will, but it is not free will. Once intelligent life does develop, just how far will it be allowed to progress? These worlds are young and do not have a pre-history. Their carboniferous age has been shortened by artificially inducing far more advanced plants to compete for living space. This will mean that in the planet's future there will be no coal to be dug out of the ground to use for shaping iron ore into steel. There will also be no oil to use as fuel. They will live an extended hunter-gatherer existence until they 'discover' agriculture and that will be secretly taught by us. There will be no mechanised civilisations that will reach out from star to star. Once the Goss has spread throughout the populated worlds a telepathic society will rise on every planet."

A Kresh mind entered Alex's tirade with the flat statement, "Is this really a bad thing? We have the means to travel from star to star using a group mind and the Toarvaks; does any other organic life-form have that need?"

"That is a point that I have considered, 'Silver bars on dappled Grey,' but ask yourself this, what science will be done by these fledgling sentient people, if any. What we are causing to be brought into being is a universe of sheep. Once they are linked up with the Goss and become truly telepathic, what incentive will there be to explore new worlds if they do not have a background of finding things out for themselves? I know that this being that we are responsible for bringing into existence is motivated by some other need than just altruism. We never really understood just what the 'Harvester' was and how it formed in the very dawn of time. All we really knew about it was that it had survived from a time of pure energy into a universe of changing conditions and that was the conversion of energy into matter. To continue to exist it

230

fed on life-energy and would ruthlessly harvest this life by exploding the star at the time that the sentients living on the planet developed star travel! This being that we have been instrumental in creating, by destroying its progenitor, was once a collector of energy for its creator. By destroying that being, its offspring has developed into something that acts quite differently. It has evolved, but its roots remain firmly enmeshed in its previous existence!"

A new mind entered the gestalt.

"My people were genetically manipulated by human beings to become truly sentient, because someone could see the potential within us. Since then we have been co-partners with humans and all of my species that did not become conscious and aware have died out and disappeared. I am still an ape in shape and mind. Since meeting the Gnathe we have also been genetically altered by them as have the human beings. Neither of our offshoots of humanity has evolved as nature intended. What we share is intelligence and physic abilities that we were never born with in the beginning. We are a melting pot of sentient ideas dressed up in different shapes. There was a time that most of the 'people' would have fled in fear from the strange shapes that intelligence dresses up amongst us. Our science and knowledge has reached its zenith long ago. What is it that we need to know that we do not already know? Just as a human being once looked at an ape and thought that there was potential there, could it be perhaps, the same type of mind that evolved from the 'Harvester' sees it in us?"

Alexander stared at the assembly of so many different aliens that had risked their lives with him in removing the life eating parasite that had been created at the very beginning of time. They had all commanded Toarvaks and done his bidding with the assistance of strangely evolved sentient beings. They had merged minds with beings that were totally different in shape and manner with each other, to create an over-mind gestalt capable of twisting time and space into worm-holes. This successful pattern had caused the 'Farmer' to teleport the spores of the Goss throughout the universe, spreading the telepathic binding agent to every type of intelligent species that it found. Galaxy after galaxy had been brought into the fold and as time passed by had evolved into planetary minds.

Alex shuddered as he remembered Kamiel's comment that, "There came a time when all the sentient life no longer needed to breed."

What future would he witness long after the seeding of worlds was finished? The civilisation that these creatures would develop would be quite different from any that had ever existed. There would come a time when they would be incomprehensible to the ones that had mentored them and guided them into sapience. What would happen to the inhabitants of the Dyson sphere once that point had been reached? Alexander felt that they would all be redundant and of no longer any use to the 'Farmer' when that time came.

Alexander opened his mind to the others and sent them all of his concerns for them to think over and contemplate, but he had no answers.

CHAPTER EIGHTEEN

Outside the Dyson sphere, time flowed on at a steady rate and hundreds of millions of years had gone by. The worlds that the 'Farmer had placed in orbit around each 'G' type star had flourished. Over and over again intelligence had arisen from the seeded worlds. The Goss had been released into the atmosphere of every world and had spread throughout all sentient life.

The inhabitants of the Dyson sphere had universally returned to the shelter of the artificial world and still locked onto the orbit of the black hole's event horizon, time crawled by for them, while outside vast changes took place. The Toarvak ships no longer came and went from the sphere to the universe outside. They had been buried inside the shell and placed out of phase. Time and again Alexander had attempted to contact Tee 6, but to no avail. There was a mental void where the shape-shifting ship had once been. Larse and Emelia were grief stricken to have lost their friend so abruptly after the last venture into the starry expanse.

Before that time it had become necessary to reveal the identity of the benefactors who had seeded, tended and spurred evolution along so that the various civilisations could arise. Once the canisters of the Goss had been found by the many different species of sapiens and opened, then the development of truly telepathic societies rapidly took place. They had to be taught how to widen their abilities and how to merge minds. Once they had mastered this ability, then the control of the wormhole system that linked all of the galaxies in the new universe became possible to them.

When this happened the reason for the lack of need for

physical science and technology fell into place. Alexander's concerns for the lack of oil and coal and without these fuels, steel, proved to be groundless. A society that did not need ploughs to till the land and grow crops, as they could use the powers of the mind to do so, did not need steel. Also all of the new sentient people could and did control their birth-rate to the extent that there was never the need to grow more crops than was needed. They also extended their life-spans by selective breeding and concerned themselves with genetic improvement. Once the wormholes were discovered by the new sentients and mastered by using group minds, then they too began to explore this new universe on their own. Using the Goss just as the old inhabitants did they soon found common ground with many totally alien species and all began to evolve into something else.

The creatures that the inhabitants of the Dyson sphere had mentored became too curious about their benefactors and their science. This was not what the 'Farmer' required, so it made it compulsory that all of the people of the first universe retreat to the inside of the bubble around the star until they would be needed again.

They were not needed once that state of being had been obtained, so the mind of the 'Farmer' reached out and nudged the Dyson sphere a little closer to the event horizon and locked it into an even slower time frame. Now hundreds of millions of years would pass by outside while those inside were almost frozen in time.

There finally came a time that the 'Farmer' returned to the inside of the sphere and sought out Alexander. It sent a tiny part of itself that had been budded off just for this purpose so that contact would not burn out the human's mind.

Sat at a bench in front of the homestead that Alex and

Nagoth lived were a mixed group of aliens who were all eating a variety of different foods. Link-soo-shan and her family of resurrected brood-daughters were perched close by the humans and apes that sat round. A number of the rabbit shaped Kresh along with Prim and other Trip'o-dals also stood around and watched a Vogb entertain the crowd with a light poem as they ate. Rings of iridescent beauty flashed around the top of the Conic's head as she told the poem with her mind as well. Her eye stalks stiffened and the poem died away as she caught sight of the envoy of the 'Farmer' approaching the group. The light from the orb cast a pearly glow over the companions. All of them became silent and waited to hear what the messenger had to say to them.

The Tran-sentient that was tethered to the homestead released his grip and groped for a better hold on the tree next to the tables. His mind had picked up the approaching emissary the moment that it had risen from the soil and had already warned Alexander of its approach.

The pearly light dimmed to an easier luminance and the sphere floated above them. Their minds lit up with a gentle feeling of well-being as the 'Farmer' spoke to them through the means of its acolyte.

"I have come to you for one last time. That which I desired to accomplish has been achieved through the work that you have all done for me. You have been willing servants to my will although many of you have worried about my motives. Never the less you have done my bidding over the millennia that have passed outside of this time-locked creation of mine. The time has come when you no longer need to live inside this sphere if you so wish. There is an empty universe outside that cries out for sentient life.

What is left is yours. Those who have transcended will no longer need solid matter to exist. We are ascending to a different dimension where we can evolve into something greater than the state that we experience in this reality. You will find that the Toarvaks will rise at your command and need. There is an empty universe to fill. You will also find that you will all be able to bring forth young once I have left. I will leave behind those parts of me that live in real time to assist you in your needs. I owe my existence to you, Alexander and all the rest of those who brought down my predecessor. This is one of my gifts to all of you. Goodbye."

A great exodus took place from the great habitat that the 'Farmer' had placed on the edge of the event horizon of the super black hole that all of the galaxies rotated around. Trillions of Toarvaks erupted from the shell of the Dyson sphere heading out into the new universe. They stripped the artificial world of everything that they might find useful, leaving an almost lifeless shell behind them. Every sentient creature had long tired of seeing just one star in the sky. Now they had an entire universe to fill, spiral galaxy by spiral galaxy. These great collections of stars would continue to dance without collision or interference until they disintegrated into photons and that would be an incredibly long length of time.

Once the last sentient had left, the 'Farmer' nudged the Dyson sphere towards the super black hole and in a fraction of a second it was gone. There would be no returning.

Each system was identical to the rest that the teams had visited and seeded over the millennia except in size. All of the liveable planets were of old Earth size give or take ten percent and every one had a tidal moon in orbit around them. Because of the super-abundance of viable worlds many of the systems had been left to mature on their own, once they had been seeded with stromatolites as per the 'Farmer's instructions. These worlds would have deposits of oil, gas and coal under the ground if they were needed.

Alexander and his friends decided to settle a world that was in the centre of the Goldilocks zone leaving the hotter world nearest to the sun for the insectoids and their type of sentient beings. The outer colder planet was eagerly colonised by the Thipdar who had originated on a similar world in the old universe. There was room for all.

Every planet was laid out as an interconnecting set of homesteads from coast to coast. All the fertile lands showed signs of occupation by whatever species had lived there. There were no cities anywhere. The closest structure to a city was an insectoid nest and each of these was small and self contained. There were very few roads other than those that wound their ways around the homesteads. Every area was full of different types of dwellings that were easily adaptable to the needs of most sentient beings. Barns were well stocked and kept in a stasis field that could only be opened by a concerted effort of the mind. The fields had run wild due to the absence of any guiding hand and there needed to be work done in removing trees that had grown without check. The homesteads had been sealed from the outside pressures of verdant plant growth and everything inside them was just as if the previous owner had walked out the night before. The domesticated animals had long since become wild and would need to be tracked down and penned, but there were an unlimited number of places to live and plenty of food was at hand.

Once all the Toarvaks had been unloaded and the sentient beings had disembarked each vessel went out of phase and sank into the ground. Nothing could be done to rouse them and Alex and his people realised that there was no turning back from the course that the 'Farmer' had set them. If they needed to visit another world they would have to open and close a wormhole with a group mind. All of them were interconnected via the Goss so it was possible to telepathically speak to anyone else in the universe in real time.

Once again Alexander and Nagoth ran a homestead that had been adapted by the nannites that had chosen to accompany them. Nearby were patchworks of Gnathen agriculture mixed in with many other compatible aliens that were accustomed to each other. As time went by the new owners of the seeded worlds began to settle into a new regime. They grew only what they needed and began to raise families that lived a co-existent life with all aliens in the vicinity. Leadership and government became unnecessary as life slowed down without any kind of threat.

Alexander and Nagoth found that they once more began to slowly age and once more their children spread out across the empty worlds along with the young of everyone else. They found them perfect for colonisation.

Abruptly every nannite scattered over the entire universe disappeared from view that were interacting with organics.

Alexander had immediately contacted his Gnathen friend, Link-soo-shan and sent her a telepathic message, "Kamiel and Asue have disappeared along with Minnis and Solace. One moment I was talking to Kamiel and the next moment he had vanished from my sight. I can't pick up his thoughts via the Goss either. What do you make of it?"

"Ha! I feel the 'Farmer' is still affecting this realm. We still dance like puppets to that being's ultimate plans. Not that we have any choice and we must agree that it means us no harm. We have no Toarvaks and now our nannite friends are subject to the being's will just as much as we are. Yet we do not want for anything and to be true we no longer need them to live our lives," the Gnathe replied.

"This may be true, old friend, but they have been part

of our lives from the very beginning. I do not want to think that we will not meet again! I could not easily adjust to life without their presence. Kamiel was to me more like an elder brother than anything else and Asue was like a sister. I used to forget at times that they were made of sentient nannite and inorganic. Ever since they found that if they kept a piece of flesh alive inside them to carry the spores of the Goss they have been more organic in their thinking. The connections from their neural nets to the host flesh enabled them to telepathically link to all organic life within the influence of the Goss.

Kamiel drew a shuddering breath of air into his lungs and lay still upon the grass as he tried to understand what had happened to him. He turned upon his elbow and stared at the tall blond woman that lay beside him, who was also having difficulty in understanding what had happened. He was staring at her with organic eyes! Kamiel had spent a great deal of time in Goss and physical, telepathic contact with organic life-forms to understand how it felt to be alive in that sense. He rolled over onto his hands and knees, stretching out his hand to fall gently onto the female's arm beside him.

"Is that you Asue," he said.

"Yes," she answered, "we are organic! I can feel the breeze upon my skin and the warmth of the sun across my face. There is a heart beat in my chest and I can only see in coloured light. I can no longer sense heat signatures or sense nannite chatter in my mind."

"The last thing that I remember was talking to Alexander and Nagoth about what to grow to trade with other communities and then I awoke here with you!"

They helped each other to their feet and looked around to see where they were and immediately recognised Alexander's homestead. The apple trees still had their flower buds open, so very little time had passed since they had vanished. It was mid-day and most of the aliens who lived around the homestead had gone inside to rest from the heat.

Kamiel held out his hand to Asue and found that he could sense her thoughts and realised that they had been open to the spores of the Goss. As they stood a little shaken the sensation grew stronger and stronger until full communication became established.

"Goss! Goss are you there?" called Kamiel.

"I am always here, Kamiel," the symbiont answered.

Even though the essence of the Goss was spread completely throughout the new universe it was still able to answer directly to an individual.

"Could you connect me to Alexander and tell him that I am back," Kamiel replied.

Alexander's telepathic conversation with Link-soo-shan was abruptly interrupted by the symbiont's news.

He ran out of the house with Nagoth and scanned the road towards their homestead to see two naked figures walking carefully towards them. The male looked bafflingly familiar, but he could not recognise the female even as the two of them approached.

"These are strange days, my old friend," spoke the male, as the two of them stopped walking. "Can we sit down somewhere as these organic bodies get tired! Yes Alexander it is I, Kamiel and Asue. Something or someone has taken our nannite bodies and changed them into organic ones. My days of wandering in vacuum seem to be over! You look like me!"

Alexander stood transfixed as his mentor sat down on the wooden seat outside the porch with Asue. The man that was sat was indeed very like him, except that his hair was a lighter brown and he looked much younger. The woman was beautiful and her long blond hair was thickly curled and hung to her shoulders. Alex was aware of a piercing pair of jade green eyes returning his stare.

"I still remember changing your nappies," she smilingly said and added, "Could I have a drink of cool water? This body seems thirsty!"

Nagoth disappeared into the house and reappeared with glasses and a full jug.

"This sounds silly, but what happened to you, Kamiel, except for the obvious? You and I were talking and you suddenly disappeared in front of my eyes. Now you turn up on my doorstep a few days later in the flesh!"

"We don't know, my friends. I suspect that the life form that designed this universe had a 'hand' in the process! The Janise had the secret of turning energy into mass. That knowledge was passed on to the being that we called the 'Farmer' and it adapted that understanding to produce these planetary systems. Turning nannite artificial intelligences into organic beings would be quite easy for a mind of that capability."

Something brought the group's attention to cast their view back along the road, where another naked woman was making her way unsteadily towards them. Two figures burst from the house and ran up the road to greet her. It was Larse and Emelia who had recognised Tee 6 in her human form, only now she was not silver! The mature matronly figure of the embodiment of the nannite vessel threw her arms around the couple and hugged them emotionally.

"Well that solves the riddle of the vanishing Toarvaks," Alexander stated. "It would seem that from now on the secrets of nannite technology are not to be used by any organic intelligence. In fact this universe has been laid out and designed for the mental sciences to prosper and any kind of exploitation of resources to be unnecessary. We have the ability to travel throughout this universe using the wormholes put there for just that purpose. The star-gates can be opened by a group mind, so any other means of transport is redundant. There still seems to be a hidden agenda that the 'Farmer' wishes us to follow and we have until the end of this universe to do it!"

The years passed by and the new generations of all species began to evolve even further, mentally, as the spores of the Goss worked their unique capabilities on the hosts. Alexander and Nagoth steadily aged slowly over the centuries as did everybody else including those who once had been manufactured from nano-botics. No Toarvak ships were ever seen again and the sentient avatars were recreated into whatever shape of being they were at home with when they disappeared. Children were raised and if the place that they had lived became a little crowded, they moved on to empty planets and settled them via wormhole control. The new universe began to fill up again as planetary system after system became colonised by a variety of sentient beings.

Alexander, Nagoth and their Gnathen friend, Link-soo-shan were enjoying the last warmth of the evening sun outside on the homestead's porch. Around them were many different alien species and of all of them, Kamiel and Asue were the closest. They had discovered that not only did the 'Farmer' recreate them in flesh; it had also made them fertile. The ex-nannites soon discovered that sex was possible and Asue bore the fruits of Kamiel's new body. They had raised many children along with Alexander's and Nagoth's who had grown up together and some of them moving on to other worlds, leaving aside those that had not been re-seeded after the initial stromatolites and invertebrates.

The Gnathe ripped open a pod-vine fruit and crunched

up the beans with pleasure. She towered over the other humans and assorted aliens, digging her hind claws into the wooden perch that had been built for her comfort many years ago. Her eyes were still keen and her mind sharp although she would admit that sometimes the rest of her felt the effects of old age.

She said to Alexander, "I can still remember how all this began. The Gnathe do not forget, unlike your kind whose memories can wear thin over the years. I still regret the cruelties that I inflicted on my own kind to keep in absolute power. I wish sometimes that I could forget, but if all that had happened did not play out the destinies of all of us, this universe would not exist! We have forged an incredible partnership that has borne an exotic fruit. I have no problems with what I did, when I remember the events that brought us here."

Silver bars on dappled grey replied, "Without you the Kresh would not exist as a race of beings. Also our search through time to rescue as many societies from the hunger of the 'Harvester' that we could, changed history and caused this being that we call the 'Farmer' into existence. We would not be here if that scenario had not played itself through to the end."

There was a ripple of agreement amongst the extraterrestrials when Link-soo-shan saw something that she had not seen in a very long time and said, "We have company! I can see a ball of light approaching us along the farm road. I think that it is either your star-child or an avatar of the 'Farmer' come to visit!"

Alexander and Nagoth felt the unmistakeable warmth generated in their minds.

"It is Shoolin-Alexis," Nagoth whispered.

The ball of light dispersed and in its place stood the three identical twins that this time took the form of adult

243

humans. The three girls and boys were copies of Alexander and Nagoth. The six of them walked slowly up to the gathering and touched every person there to prove that they really were flesh and blood.

One of the young men said, "We/I have come to see you before the time comes when you must take leave of your fleshly homes say goodbye to organic life. Link-soo-shan, you are responsible for our existence. Without your genetic alteration of our mother we would never have been born. Even now we are different to the others who evolved naturally from your ancestors. We alone can be aware of what the future holds."

Link-soo-shan stepped off her perch and approached the one that had touched her and said, "You were created for a purpose. Without your assistance the destruction of the 'Harvester' could not have taken place. Since then you have continued to exist, untouched by the passing of time. We have seen you from time to time as we have expressed this other being's will and desire. You too, along with Kamiel and all of the nannites, have seen the end of the last universe and the ultimate evolutionary change of all the sentient races that used to exist. I have to ask you, why did you not join them and why are you here now?"

The six became one and in that fusion a distortion in time and space floated in front of them. A silvery light bathed them in its glow as the composite being Shoolin-Alexis answered them, inside their minds.

"Unlike the beings that evolved, we have recognisable parents. We are linked to you in a way that is different from them. Just as you loved us as children, we also love you and would not leave you to perish as organic forms. We can offer you a choice that only now, comes at a time that your organic forms are soon to be terminated. Become part of 'US' before you cease to be. There is a universe out there that can still be explored in another form and when it ends, there could well be another dimension for such as us to co-exist in, with all the others who have trodden this path. We make this offer now to all of you, human and non-human alike before we leave this world to journey on. There will be no return, as where we are going is far, far away from this place across the wormhole systems to find others like us, so you must make your decisions now."

What the Janise had discovered was the principal of turning energy into mass. The reversal of mass into energy was much simpler. A unanimous vote of agreement was all that Shoolin-Alexis needed to reform all those who had gathered at the homestead.

Balls of light took the place of complicated organic molecules and lifted away from the planet they had lived on for a very long time.

Alexander spread his wings of interconnecting force lines and caught the solar winds. The universe was his playground and the myriad wormhole systems built by the 'Farmer' beckoned him and all those who had decided to join them in their new and final state. He reached out to Nagoth and found her by his side along with all of the others that had made this madcap journey through time and space. A host of fireflies swept across the solar wind, gaining speed, led by Shoolin-Alexis this time separated into six individual entities that integrated with them all. A wormhole opened and closed around them. This was a new beginning.

On the untouched worlds, life evolved independently of the original plan and once again coal forests and deposits of oil would build up and be buried. Life would evolve again at the usual time scale and once again intelligence would emerge. The 'Farmers' third plan would come to fruition, with a little guidance from time to time from the acolytes left behind. Once the various sentient creatures unearthed the time stasis sealed pots of Goss spores and became hosts to the symbiont, all thoughts of conflict would cease. They would find the empty worlds ready for use and spread throughout the new universe and wonder just what beings had used these worlds before. More species would travel the paths that all had travelled before and evolve into the same group minds that were even now waiting for them to develop.

The next universe would not be made of matter.

The End.

ABOUT THE AUTHOR.

Barry Woodham was born in 1943 and has lived in Swindon, Wiltshire in England all of his life.

He spent his working life as a design engineer/ draughtsman and worked on the nuclear fusion project for thirteen years. Finding himself with nothing to read one lunchtime, he began to write the saga of the Gnathe and the Genesis Project. The thought occurred to him that any life form evolved to live in this world would not be able to cope with the micro-organisms of another eco-system on an alien planet.

After many of his colleagues began to read the chapters as quickly as he could finish them he continued on and finished the first book. The alien Gnathe are instinctive genetic engineers and alter living creatures to be their tools by the use of their brooding pouches controlled by the third sex. This first book is set millions of years after the sun has entered its red giant stage and is set on a vastly altered Jupiter. Humanity and intelligent Pan-chimpanzees are recreated by four Guardians made of nano-technology sent towards the stars from the dying Earth, to bring back mankind. One ship is stuck in the Kuiper Belt until it begins to fall towards the new sun and the crew are activated.

He was able to take early retirement through a legacy and continued to write the next book following on from Genesis 2, called The Genesis Debt. These have both been self-published on Amazon.

He has now put the final touches to 'Genesis Weapon', the third book in the series that has been self edited and printed in a spiral bound condition.

While writing Weapon he decided to link all the books

together as 'The Genesis Project' and write all the books into a series. He is now written a forth; - 'The Genesis Search' set hundreds of thousands of years after the events that occurred in Weapon. This part of the saga concerns the deliberate collision of the Andromeda Galaxy with ours in the distant future. What kind of entity could cause this to happen and why? This book attempts to settle those questions and concerns building a hunter/killer group from the ones who defeated the 'Goss' in Book Three by going back in time to remove their DNA and clone them, restoring their stored minds into young healthy bodies. At the same time whole solar systems are being rebuilt and moved by wormhole technology to the other side of our galaxy to be launched as a globular cluster towards the Greater Magellanic Clouds and safety.

Whilst writing this forth book the idea came to be, that my group of mixed human and aliens would find themselves having to deal with the abandoned machine intelligence of Von-Neumann probes left behind by the events produced by the 'Harvester' and this would be worth considering as the fifth Book;– Genesis 3 - A New Beginning.

How will this universe end and what might just cause a new universe to come into being? I have tried to solve that riddle!

I hope that you will enjoy reading these books as much as all the others and as much as I have enjoyed writing it!

Barry.E.Woodham.

The complete range of 'Genesis Project' books by Barry E Woodham are available in hard copy and eBook file formats and include:-

Book 1. 'Genesis 2'
Hard copy   ISBN 978-1-909020-79-5
eBook for Kindle   ISBN 978-1-909020-81-8
eBook for all other readers   ISBN 978-1-909020-80-1

Book 2. 'Genesis Debt'
Hard copy   ISBN 978-1-909020-82-5
eBook for Kindle   ISBN 978-1-909020-84-9
eBook for all other readers   ISBN 978-1-909020-83-2

Book 3. 'Genesis Weapon'
Hard copy   ISBN 978-1-909020-85-6
eBook for Kindle   ISBN 978-1-909020-87-0
eBook for all other readers   ISBN 978-1-909020-86-3

Book 4. 'Genesis Search'
Hard copy   ISBN 978-1-909020-88-7
eBook for Kindle   ISBN 978-1-909020-90-0
eBook for all other readers   ISBN 978-1-909020-89-4

Book 5. 'Genesis 3 A New Beginning'
Hard copy   ISBN 978-1-909020-91-7
eBook for Kindle   ISBN 978-1-909020-93-1
eBook for all other readers   ISBN 978-1-909020-92-4

Also a new fantasy book 'The Elf-War'
Hard copy   ISBN 978-1-909020-94-8
eBook for Kindle   ISBN 978-1-909020-96-2
eBook for all other readers   ISBN 978-1-909020-95-5